THE VOLCANOES OF SAN DOMINGO

The Volcanoes Of San Domingo

ADAM HALL

A FOUR SQUARE BOOK

Para la familia famosa
VARNEY
– Saludos, amigos!

© Copyright Adam Hall, 1963
First published in Great Britain by Collins in 1963

*

FIRST FOUR SQUARE EDITION APRIL 1967

*

Four Square Books are published by The New English Library Limited,
from Barnard's Inn, Holborn, London, E.C.1.
Made and printed in Great Britain by C. Nicholls & Company Ltd.

CHAPTER ONE

THE skyliner 12 crossed latitude 5° north at her cruising ceiling, alone and remote in a noon sky. The whole of the visible world was blue. From the cabin it was impossible to tell where the sky met the sea's horizon; nor was there any cloud to break the scene. The world had become a colour: blue.

The air-hostess made her way between the seats, and found the man she wanted. "Mr. Rayner . . ."

He looked up, his thought-train broken. "Yes?"

" We shall be coming within range of 5-Island Beacon in just a few minutes now."

"Thank you."

He had these few more minutes in which to think. Mostly, in his mind, he listened to the voice of Gates again. Gates had called him to the boardroom of Transocean Airlines at short notice, and the taxi had ploughed through London's January rain, barely twenty-four hours ago.

By the atmosphere in the boardroom Rayner had immediately sensed a crash. In a way he was right. The chairman of T.O.A. had got to the facts the moment he had sat down:

"Well, gentlemen, I wanted you to be here when I told Rayner about this thing, because you may like to go over the facts again in your minds. We've called you here, Rayner, because you were our station-super in San Domingo, Aguador, two years ago when we lost the new Skyliner 10 over the Pacific there. You may remember the exact date: March Fourth, 1961."

Rayner nodded. So it was, in fact, a crash. But not a new one. He could relax.

"Quite apart from the normal desire," Gates said, "to find out what happened to that aircraft – the *Glamis Castle* – we've been anxious because she was the first model of the then new series, and we are still flying thirty of the same type. The crashes at Munich and Bombay were found to have been caused by technical failures." He gazed along the table, meeting no one's eye. "We all know how much those disasters cost the airline in reputation, but the present fleet is now flying with a clean sheet after grounding and modification. In the case of the *Glamis Castle* there was no trace of wreckage and no survivors." He slid the sheaf of papers towards him. "Let me read for you the evidence – such as it was – given at the Air Ministry inquiry."

Rayner listened with half an ear. He knew the evidence by heart: he had presented most of it himself, as station-super San Domingo, the Skyliner's destination at that time.

The report took twenty minutes to read; Gates spoke the final item from memory: "Captain Lindstrom's last signal from the *Glamis Castle* was received clearly by the San Domingo tower: *'GLX at QNH nine nine zero – Out.'* And from that time onwards, there was silence from the aircraft."

Rayner waited. Gates had something more, apparently, to say. In the few seconds of silence, Rayner recalled whole hours of the action that had followed his receipt of Lindstrom's last signal at San Domingo tower. The Aguador search-and-rescue organisation was alerted twenty minutes later, and this alert phase began at 16.25 hours local time. The Rescue Co-ordination Centre alerted SAR services for immediate action a few minutes afterwards. With still no further signal from Lindstrom's plane, the distress phase began at 17.00 hours, following the absence of any news from widespread communication checks. Actual search-and-rescue operations went into action at the same time: three helicopters were sent up by the North Aguador Mountain Rescue Base; an Army seaplane took off from Lago Azul; and two sea-going cutters put out from Puerto Fuego on the coast. By nightfall, 18.00 hours, nothing had been sighted. A sea-search operated all night and the air-search was remounted at dawn. Two days later, all these operations ceased. The new Skyliner 10 was listed as missing. Crew and passengers were presumed dead.

It had been the first time that Paul Rayner had had the task of reassuring – falsely, as he knew – the friends and relatives who had come to the San Domingo airport to meet those passengers. His memory of the events was still brutally clear.

The chairman was saying: "Rayner, you'll know a flight steward of ours, called Marsh."

"Yes, sir."

The next instant, Rayner knew that Gates wanted his reaction, cold, because he threw the shock at him deliberately:

"Marsh has just come back from leave in Puerto Fuego, Aguador, where he did some shark-fishing. He says he has seen Captain Lindstrom there, alive." He watched Rayner steadily. "You seem unready to believe that." He waited.

Carefully Rayner said: "No. But I'm shaken."

"So was I. We've grilled Marsh without mercy, but he won't budge – he won't admit he was mistaken. As you know, a steward has to be very observant. Out of some hundred photographs of pilots in uniform that we showed Marsh, fifteen were of Captain Lindstrom. He picked out fourteen of them without hesitation."

Rayner said: "Marsh was flying the Atlantic routes for a goodish while, sir. So was Lindstrom. They would have seen a lot of each other."

"And even after two years – since Lindstrom crashed – you think Marsh would still recognise him, out of uniform?"

In a moment: "I do. Where did he see him?"

"In a bar. He spoke to him, but Lindstrom went out right away. And Marsh never saw him again. Now, Rayner, you'll be given the chance of talking to Marsh yourself. But at this moment it would help us all if you could give us your immediate reaction. Do you think it possible that Lindstrom is still alive?"

The silence lasted some half a minute.

"Yes. Possible."

"Thank you, Rayner. Now you see why we've called you in. Willis is working on the Singapore drug leak" – Willis was Transocean's security man – "otherwise we would send him down to Puerto Fuego. You see, this is a pretty slim piece of evidence that's come up. We can't re-open the Air Ministry inquiry just to add this late and very odd item to the reports. And we can't start any official kind of search for Lindstrom, because we wouldn't get much assistance from the police in Aguador, in face of the strained political relations with Britain since President Ycaza seized power there." He looked along the table, this time meeting the eye of each director and adviser. "So we've decided to send our own representative, to try to find out if in fact Captain Lindstrom is still alive in Puerto Fuego, and if so, what happened to his aircraft and its total complement of ninety-nine passengers and crew."

Rayner saw it coming, and wished he could duck. Puerto Fuego, on the Equator, was just another name for hell-on-earth.

"You were in Aguador for eighteen months. Rayner." The steady voice became persuasive. "You know the country well – and better even than Willis. You speak fluent Spanish, and you would recognise Captain Lindstrom as easily as Marsh, if you saw him there." Pause.

"Yes, sir."

"It's an unusual service I'm asking of you. I know that." And Rayner noted that the use of "we" had changed to "I." In other words, he was to be in the personal service of the chairman of T.O.A. A compliment: and an incentive.

The sharp January rain lashed the windows. The ventilation system purred in the background, as softly as the chairman's voice.

"And I realise that we shan't be able to replace you very easily as station-super London, even for a short time. But I hope you'll help me."

It was the smooth routine of the soft-sell, and Rayner heard himself saying, "I'll do what I can, sir," and knew as he said it that he was going to miss this cold winter rain within a matter of hours, and would be longing for it as a man longs for a drink in the desert.

And now the world was blue, and the sun blinding along the metal skin of the mainplanes. He put out his cigarette and went forward and through on to the flight-deck. The crew looked up. He said: "You've got the instructions, Captain Mayhew?"

"Yes, sir. To copy the coastal approach made by Lindstrom two years ago." He checked the sheet. "Be another two minutes. Like to sit down, Mr. Rayner?"

The navigator flipped down the spare swing-seat, and Rayner took it, looking directly ahead through the forward observation-panel.

"Coming up now, sir."

The radio operator began sending their position down to San Domingo Tower: *5-Island now one seven at two one zero zero feet. Estimate 6-Island at two four.*

Rayner sat perched stiffly, listening to the exchange of signals between the aircraft and San Domingo Tower as they reported over 6-Island. Then they were on the coastal GLX station and receiving the prelim. pattern. San Domingo came in: *Check GLX at QNH nine nine zero – Over.*

The response went back. It was Lindstrom's last signal, word for word. *GLX at QNH nine nine zero – Out.*

The pilot looked round at Rayner and he nodded, leaning forward on the flip-seat and staring ahead through the Perspex panels. The blue was bright and unbroken. At seventy miles from the coastline, nothing of it could be seen; not even the haze-belt where the sea met the land that they would pick out soon.

This, then, was the area where it had happened. Out of sight of land. A mote of machinery floating in a waste of blue, alone, never to be heard of again.

Hello San Domingo ... Have checked GLX at QNH nine nine zero ...

8

It was the signal that Captain Lindstrom had never sent. The patterns split just here. Rayner felt the continuing lightness of his body on the flip-seat as the aircraft increased its descent. She was going in on course and on schedule with all checks normal.

*

On the way in, he asked the captain: "From that point, where you were checking GLX, have you ever seen the coastline?"

"Twice, in the past year, when there was ten-tenths visibility and freak light after a rainstorm. We could even see the volcano range."

"And below? How did the sea look?"

"Just glare. It was about noon, both times."

Rayner nodded. That would be right. With the sun at its zenith on the Equator the light would spread almost vertically, and the surface of the sea would be opaque.

"Thank you."

The coastline became sketched across the blue in a thin ashen line that darkened gradually and then broke up into detail as the township of Puerto Fuego took shape, red and white and green: roofs, walls and the avenues of trees.

The plane sank heavily and vibration set in, fluttering along the mainplanes. The captain's attitude became more precisely composed as the radio operator went into the approach exchange with San Domingo Tower.

Repeat procedure, please.

Rayner thought: it could only have been an explosion inside the *Glamis Castle,* nothing else. Something that had wrecked the aerial or killed the crew or both. Sudden fuel-blockage or a slow fire or even the breaking-up of the machine would have given plenty of time for distress signals by radio.

Repeating: No delay expected. Runway 9. No surface wind. Visibility five miles. Cloud two oktas at three thousand feet. Addition: Touch-down elevation 32 feet. Report your altitude please – Over.

The sound of the radio and of the vibration became deadened as pressure began on the ear-drums, soft needles probing inwards.

But an explosion would have been heard by fishing-boats and reported.

Beyond the town, the hazy green of the rain-forest to the east and the metal-grey thread of the Xapuri River. The salt-pan east of the town, a blotch of dirty white among the dun-brown and mould-green of the thorn and savannah scrubland.

Already the appearance of flowing heat across the landscape that became slowly magnified.

At two thousand outbound on WILS front beam.

Improbable, an explosion. It would have been heard and reported. A progressive break-up would have left time for at least one signal. Improbable. A sudden and total break-up would have led to a fuel-explosion either in the air or on the surface. Improbable. Most improbable of all: the steward's story of having seen Lindstrom. In a bar. How drunk had Marsh been?

Starting procedure turn one five zero zero feet.

Beyond the salt-pan and the savannah, the rising flanks of the volcanoes, seventeen of them in an unbroken range, scalloped by the intermontane basins. A long dark roll of smoke curling out from the head of Catachunga and drifting across the escarpments and canyons and plateaux to the north where volcanic lava had dammed the river and formed a torrent.

Cleared to final approach. Report at outer marker.

Outer marker at one two zero zero feet – Over.

The heat flowed in waves across the salt-pan and the dry-weather road and the first scattered buildings of the capital where the sun sent up a gibberish of heliograph signals from reflecting metal and glass.

The soft needles hurt the ear-drums. The vibration had eased. The mud-flats and the machines where men were extending the runway and the groups of marker posts and radar scoops began flashing beneath the observation panels.

Cleared to land. No surface wind – Over.

The heat was already oozing into the cabin.

Roger – Out.

As the wheels hit the runway and the plane shook to the impact, Rayner felt that he should never have come here, because he was sure that Marsh had been drunk and that Lindstrom was dead.

Half-way down the steps from the aircraft he was staggering under the heat's shock-wave. This was San Domingo, where the rich came for the cool. The soft whine of the jets was dying away and voices sounded faintly through the pain in his ears.

There was a relief from the glare inside the airport building where green glass made the place look like an aquarium. The huge portrait under the main clock had a different face: that of José Maria Ycaza. *El presidente.* Not a bad face; less flaccid than the usual face of the murderous spoiled child that so many of the dictators seemed to have. In this one there was even a hint of gentleness in the eyes but perhaps that was a trick of the light, since *el presidente* had sacked the Government Palace with a traitorous contingent of the secret police four hundred strong and armed with bayonets and grenades before ordering the immediate execution of President Maya and fifteen of his political staff. The firing-squad had been rattling for months after the *coup d'état*.

Rayner checked in at the T.O.A. office and found there was a branchliner flight down to Puerto Fuego in two hours. To make use of the delay he drove into the capital to search the files of *El Diaro*, the San Domingo daily, bringing away some dozen photographs of people who had been reported missing on Flight 696.

The branchliner seaplane took off from Lago Azul and put him down in Puerto Fuego harbour just before sundown, when the last of the day's heat was choking the streets and withering the air. The smoke from the dredger and the wharf furnaces clung in thick wet webs across the masts of the shipping, and from the cutter that took him to the jetty it looked as if the whole town had been struck by a plague. A few fishermen moved along the curving sand beach, preparing their gear for night sailing; apart from their movement – as dull and as heavy as if they worked under water – there was no sign of human life along the quays and jetties where prone figures lay with their dark arms crooked below their heads in the sleep of the marijuana.

The smell of the drug came to Rayner as he passed among them; and it was this that recaptured all of the heat and the stink and the feel of those eighteen months he had passed in this loathsome land he had hoped never to see again. His own fault; he had kept on saying, "Yes, sir," like a fool, committing himself to his fool's errand.

Before the dark came down and the town came alive along the lighted streets, an Indian porter had found him a *pension* among the heights of the harbour quarter, not far from where the badly-printed plan showed Ventura's bar; and when he had stood for ten minutes under a trickle of rust-brown water from the shower and had double-checked the mosquito-screens and the net over the bed, he switched on the ceiling lamp and spread on the table the photographs from the files of *El Diaro*, together with the batch he had brought from London.

Of the forty-two photographs so far collected, fifteen were of Lindstrom. These were the ones Marsh had been given for his identity-test. Of the rest, five were the crew of the *Glamis Castle*; many were Aguadorean nationals; and the total was made up of British, French, Spanish, American, and Peruvian passengers. There was only one V.I.P. – Platt-Fellowes, British Foreign Office. There were six children.

Sitting in the quiet room, high above the awakening life of the evening and the sounds of voices and the surge of traffic along the Avenida del Mar, he began, in the harsh glare of the ceiling lamp, to study the faces of the lost.

CHAPTER TWO

As he climbed the sloping alleys and the steps from the harbour the drum of traffic along the big streets became faint and in its place there grew the din of voices from the bar.

The great blue stars seemed at roof-level; you could raise a hand and gather them. In the corners of the steps, unseen rubbish stank and there was the constant hum of flies. Outside the bar three human bodies lay in a heap, cast there by the drug that any man could buy for very little, anywhere in the ports along this coast. One man was on his back with his eyes wide open against the unseen stars; in his fingers was a crumpled lottery ticket, his stake in the universal dream.

Rayner went into the bar and asked for Pernod and sat at the end of the long smoky room. From here he would see people coming in before they would see him. This was important. Assuming Lindstrom to be alive (and Rayner meant to finish this game according to the rules before he cabled, in the morning, for permission to go home), he must not have a chance to see Rayner first.

From Marsh's description, this was Ventura who added water to the Pernod for him.

The thick-bodied and gentle-eyed Spaniard watched the drink turn milky; in the yellow light of the mosquito-encrusted bulbs the drink had the colour of pearls.

"Is expensive, Pernod, señor. Is imported."

In Spanish Rayner said: "It's my only vice."

"Is good vice." Ventura was proud of his English.

"There are worse." He had not spoken a word of English since he had landed from the seaplane a month ago. By day he had worn sun-glasses against the glare and against the thousand-to-one chance that Lindstrom was alive and saw him on the street and recognised him. Dark glasses were better than a beard: the eyes were nine-tenths of a face. Also he had let a shadow of stubble grow between shaves; a beard changed the appearance but stubble changed the whole character from that of a careful man to a lazy one, even from that of an Englishman to a Latin.

For a month he had not gone near Ventura's bar, because Marsh had said that Lindstrom had cleared out the moment he was recognised. He would need time for reassurance before showing himself again in that place. Rayner had spent those hours of the day – when one could walk in the open without blistering – along the streets and among the waterfront slums and the fishermen's shacks on the beach beyond the town, talking with Spaniards and the coastal-strip Indians, the Negroes, mulattoes, creoles and mestizos and the few whites: American, English, Canadian, French, who worked among the fisheries and on the boats or moved like penitents along the bright sand with their eyes cast down as they combed the beach for any treasure worth a crumb or a marijuana cigarette.

He had asked questions, moving on again the moment he drew blank, never pressing to arouse their curiosity; and in this way he learned a great deal: that in Puerto Fuego few people had even heard of the aeroplane that had gone down over the sea; because it had been making for San Domingo, and San Domingo was fifty miles away on the far side of the world. He learned that the only dead bodies washed ashore here two years ago had been those dead bodies that could outswim a shark, just as in any other year. But he learned nothing of Lindstrom.

By night, he had sat alone in the cafés and along the pavements, watching the passing faces and never, once, seeing among them a face among the forty-two photographs that he studied for an hour every night before sleeping, sitting alone in his room at his macabre game of patience with the photographs spread in rows on the table under the light.

Now he sipped his Pernod, watching the men coming into the bar. The place was crowded, mostly with fishermen up from the port. Among the blue cotton shirts were the red ponchos of the Indians and the clean white linen of the Negroes: to-day had been a market festival and to-night was for drinking.

An old man with the wizened face of a new-born infant was lurching to his feet and sinking periodically to the floor, heaving himself up again and pawing the air for the feel of his good friends; they found his glass for him and helped him to drink and let him sink again, singing.

13

"Is celebrating, señor," Ventura said. "Catch very big swordfish last night. Ten pesaldos. Five hundred pounds weight. Very happy."

Rayner sipped his Pernod.

"Very happy."

Ventura looked relieved; sometimes strangers, especially English, did not like to see drunken men here, and would not come again.

"English," said Ventura.

Rayner looked again at the wizened face of the drunk, whose skin was the colour of walnut stain and whose intermittent song told the hoary story of the Girl of Pamplona who was tossed on the horn of a bull. He didn't look English at all.

"Really?" Rayner said.

Ventura wagged his great maned head of gunmetal-blue hair.

"You, señor. *You* English."

"Oh." He saw a man coming into the bar. "I was born in a lot of places."

He watched the man who had come in. It was not Lindstrom. He had been looking for a clean-shaven Lindstrom, as well as a bearded one, all these weeks; because after Marsh had scared him off he might have cut off the beard to make things difficult. This man who was coming towards the end of the room was short-bodied and had a square head with a nobly-sloping brow that was slashed across by a dreadful scar. One sleeve of his white silk shirt was pinned above the elbow. He stood for a moment to gaze down on the singing fisherman, who had now stopped singing and was sleeping soundly while his friends formed a group around him so that nobody should tread on him.

The man stood square on his feet, and Rayner remembered that an arm was heavy and that the man must have developed the square stance in finding his balance again. At Rayner's prep-school there had been a boxing-instructor who had sparred with his right arm held behind him so that the smaller kids would feel they had a chance; and it was the same with this man: there was the suggestion of implicit strength because of the lost limb. Where others needed two good arms for the fight with life, he needed but one. You were one of the smaller kids and the fight would be fair.

"Luis!" cried Ventura, and came lunging round the bar to greet him with his golden smile. He threw an arm round the man's shoulders while Luis looked about him idly, as unconcerned as a man who, preoccupied with his return home,

14

finds his dog leaping at him after absence. "You have been gone too long, Luis!"

The man moved again, towards Rayner, to look at him. He had already looked at every man in the room and now he wanted to study the stranger.

"You have been gone ten years!" Ventura cried, and hurried to fetch a bottle of white Venezuelan rum.

"A month," the man said, looking at Rayner with blank brown eyes.

"How is Pepito? How is your son, Luis?" The rum gushed into a tumbler of chipped ice until it spilled over.

"I haven't seen my son." Luis looked away from Rayner, hearing a woman's voice and noting that it was the voice of a tart who had come in. He looked at Ventura, who was telling Rayner in rapid Spanish:

"His son is in prison but the president is going to let him free soon now because all political prisoners are to be pardoned as a sign of the president's generosity towards his former enemies!" He slid the tumbler of rum across the bar and Luis stopped it within an inch of the edge while Ventura mopped the spillings away.

Luis drank, swallowing some of the ice chips. "They will never let him out."

"Of course they will let him out!"

"They will let him out when they let the president in. If either of them lives long enough."

Rayner asked in Spanish: "How old is your son?"

Luis drank again and looked at him without expression. "You live in Spain?"

"No."

"You have the Castillian accent."

"A poor one."

"He is nineteen years old."

"Young, for a president's enemy."

"He was trying to blow up the *ferrocarril* with some students as a demonstration. If you are not from Spain, then tell me where you are from." For the first time he had spoken in fluent idiomatic American English.

Rayner drank some Pernod and said: "I came here for some fishing."

"Shark?"

"Yes."

Luis was regarding him with his inoffensive, expressionless gaze, perhaps even thinking about something else or listening to the harsh rich laughter of the tart at the far end of the room. It was then that Ventura exclaimed softly: "*Ay de mi!*" as a trembling began under their feet.

It came rhythmically, and over the seconds the hubbub of voices died away and there was silence but for the tinkling of the glasses and bottles along the shelves as the vibration filled the whole room until the doors rattled as if to a wind and the lamps swung slowly as if to the same wind; but the air was still. Men stood avoiding one another's eyes and pretending to drink while the long rhythmic shudders passed under their feet and the dust rose like smoke from the cracks in the floorboards and Ventura's great shadow, cast by one of the swinging lamps, began a ghostly bear-dance on the wall.

Ventura looked at nobody, his eyes down, the sweat bright on his face, standing subdued like a child about to be beaten, while the shadows swung against the wall and a glass fell from the bar with sudden violence and he closed his eyes as if that had been the first stroke of the beating.

The drunk who had caught the big swordfish was moaning in his stupor but his friends did not pay attention to him; they stood very still, as if they feared that any slight movement added to this terrible shuddering would bring it to such anger that it would break down the building and destroy them all.

In the near-silence, mosquitoes sang their thin song as they wreathed about the light-bulbs, swarms of them clouding and flowing back and forth to follow the swing of the lamps, their smoky shadows blowing and drifting about the head of the dancing bear; and from far away, the sound came of a kind of music and a lost voice singing, jerking into cracked rhythms and singing on, the song of "Sonny Boy."

After a long time the vibration diminished, and the glass along the shelves became silent again; gradually the lamps grew still, and a man spoke, and then another, until the din was at its height again and they were banging their empty glasses on the bar and demanding of Ventura if he were going to stand there like a whore with sores until doomsday while his customers died of thirst.

"Is the will of God!" cried Ventura, his eyes still hurt by the beating. He began pouring the liquor for them all.

In English Luis said to Rayner: "Every night, around this time, around this season." He finished his drink.

Rayner nodded. These tremors had been felt often in San Domingo, though they were shorter there where the ground was high and the rock more massive.

Then Luis put his glass on to the bar and said: "I will see

you again," and went down the long room nodding to his friends as they called his name until he was in the street and out of earshot. They had not sounded like the polite words of parting, but a simple statement. But he was wrong, Rayner thought.

After four weeks of steady searching he had not picked up the scent. Lindstrom was a skeleton, seventy miles from here and fathoms deep below shark water. He could come here every night, to listen for a chance word from a stranger and finally to see significance in innocence itself.

Marsh had been mistaken.

He left the bar soon after the other man, and went down through the stifling streets until he came to the long bright avenue along the waterfront, the Champs-Elysées of Puerto Fuego, the Avenida del Mar. Here it was cooler and the pavements were as wide as the roadway, and you could walk alone at this late hour, with elbow-room for your thoughts. He was already conscious of the relief that he was soon leaving here.

Traffic was still moving along the paved roadway and he kept close to the face of the buildings and the galaxies of bright shop-windows, preferring the reflected heat of the stones to the waves of exhaust-gas.

There was a Western Telegraph bureau at the end of the Avenida del Mar, and he was going consciously in that direction because it was open all night for overseas cables.

He would simply send: *No luck. Request permission to return.*

An ivory-coloured sports Mercedes was parked at the kerb and the woman who came from the doorway crossed to the car, hurrying a little under the mottled shadows of the leaves where the light fell from the tall standards; and Rayner, stepping aside to avoid her, saw her face as clearly as if one of the forty-two photographs had been held suddenly in front of him; so that he knew that the cable would never be sent.

CHAPTER THREE

HIAWATHA Moses sat near the boat and watched the sun come up across the volcano range. Seeing it, he forgot the world, so that there were only the two of them: himself and the sun. It was more beautiful than the shrine in the Church of San Domingo that he could still remember. His mother had taken him there a long time ago when he was not old enough to know what a church was; and he had seen the shrine in a beam of

17

sunlight and he had cried with the beauty, even so young as not to know what beauty was.

Many things awed him: the shrines; the coming up and the going down of the sun; the red rage at the head of Catachunga by night; his priest; and El Angelo.

He sat naked on the sand, watching the great orb of the sun until tears came to his eyes and he must look away. A man was coming across the sand, with a palm-frond in his hand to keep away the flies. The voice of El Angelo came ringing.

"Hiamo! Garb yourself! Be ready!"

"*Capitán!*" He struggled into his denims. The day was begun.

Nobody in Puerto Fuego ever took his boat as far into the ocean as El Angelo, when he had the mood on him. There was no need; you could find shark twenty feet long within five miles of the coast and you would not have to cut your profit with the cost of much diesel oil. You would not, within five miles of the coastline, be far from the help of other boats if you met with a giant manta ray or ran foul of wreck-timber or had a man injured by the catch.

But El Angelo would go fifty, a hundred miles, once in a blue moon; and he would be thought of as lost. It was as if a great wind caught him and took him horizonwards until the land was gone from his mind. When he came back he was as gay as a buccaneer home from a prize on the main.

Puyo had said: "He goes because he must; he goes to be with nothing but the sea and the sky; and he is healed."

Only twice had Hiawatha Moses been into the deep ocean with the *capitán*, and to-day he was uneasy; he did not care to be with nothing but the sea and the sky, beautiful though they were. He had heard many tales of swordfish that formed a pack and attacked a boat and stove its timbers in; of the deep-water octopus that sometimes came to the surface from its cave five hundred fathoms down, to seize upon a boat as small as this; of the manta whose wings could be thirty feet across and black as night, most dreaded of them all.

But El Angelo was the wisest and the strongest man in Puerto; with this captain you were safe, even here in the midst of desert water, under the desert sky.

I am safe with El Angelo, Hiamo kept saying to himself, and was by a little reassured. They had sailed four hours from land and now drifted, with the lure trailing and a bullock's thigh cast over the side, its blood spreading across water as clear as glass.

18

They had eaten the small green fish they had caught on the journey; and now El Angelo slept for an hour in the deck-house while Hiamo sat crouched beneath the awning to keep watch. Often he looked through the hatchway and saw the *capitán*, whose shadowed face with its white beard reminded Hiamo of the face of God he had seen in the paintings of Layuzgo on the ceilings of the churches.

He shut his eyes, for the glare of the noon sun was blinding; and he knew that he must have fallen asleep under the awning, for now, as he opened his eyes, the hard glare of the sun was gone from the sea, and the sky was grey, like a sheet of metal, and the pool of blood from the thigh of the bullock was immense, and of a faint rose-pink on the flat surface of the water. He started up.

By the shadow of the mast it was still not far beyond noon. A haze had come upon the ocean, as it does before a storm; and Hiamo was afraid; but he was more afraid of waking El Angelo, who had the sleep of God upon him. He sat watching the water. Despite the lure they had towed here and the thigh of the bullock whose blood had now seeped away, there was no sign of any shark, even here where he could see fathoms down through the clear water.

He had never seen the water more clear. It was because of the change that had come to the sky: the glare of the sun was gone, so that there was no hot light silvering the surface, and one could open one's eyes without hurt.

Nothing moved, anywhere. The sky was joined to the sea by a copper band that ringed the world of water. Not even a flying-fish broke the surface, and the surface was like hard flat glass.

Hiamo now saw the miracle.

He made to cry out but could not. He did not even turn his head to look at the shadowed face of God through the deck-house hatch, for he could not look away from the miracle, the sign of the cross, deep, deep in the sea. He stared and his body shook as if in fever. The sea was pale and clear, the colour of an opal; and set in the pale clear water was the shadowy sign of the cross. He stared until tears ran from his eyes, and his heart quaked.

A voice came, speaking between the sea and the sky.

"*Capitán . . . Capitán . . .*"

It was his own voice, and when the *capitán* heard him he came from the deckhouse, his eyes as clear as if he had never slept.

"*Capitán . . . Look. Look . . .*"

19

El Angelo stood in the boat with his legs braced apart and his hands on his hips and his thick beard jutting as he looked down into the water. Hiamo stared again at the sign, comforted that his *capitán* was now watching it too and could share in the miracle and, in so doing, could take away some of his fear of it. The unseen movement of the water stirred the edges of the shadowy sign; but its main shape remained still.

"I see nothing," said El Angelo.

"There, *Capitán* . . . there. It is the cross!"

El Angelo turned away and said: "I see nothing. It is a trick of the light." His face was calm and he did not seem angry that Hiamo should show him something that was not there. He did not seem interested.

The boy looked at the *capitán*, who was taking a sounding as he sometimes did, so that he could add figures to the great chart he had made on the wall of his shack. Then he looked up at the misty blob of the sun, and checked the compass, and said:

"We will go."

He commanded Hiamo to start the engine and set it at exactly three-quarter speed. They would steer east by ten degrees north, he said, directly for Puerto Fuego. As they cut away the bloodless thigh of the bullock and turned into their course, El Angelo looked at the little brass chronometer that was set in the deckhouse, and made a note on the paper beside the figures of the sounding he had taken.

He spoke only once of what Hiawatha Moses had seen.

"Tell no one of it. No one. They would not believe such a story, and they would laugh at you."

Hiamo said that he would tell no one. He sat in the bows, awed by the mystery of what he had seen. Yet, had he seen it? El Angelo said that there was nothing. El Angelo was almost God. Therefore, Hiamo had seen nothing. It had been a dream, and he would tell no one of it.

CHAPTER FOUR

IT was anger that cost Rayner caution and caused him to drop his careful plan. This onset of anger, that had begun at dawn the day after he had seen the woman of the ivory Mercedes, surprised him. His hand had trembled as he had shaved.

Because there had been ninety-three passengers in that plane and it was impossible that all had survived whatever

20

accident there had been. He could imagine no circumstance in which so many people could have remained alive without some knowledge of it getting through to the outside world.

Rayner noted his instinctive choice of the word "outside." Whatever had happened to the Skyliner 10 over the Pacific Ocean two years ago, the cold fact that it was missing from human knowledge had enclosed it within a dark pocket, a region of the unknown in people's minds. Assume, he thought as he stared at his angry eyes in the mirror, the lather growing stiff on his face – assume that every one of us has at the very least ten people who are near to us in our private environment: parents, children, friends: ten people who would be, for a time, shocked at our dying.

Ninety-three passengers and a crew of six: call it a hundred. A thousand, then, thrown into grief by that single event over the ocean. He had seen some of them himself at the airport in San Domingo, when the plane became overdue.

Two had survived the accident. Certain as he was that the woman was the woman in the photographs, he had come immediately to accept the testimony of the steward, Marsh. The woman and the pilot had survived. How, then, *dared* they keep their secret?

He resumed shaving, and made a bad job of it because emotion affects the skin. He watched with distaste the red-stained lather swirling away in the basin as his anger passed to a mood of deep and energetic thought. But his imagination, running at full gamut, fogged his mental view of this thing.

Most of those passengers had been strangers to one another. They had never met before – or had they, briefly? The names were on the reverse side of the forty-two photographs. Scott, Waring, Brown, Fouillet, Ibarra, Delano.... Had Mr. J. G. Scott ever lunched in the same restaurant in Oxford Street as Miss Alice Waring; had their glances met, just once, by chance, across the tables, to pass on with the flick of an eyelid, without interest? Had Mr. Clive Brown ever caught a passing taxi in Belgrave Square or the Place de la Concorde, leaving M. Georges Fouillet waiting on the pavement for the next? How often had the paths of these many people crossed, during their lifetime, without their knowing that one day they were to occupy the comfortable foam-rubber seats of the Skyliner 10 in close proximity and to be carried on their precisely-timed journey to a place known as Longitude 82° 9′ by Latitude 1° 4′ Pacific? There to observe one another in the precipitate intimacy of horror and alarm, to watch a stranger in the throes of pain and death, awkward and uncivilised as the animal

21

took over and fought for its life regardless of the decencies; there, perhaps, to make a sacrifice of heroic proportion in helping a stranger whose glance had only once caught the other's in a whole lifetime across the white-draped tables of an unremembered restaurant in a city five thousand miles away from this, the meeting-place.

If, Rayner thought, there were any pattern in these events, then one could say that nearly a hundred people had been called together to share the greatest moment of truth in their life: their death.

And if some of them, like the woman and the pilot, had escaped, then here in this town on the Pacific coast was to be found the most exclusive club in the world. Its membership was limited and closed; and its one rule was that of silence.

He dressed and left the hotel. He had moved here from the *pensión* last night, to the surprise of the management, so that he could have a better view of the town and the port, and of the long peninsula that reached out from the mainland two miles into the gulf. Along the peninsula there were the most sumptuous houses in Puerto, Spanish colonial buildings set in shade-covered grounds along the single roadway. It had been along that strip of road that he had seen the ivory Mercedes moving, a pale mote in the distance across the water of the harbour, before the dark leaves of the banana-palms had hidden it from his sight.

The Hotel Miraflores was higher than the little *pensión*. From its terrace he could keep a better watch. But now he climbed the steps through the rising heat of the morning to Ventura's Bar, his anger and his need for action cancelling his earlier plan of cautious inquiry and tactics. As far as he could, he would work in the open. Even in the heat and the white glare of the stones he felt the relief of this decision cooling his mind.

One question was paramount; it had risen from his thoughts of the "exclusive club." Did the woman and the pilot know of each other's existence? Or was the club so exclusive that even its members were unknown to each other?

The name on the back of her photographs (of which he had three from various sources) was Mlle. Giselle Vidal. It was all he knew of her.

Ventura was trying to repair a vase – one of the cheap garish Indian pieces one saw in the markets here – that he said had fallen down during the tremors of a week ago. The bar was open for business but the only customer was a seller of tagua carvings slumped in a corner and half covered with

22

his huge straw hat. Whether it was whisky or marijuana that had felled him thus, Rayner did not know. He watched Ventura studying the set of photographs. From the harbour there sounded the steady dungeon-rattle of the dredger.

Ventura hit out haphazardly at the flies with a savannah switch while he looked at the photographs.

"I am not knowing this man," he said in English. He looked gloomily at Rayner. "It fall like *that*." He brought the fly-swat down with a slap. "Like bomb." The glue was oozing from the tube because of the heat. "Now is see-saw puzzle."

His big hands moved the pieces of the vase hopelessly.

"This one," Rayner said, tapping the photograph in the middle. He had spent ten minutes last night with a ball-point, sketching in a beard round the face. "This one with the beard." He used Spanish, so that Ventura would have no cause to say he misunderstood.

"I am not seeing this man, never, señor. You wish for drink? Is Pernod. I remember is Pernod, for cooling." He reached for the bottle and went to the big refrigerator for ice.

"Ventura," said Rayner while he drank his Pernod, "I need to find this man because he owes me money. It is so much that I will give you five hundred pesos if you help me to find him. Five hundred."

Ventura could not take his eyes away from the puzzle of the pieces; or he could not look at Rayner.

"I very much like five hundred pesos, señor, but I am not knowing this man."

"You know a man with a beard –"

"Many men! There are –"

"An Englishman with a beard –"

"But you show me pictures with no beard –"

"He might have shaved it off. There was a man with this kind of beard in here a month ago and he was English and his face was like this. He was wearing white cotton trousers and a dark blue singlet; his hair and his beard are gold-coloured. Red. Now."

He put down five one-hundred peso notes and saw Ventura looking at them like a bear looking at a barrel of honey.

"I very much like to take, señor, but if I am not knowing this man, I can not take."

"All I want is the address."

Ventura was silent but he could no longer pretend to concentrate on the pieces.

"Tell me someone who knows his address, or even someone who might know it."

23

He turned away and stood at a little distance, leaving the notes on the bar. Ventura was sweating hard and stood motionless with his big hands resting among the broken pieces, his face puckered like that of a child with a smashed toy. Then Rayner said:

"Tell me his name, then. Only his name." Lindstrom would have troubled to change his name; he had troubled to grow a beard. "For five hundred pesos."

Ventura brooded with his black eyes half-closed, not looking away from the pieces. Flies skated nervously across the surface of the bar; he did not reach for the switch of savannah-grass.

"Tell me what made him dumb."

Ventura swung his leonine head up to look at something on the wall and in the mirror Rayner could see that the only thing on the wall behind him was a portrait of President Ycaza. The black eyes were narrowed.

"Take," he said, looking down and pushing the notes to the edge of the bar. "You can not give me five hundred pesos for nothing. For nothing."

Rayner finished his drink and put the glass down near the notes.

"I am staying at the Hotel Miraflores here in the Calle 30 de Agosto. Here is my name." He wrote it along the white edge of one of the notes. "Send someone there with a message, someone whom I shall not even see. Let him leave the message there for me at the hotel. Then I shall never be able to say it was you who told me." He went out of the long room and was going down the steps where the lizards ran and flicked in the brass heat of the sun before Ventura caught up with him at a shambling run.

"I am not knowing this man." He pressed the notes at Rayner, who found a peso coin and gave it to Ventura.

"Then at least I will pay for my drink."

He continued down the steps. The report made by Marsh was confirmed. Ventura knew. If he were corrupt he could easily send a message – any message with any address where Rayner could look for the Englishman and find that he must have moved on. If he were honest he could have earned himself at least one of those notes by being helpful: "try the harbour authorities in case the man has a boat – a bearded Englishman may be a man of the sea, it is often so. Ask Luis or N'Gami the Negro or Tycapa the seller of lottery tickets, because they are here every night and they might have seen this man if you say he was here. And I will ask others, myself."

24

Instead there had been the insistent denial and the hurried return of the money – perhaps before he could weaken. It was a big sum; the price of his loyalty to Lindstrom must be higher.

Rayner went down the steps to the Avenida almost at a stumbling run, reaching the shade of the trees with his eyes throbbing and his sweat soaking into his gaberdine suit. He found a bar and drank two glasses of fruit-juice, saying to the barman:

"*Progreso!*"

"*Viva!*" The barman looked at the picture of *el presidente* on the wall, his smile prescribed. Rayner was not thinking of the progress made by *el presidente*, but of his own. When he left the bar he walked as far as the Western Telegraph bureau. Earlier this morning there had been a cable for him, from London: *If no luck please return.*

He sent his reply. *Progress. Staying.*

Half-way along the waterfront drive he had seen a shop that sold optical instruments and he went there now, bringing away a pair of 10 x 50 Bleicher Verikon field-glasses with bloomed lenses and glare-hoods. He took them to his hotel and settled down on the terrace in the shade of the awning. The shutters were across every window; no voice sounded from any room; across most of the town the traffic had stopped; no one moved along the pavements under the trees; in the harbour the boats were calm. Nowhere was there any shadow, except below horizontal planes such as the trees and the awnings: the buildings had no shadow. It was noon on the Equator.

He swung the glasses methodically across the streets and the harbour, passing over the squat round shape of the bull-ring beyond the church. At the river's mouth where the water came sluggishly like molten silver some women had put their washing to dry, bedecking the scrub with fragmentary colour, from this distance as small as the pieces of Ventura's broken vase. Higher along the Xapuri a circus of condors wheeled with their black wings catching the light as they turned and drifted, on the watch for carrion.

From near the river's mouth, to the north of the town, ran the long peninsula southwards into the gulf, a ribbon of green and white where the road ran for two miles between the trees and the bright fountaining leaves of the banana-palms. Many of the houses were beautiful, their walls white and laced with balconies whose ironwork was as delicate as a web.

He studied each house carefully for minutes at a time; then he rested the field-glasses on the little iron table, lowered the deck-chair and began his vigil proper. The circular field of vision was traversed by the strip of road along the peninsula where he had last seen the ivory Mercedes. It was a liquid ribbon in the lens, flowing and rippling in the waves of heat that filled the air. Within the first minute of the vigil, sweat was coursing down his face and into his eyes.

He watched for three days, and after the dusk of each day he walked down the peninsular road hoping to see the car in the drive of one of the houses. Only his certainty that the woman he had seen was the woman in the photographs gave him the energy to force his eyes to concentrate through the torpor, hour after hour, and to walk six miles in the evening, without a glimpse of the quarry.

There had been one cable from London: *Willis arriving. Please give all help.*

So the company had decided it was now worth calling the security man off the Singapore drug leak. He was of two minds about the cable. In his own sphere of the airport he had long been used to running things himself; on the other hand he would need help down here when the whole situation began blowing up. Even his evidence of having recognised a passenger of the Skyliner, added to the evidence of Marsh, was enough to reopen the public inquiry and bring in the Air Ministry Accident Inspectorate.

In the late afternoon of the third day the sun became lost in haze an hour before dusk, and a coppery hue tinged the horizon of the ocean. The air became clogged, and the smallest exertion made breathing difficult. He was constantly troubled by the steaming-up of the field-glasses, and his eyes were bloodshot from the strain of the vigil.

By five o'clock the sky went the colour of a bruise, and the insects came clouding up from the lower reaches of the town. Now that the sun's glare had gone it was easier to keep his eyes to the lens for longer periods; but from his experience in San Domingo he reckoned he had another sixty seconds out here on the terrace. The first raindrop hit the iron table with the sound of a bullet, splashing his face, and more began falling as the white spot moved into the field of vision along the ribbon of road.

There were two other cars of this colour that he had seen in the last few days: a large American sedan and a Ford station-wagon. Refocusing the lens with great care, he made quite certain that this one now on the peninsular strip was an open sports.

A shutter banged and one of the doors of the terrace came open and a servant came out at the trot – "Señor! The rain, señor – the rain comes!"

"Yes."

The white spot moved steadily, vanishing for seconds beyond the banana-fringe and reappearing. The man behind him was still shouting about the rain as the great drops began pattering on the stones to leave patterns of smaller drops on the film of dust. The man was working frantically at the awning-winders, rolling the canvas in before the rain could reach its full force and tear it from the framework.

"You must go inside, señor! The rain!"

"Yes."

His head was now exposed to the sky and a raindrop hit the nape of his neck, stinging hard. The white spot was slowing, and now stopped, near where the peninsular road met the curve of the Avenida del Mar. Troubled by the hitting of the rain and by the servant's entreaties, he was still able to see movement immediately above the car; and a patch of black appeared there. The hood was being raised. Then the car moved again.

In choosing the Hotel Miraflores he had noted that the terrace commanded a view of most of the lower town, all of the Avenida, the whole of the peninsular roadway, and that stretch of the Avenida where the ivory Mercedes had been parked four days ago. The rest was up to luck.

"You will be overwhelmed, señor!" The man was running to close the canopy of the swing-chair at the end of the terrace. The rain was now beating on their heads and the stones had turned dark.

"Yes."

When the car was half-way along the curve of the Avenida he had to stand up and brace himself against the wall to steady the weight of the glasses. It was now possible to identify the car with certainty as the Mercedes; the black hood was already shining with water and a haze fanned out from the wheels. It was being driven fast.

The Calle 30 de Agosto, where the hotel stood, ran straight down to the Avenida; it was half a minute's run from the terrace if you took the garden steps to the street. The Mercedes was much the same distance – in time – from the intersection where the street met the Avenida.

If he stayed here he would be able to see how far the car drove on, if it didn't park in the place where he had seen it

27

four days ago. But if he started now he might reach the intersection first and in time to stop it.

The rain hit the stones and sent the crimson blooms of the flowers dipping and fluttering. The sky was turning black overhead. It was a difficult choice with the chances even.

"Señor! You must go inside now! The rain will – "

Rayner moved at a run and thrust the field-glasses into the man's hands for safe keeping as he reached the top of the steps and went down two at a time with his hands hitting out at the stones of the wall to prevent his shoes sliding on the rain-film. The gutters of the street were already gushing and a man was trying to whip his mule up the hill, afraid of the deluge to come.

He stopped his momentum with his hands flat against a tree-bole in the Avenida where flower-petals were flowing from broken blooms across the paving stones; under the big leaves it was still dry and the roar of the water falling on to the leaves was louder even than the car's engine as the Mercedes came past. He made a jump for the roadway but the car was already abreast and even if he could have stood in its path with his arms waving she could not have pulled up without killing him or sliding and hitting a tree. Grey mud, a mixture of rain and the volcanic dust, struck in a wave across his legs.

He began running steadily in the roadway so that he could keep the car in sight as long as possible through the immense avenue of trees; and as he ran he repeated the number in time with his feet. *14 – PF – 60 . . . 14 – PF – 60. . .*

The enormous leaves were dipping under the weight of water and sending the rain down in cascades as he ran from one dry patch to the next until the whole roadway was flooded and the gutters were filling and spilling across to the pavements the water they could not cope with. The number had faded and now the shape of the car itself became smaller and less distinct as he ran steadily, half-blinded by the rain-screen and soaked to the skin.

For seconds he had run with his eyes shut and now the car bloomed from the rain-haze like a soft white explosion and he ran harder, hearing the door slam as she began crossing the wide pavement, flitting palely through the haze towards the buildings where the lamps had come on in the windows and the neon signs were turning the street into a rainbow.

This was the place from which he had seen her come the other night: a restaurant-bar, the La Ronda. Slowing to a walk before he reached the doors he steadied his breathing;

28

she would not have seen him running after the car. He was a stranger seeking shelter here, as she was.

Two waiters moved like moths in their white jackets from the shadows between the soft glow of the lamps; there was only one other figure: the woman's. She was leaning her back to the bar, shaking the rain from her pale hair and calling something to one of the waiters above the heavy surf-roar of the rain outside the open doors.

The place was like a great cavern, its gloom relieved by the pools of amber light from the lamps along the walls; one of them shone upon her long pale hair and lit the kingfisher-blue of her eyes as she turned, aware of the stranger.

He drew nearer, and looked for the second time in his life at the cool haunted beauty of her face.

CHAPTER FIVE

SHE had gone to the table by the dais where the band had left its instruments, and sat with her back to the half-seen shapes of the guitars and the glow of the flamenco dress that was draped across a chair.

She had been there for an hour, watching the avenue through the open doors; and Rayner, still distant from her, at first thought she was waiting here for someone; but when a car went past or a man ran through the deluge she did not appear to notice them.

Water from his suit had dripped and formed a pool that was still spreading towards the doors, a bar-ticket afloat at its edge. The sound of the deluge was deafening; to order another drink he had to go up to one of the waiters and speak into his ear. A fast tide of rainwater was racing down the pavement, the choked gutters throwing up the coloured paper of the last carnival and spreading it across the roadway; a black pariah dog was trying to wrest something alive from the guttering, perhaps a bird caught by the rain and brought to the ground.

Once, Rayner had stood close to a waiter. "Who is the lady?" But the man had shrugged and his quick Spanish smile said: "Courage, and she is yours."

Rayner had not gone over to speak to her because he had hoped she was here for a rendezvous, and he might see another face from the forty-two photographs. Now he was simply at a loss: she had a drink on the table but had not touched it for an hour; she had no cigarette, no magazine.

She stared through the doors as if mesmerised by the racing water.

She had not looked at him directly; but sometimes, as he had returned his gaze to her after watching the scene of the deluge, he believed her head was turning away, as if she had been watching him.

He would never now forget her face, or the way she sat. If she had not been among the photographs he would still have been content to stay here and watch her as he was doing now.

Somewhere, five thousand miles from here, perhaps near Paris, there was a memorial-stone in her name; surely she could not know; and yet she must.

She looked up at him, startled because she had not heard him coming, in the rain's sound.

Sitting at the table and folding his arms on it and watching his fingers he said:

"I didn't expect to see you again."

He waited. His carefully-chosen phrase had been designed to mean: *I was there too.*

Because, during this hour while he had watched her and gone over everything again in his mind, he had realised one thing that was very important. The passengers, sharing their moment of truth though they had, must have remained strangers. The crew would have had no more than a passing sight of the ninety-three faces as they had walked the length of the cabin to the toilet and back. Neither crew nor passengers would have recognised one another if they had made a normal landing and walked to the airport building.

Her face, with this much beauty in it, would have been admired more often than some others on board; but in the tunnel-like cabin no one could have looked at her for long, without embarrassment.

His own face was unremarkable; it would be called "English" and nothing more; and she would not have recognised him even in the customs after a normal landing; or now.

Her voice was low but he heard it clearly against the rain's sound.

"Who are you?"

He had expected a stronger French accent. On his way to her table he had thought of addressing her in French and by name; but it might show his hand too much. Better that they remained strangers for a time.

He said with a smile, "We don't know who any of us are, do we? It's so dangerous." Her look of defence had formed

30

a long time ago and was now part of her expression; her hands too had tightened together.

"Did you follow me here?" she asked brusquely.

"We all followed each other, didn't we? Or did you lose your memory when it happened? It was all very violent."

He saw that her hands were held tightly together to stop them shaking; her mouth was quivering as though she could not trust herself to find the right words, the undangerous ones. Had he observed her less alertly he might have been taken in by her general appearance of calm: her eyes were steady on his and she had not moved her position since he had sat down. He realised that she might have had to make this kind of effort for two years; yet she had sat here for an hour without a cigarette.

He took a shot and scored a hit.

"I'm leaving this country soon."

"How?"

The question had leapt at him.

So they were prisoners.

"I'm not sure," he said, smiling a little so that she would not think he refused her the truth.

"When are you leaving?"

"I'm not sure," he said again, and was aware of an odd thing: he no longer wanted to leave this hellish place. Her saying, "When are you leaving?" had saddened him, and the brief emotion had leapt into consciousness. "I expect you've tried, haven't you?" he asked casually.

He didn't know where he had gone wrong; but he had made an instant enemy. Her eyes were cold on him and her voice cut through the beating of the rain.

"I have never tried. I have no wish to leave."

He said: "Have you ever seen my face before?"

"No."

"Then why be afraid?"

"I am not afraid. In this town one does not accept a stranger who follows." There was deep contempt in the last word and he believed she had said it in a rush of anger and unwisely, for she added: "Perhaps you did not follow."

"The world is round," he said, "and ours is small."

She was staring through the doorway and the door of a car slammed like a shot in the deafening beat of the rain. She got up so quickly that her drink went spinning and the glass crashed as she moved between the pools of amber light. A man came through the doorway taking off his chauffeur's cap and she halted, waiting while he paid the barman; then she walked out slowly, even across the pavement with the flood water rushing against her shoes. The chauffeur ran past her to open the door of the Mercedes and she got in and drove off.

Rayner was in the doorway and read the number of the white station-wagon as it followed the coupé. He wrote it down and from memory also wrote the number of the Mercedes.

Going back to the table he sat as he had sat before. One of the barmen had wiped away the spilled drink and was picking up the glass fragments, their tinkling music making it seem as if he were touching some instrument in the shadows along the floor.

When he could no longer smell the scent she had worn, he went out and began walking back to the hotel under the black clouds of the trees, his shoes pushing against the water.

He found Willis, the airline's security man, sending a letter from the porter's desk at the hotel. The porter licked the stamp, which was a new issue with the face of President Ycaza on it.

Willis said in Spanish: "You are lucky to have such a man as the president to lead your country."

"Very lucky, señor." He brought his fist down on the stamp to stick it securely.

"Hallo, Willis," Rayner said.

The security man looked at his drenched suit and gave a lop-sided smile. "Forget your umbrella?" They shook hands. Willis was tall and thin and stooping, with small eyes high in his face; he seemed always to be peering over an unseen wall, undecided if he should climb it and take a closer look. His mackintosh had only a few large spots of rain on it; he must have come here by taxi from the seaplane jetty.

"Let's have a drink," Rayner said; and they sat under the light in a corner of the lounge. Willis gave him a letter for him to read. It was from the chairman.

From all accounts you have done extremely well down there, and we have decided – as you see – to send Willis to take over from you. Please return by the next convenient flight. I shall look forward to offering my sincere thanks to you for your good work in what I know to be the most trying conditions.

It seemed quite natural. He had been taken off his normal duties – which he enjoyed – at London Airport, to begin what

32

might have been a goose chase during the hot season in a town on the Equator in a country he was known generally to detest. A few days ago he would have waved this letter in the air and packed his bags with a will.

Even the expressed gratitude in the letter was not out of the way: it was Gates himself who had persuaded him to come out here.

"You're taking over from me," he said to Willis. "You obviously know that."

"Yes. You don't seem happy." Willis had been peering over the top of his wall at him.

"I'm a bit wet." He left the letter on the table. "If you don't mind I'll go and wring myself out."

It gave him fifteen minutes to think, while he showered and put on dry clothes. Willis was studying the big map on the wall when he came down the stairs.

"Is that the place?" Willis asked, his long pale finger on the map.

"Yes. Ventura's Bar."

"And where is the place where Marsh set out for his fishing?" He didn't mention the name of El Angelo because the hotel porter was just through the alcove.

"Here."

"Good. Where can we talk?"

"In here if we're careful."

"Good." They sat down again and Rayner found himself disliking the man's professional attitude and his intonation: "'Is this where the pain is? Good." He might lose some of his calm when he had to go reeling up those steps to Ventura's in to-morrow's sun.

Willis spoke very quietly, bending his long body across the table towards him. "They didn't put it in writing but I am to ask you on their behalf to divulge nothing – absolutely nothing – of this situation to anyone – anyone." A wintry smile. " 'Top secret.' "

"Have the Press got a smell of it yet?"

"Er, no. Absolutely nothing to anyone. Gates's words. Now you'll be wanting to get away from all this." He looked at the shuttered windows where the rain was bouncing through the slats and on to the glass. "Though I must say it was much the same in London when I left. Will you please give me all that you have?"

Rayner astonished himself by doing an odd thing. He told Willis about Ventura and the attempt to bribe him, and about the woman he had seen crossing the pavement in the Avenida del Mar four days ago. He did not tell him of the scene in the restaurant-bar of an hour before.

It was Lindstrom they wanted.

"You say you have the number of the Mercedes."

Rayner gave it to him. He did not mention that he had seen the coupé going along the peninsular strip-road.

It would depend on Gates's reply to the cable he was going to send. Until it came, Willis could do his own ferreting. He was a most able man.

"What are your conclusions, Mr. Rayner? They'd be valuable to me of course."

There had been no need to add that. Willis and Gates were being very nice to their good Mr. Rayner.

"I'm pretty certain Ventura knows where Lindstrom is. I think he would have told Lindstrom about my interest, following Marsh's. It's unlikely that Lindstrom has shown up at Ventura's Bar since Marsh saw him – or will show up there again. I'm not sure about a man called Luis. He has a bad scar right across his forehead and only one arm. His son, Pepito, is still in prison after being caught with a bunch of students trying to blow up the railway here. Luis is very bitter about that." He looked around idly. "The big cheese doesn't seem to be awfully liked, at least in this place."

"No." Willis thumped the table as if sticking down a postage stamp.

When Rayner had told him all he could, omitting only the scene in the La Ronda, he got up. "I suppose it wouldn't bother you if I stayed down here for a while on this job?"

Willis peered at him with his small clear eyes. "I should be delighted."

Rayner went to send his cable. Obviously Willis was relying on London's authority to pull him out of Puerto Fuego, and could afford to express his "delight."

There was nothing Rayner could put his finger on to justify his feeling that he was being recalled before he found out too much. Gates's letter had been natural; Willis's two little spoken courtesies might simply be a sign of a good liver or of his relief at a change of scene from Singapore to Aguador.

He cabled: *Request permission to stay few days. Feel urge to follow through.* The first copy he had written on the form had said: *Touch of sand-fly fever*, as the excuse to stay; but he changed it, to find out how determined they were that he shouldn't do any following through.

After the cable had been sent off he almost went back and told Willis about the scene in the La Ronda, because this inquiry would after all affect some thousand people if any further progress were made public. But there was a doubt in his mind, too appalling to consider very deeply at this stage. He would wait for the answering cable from London.

It reached him at the hotel before midnight, when the rain had eased and the head of the volcano was visible again through the haze, as a distant blood-red stain on the dark sky.

Please return immediately.

However difficult it was going to be, he knew now that he would stay.

CHAPTER SIX

Two male swordfish leapt and flashed in the noon heat, fighting to the death in the middle of the harbour water; the female was out of sight. They ripped through the slack surface, slashing it and bringing up white water, looking from this distance like two knives ripping at an eiderdown.

The sun reached its zenith and the shadows ceased, except beneath the horizontal planes of the trees and awnings. Near the drift of volcanic ash that the rainwaters had piled against the jetty wall last night, Willis stood shadowless, thin and still as a stork, watching the group of hotel and casino and brothel touts who waited for the seaplane tender.

All of these touts – Indian, Negro, mestizo, mulatto, creole, Spanish – would be bribable; Willis was looking for the most intelligent among them. He would learn more from a tout than from any other source, on his arrival in a strange town. This was probably his thousandth arrival in a strange town, and he was going through the routine of picking an informant while thinking of something else.

He was thinking about Rayner, who had upset him acutely. It was not to be countenanced that Rayner should remain in Puerto Fuego. He was needed back in London. The man's efficiency and devotion to duty was well known in T.O.A. Further, his job was nothing to do with the security of the airline. Moreover, Willis deplored his obstinate decision to prolong his stay. The chairman had told him:

"Rayner has done a good job down there, but we're recalling him for two reasons: he's found out enough to warrant your taking over, so that he can get back to his own work; and it may be that we shall have to keep a very still tongue in our heads, the further you go into this thing. You appreciate the need for discretion, and he doesn't – naturally. Please be sure to tell him from me that he is to divulge absolutely nothing to anyone. This airline has taken quite a few knocks with the Skyliner accidents, and competition is more intense than ever before. We don't want any leaks on this case before we can present the sum of the facts to the Air Ministry – if indeed we feel it expedient in the interests of all concerned."

Taking the few basic words from that rigmarole of chosen clichés, Willis had got the point. It was his job to report his findings to Transocean and leave them to take whatever action was indicated. But Rayner might not see that. He could make things very awkward for everybody.

Finally, Willis always preferred working alone except for reference to Interpol and the T.O.A. airport bureaux for information. Rayner would get in his way. It was not to be countenanced.

He moved with short deliberate steps along the burning stones of the jetty towards the Indian tout with the clean shirt and the neat haircut.

The water in the middle of the harbour was still, save where the dorsal fin of the first shark came cutting through it towards the dead swordfish.

The fisheries' truck went bumping on to the beach road low on its springs with the dead weight of the catch. El Angelo was driving his boy back to the boat with a gesture worthy of the wrath of God; for they must swab it clean and stow the gear ready for the next voyage, even now when the noon sun beat at the sand that it had pulverised from solid rock throughout the million noons before.

Hiamo ran into the sea and out again to cool his body, even though El Angelo was bearing down on him and though there was often a blue shark couched in the roll of a wave within its own length from the shore, on the watch for stale bait and entrails cast from a boat. He came back shedding the water-pearls as he ran, exhilarated by the cool plunge and his own daring.

Rayner came on towards the boat and spoke in Spanish to the huge bearded man, who replied: "We will talk in a little while. Wait in my house where there is shade."

Rayner went up the hot sand to the shack, which was built of wood and adobe and had one big room festooned with nets and cork floats, and no other room. He knew that El Angelo meant "house" to mean less a building of many rooms than his own abode upon earth and probably that of his father, of his own birth and perhaps, one day, of his death.

There was shade, but the sun's heat fell straight from the

centre of the sky in this, the middle of day; and he had to breathe consciously, dragging the heavy air into his lungs and pressing it out. He had come here to find the Indian boy, Hiamo, after a line of inquiry that had begun at Ventura's Bar on the day when he had tried to bribe its owner. Ventura – Luis – Pepito, son of Luis – the students who had tried to blow up the *ferrocarril* – among them the boy Hiawatha Moses.

He would like to know more about Luis, whose other name he had learned was Puyo. The boy might help him.

He had said to Willis at the hotel this morning: "I'll be here in the town for a bit longer, if you need me."

"What bad luck. I know how you hate this country."

Willis had turned away, avoiding the direct question and showing no surprise. Rayner had left the hotel before him and intended to keep out of his way. If he were going to dig out any more of the truth before Willis got to it, he would have to work hard.

Standing here in El Angelo's house he wondered if he were wasting time. It would be more useful to find Luis Puyo and talk to him and listen for the slightest clues; but he might cross paths with Willis, and there were two reasons why he should not. One of them was that Willis was a professional and would want to work alone.

He looked at the big chart that stretched across the wall of El Angelo's shack. It was not printed, but had been made painstakingly by hand: probably El Angelo's. The scale was indicated in the corner, but indecipherably; it looked about one inch to the mile. The coastline had been drawn in roughly except where there were creeks and moorings of special interest to a fisherman; it was the ocean that was more precisely marked, and by the difference in these markings – some in ink, some in pencil, the size of the figures varying – it was clear that the chart had been drawn up by small degrees over perhaps many years. It was probably a design embodying the whole sum of El Angelo's experience at sea in these waters: a full day's voyage, perhaps involving an encounter with a storm or the loss of tackle, had become a tiny figure on this chart – the result of a sounding made or a current crossed.

A great part of the chart was stained where torrential rain had soaked from the roof of the shack; the whole of its canvas was fly-marked; many of the references were indistinct; but Rayner knew that the chart might well be the most valuable possession of El Angelo, even before his boat. A boat was built and bought more easily than a map such as this was made. This was his house, but there was his home: the ocean.

He noticed the tiny cross by chance. In a dozen places were the marks of sunken wrecks: an inked ring with a few words in Spanish to define it – *Broken timber 50 fathoms, maybe La Firenza, 1908 . . . Plumb fouled and winch-gear salvaged, marking Collet & Brown, Hull. Unknown . . .* Most of the wrecks were grouped near the lines denoting a long reef north-south and parallel with the coast some thirty miles out. Beyond the reef was deep water with soundings of two hundred fathoms and more, showing El Angelo to be no mean oceanographer; and beyond the deep water ran a submerged plateau at an average depth of sixty-five fathoms.

The small vertical cross was just inside the area of the plateau, some fifty sea-miles almost due west of Puerto Fuego.

"Now we will talk," El Angelo said as he came into the shack. He swung a coil of line from his shoulder and hung it from the rack on the wall. "You are not Spanish, yet you speak the tongue well. How is that?"

"It's not so elegant as yours, I'm afraid." El Angelo's phrasing was almost biblical, and it had none of the patois about it. Rayner moved away from the chart and added: "I thought of doing some fishing." To have said: "I am here to do some fishing" might have been a mistake, because Ventura knew he had been here for over a month already and had never stepped into a boat. Ventura – Puyo – Pepito – Hiamo – El Angelo. . . . You never spoke to one man but to many.

El Angelo moved towards him from the rack on the wall and stood with his huge arms folded, so that within seconds the sweat gathered where they joined, and formed trickles over leather-brown skin. "I had a man here not long ago, another Englishman, with the name of Marje. Do you know him?"

"What name?"

"Marje."

"No, I don't know him."

He felt the urge to turn and look again at the chart; but he resisted. What would Willis have done about that small vertical cross? Something pretty smooth. Willis was a professional.

"Have you fished before?" the Spaniard asked. "The big ones?"

"No." Useless to lie, because once in the boat his ignorance would show.

"Why do you want to fish?" The splendid beard was glis-

38

tening with the sweat that ran from his temples.

"Why do men climb mountains?"

"To master them."

"Then . . ." Rayner shrugged.

"You already know something of the shark," El Angelo said, as if impressed. "You know that if you do not master him, he might master you. It is the same with the bulls."

"Less dangerous, I'd say."

"You wish me to take you in my boat for shark?"

"Yes."

"Then you must understand that there are dangers out there. I always insist upon this: that my guest knows of the danger. To-morrow, you will see; but you must first be told in words."

"I appreciate the warning." He turned and looked at the chart. "How far from land will we be going?"

"We shall run where the fish run. It may be anywhere. At dawn my boat will be ready. Is that a good hour for you?"

"Perfect." He turned away from the chart, because El Angelo was not inclined to refer to it. If they were going "anywhere," it could not be indicated on a chart except by a sweep of the hand.

"I ask one hundred pesos for the day," El Angelo said. "We return at sundown." He looked at Rayner critically. "Or before, if you wish."

"As soon as the catch is too heavy for the boat."

By the mere unfolding of his arms and the slightest turn of his great body, the host indicated that the time had come for the guest to leave; and Rayner was almost felled by the force of the sun as he went out into it and walked up to the beach road.

It was impossible to think, in the open; later he would try to devise some way of getting El Angelo to talk. There would be no hope of persuading him to set his course due west of this shore and hold it for fifty miles. Whatever he had found out there he had marked on the chart with a cross for his own private reference, instead of an inked ring.

Once during the late afternoon Rayner caught sight of Willis, coming away from the town offices of Transportes Aéreos Naciónales in the Avenida del Mar. He walked with short purposeful steps to the other side of the road, his new Panama hat bobbing absurdly on his long thin body. If he had seen Rayner he gave no sign.

Under a tepid shower at the hotel, Rayner faced the question: was he determined to stay in Puerto because he had tasted the savour of this chase that would soon grow to unknown proportions, or because he had gone into the La Ronda from the rain to stand for an hour watching her before they even spoke? Giselle . . . even her name was beautiful.

But the idea was absurd, and he must dismiss the nagging reminder that it had been last night, when he had come up to this room and had stood for a while at the open window to look across the shore of this hated country, that he had thought for the first time that the head of Catachunga, burning in the black sky, looked beautiful.

CHAPTER SEVEN

SIX miles off shore there was a dead calm sea. When the sound of the engine stopped, the silence was so deep that the ear was benumbed. The long wake of the boat widened across the water, half-seen through the heat-haze.

El Angelo had spoken only once on the way out, when Rayner had asked him the name of the island southwards.

"It is the Isla de la Paz."

A barren-looking rock the shape of a man's hand lying on the sea. Rayner had heard of it, but had never been close to it.

"How many are there on the island?"

"A thousand souls."

In a newspaper yesterday he had seen the report of President Ycaza's promise to investigate the conditions of the island, because a month ago there had been rioting among the convicts and fifteen guards had been killed, and the news had reached the mainland. To-day, passing within a mile of the rock, Rayner and El Angelo and Hiawatha Moses had heard nothing of any disturbance there. It had again become – as was its name – the Island of Peace.

Hiamo, crouched on the foredeck of the boat, was watching the water near the red knot of entrails that had been thrown overboard a minute ago. They had stood off three miles from shore, earlier, sometimes sending the boat in a slow circle with the lure trailing; but apart from a group of flying-fish there had been nothing to be seen: the ocean was silent, and inert, and dead.

Rayner had not realised how difficult it would be to talk with El Angelo. When the man was not preparing the lines and setting the boat, he was gazing across the water as immobile as a great carved figurehead; to call a word to him

40

would be like throwing a stone at a statue. Nor did the boy speak, even though he knew the Englishman understood Spanish; he crouched silently, in awe of the presence of his captain.

Looking over the stern, Rayner saw that the water was luminously clear, as if the white heat of the sky had drained to the ocean bed. Nothing moved in the depths.

Sometimes a ripple slapped below the bows; sometimes it was so quiet that he could hear El Angelo breathing as he stood balanced on parted legs, his massive head turning as a hunting animal's will turn, the senses tuned to catch a hint of the prey. Once during this hour an aircraft crossed the sky invisibly, its high faint sound like that of an insect caught in an unseen web.

The sea was still. The sun pressed down on it. The boat was becalmed.

"Ahead of the lure," El Angelo said, and Hiamo moved and shielded his eyes with a hand as Rayner moved too, coming for'ard, aware of his ignorance, not even knowing whether he should stay still and make no sound or join the other two on the foredeck.

He was half-way there when the water darkened within feet of the starboard side and he saw the length of a shark go sliding past below the surface and with the fin submerged. It was half as long as the boat. The air whined as El Angelo cast a line with a steel grapple-hook bigger than his fist and the white water came up as the bait struck surface and dyed the water red.

"Take it!" El Angelo called to him and threw him a loose loop of the rope. "Brace your legs by the hatch and stand hard when he comes."

The boy was spreading the line free and scrambling aft for the six-foot gaff, and as Rayner lodged himself against the hatchway he saw a great flurry on the surface ahead of the boat where a pack was moving in to worry the lure. The water was cut with fins and now the white underbellies flashed just below surface as the fish began turning for the kill. The knotted lure of entrails, ripped from the catch of the day before, had been taken below by the first shark, and the deeper water was turning grey with the last of the blood from it – then Rayner's line went taut and he was jerked against the foredeck timbers with a force that brought a grunt to his throat as El Angelo called to him:

"Let him take it – give him a run!"

A second line had gone over the side and the boy leapt clear

41

as the hunk of bait was taken by a crescent jaw before it struck water as a fish broke surface in a curving length of metal-blue hide and tightened the line until it quivered. With two shark running and a pack at the loose bait the sea was churned into spume, and Rayner's line, tautening as the great fish carried the hook to the depths, shivered like a bowstring as one of them fouled it head-on –

"Give slack! Let him have room!"

El Angelo was hauling in, letting his shark run and then bringing a loop of line aboard and then another and a third, until the long dark shape neared the surface ahead of the bows and the water began breaking up as the tail thrashed. Rayner was still fighting his fish when Hiamo gave the harpoon-gaff to his master and El Angelo took it and hurled and struck and took a turn with his line round a stanchion while he and the boy waited for a chance of giving the death-stroke. For a moment the fish lay on the surface like a floating torpedo, and the gaff went into the eye, burying deep.

They used the winch-arm, slinging it out from the foremast and hauling on the harpoon-rope. Rayner stood clear with slack on his line as El Angelo's shark came inboard, the sun flashing along its great length and the water streaming gold from the blue body. The boat's timber creaked as the weight dropped across the foredeck and it was then that the tail of the shark lashed in its death-throes, skinning Rayner's arm from wrist to shoulder. Staggering against the mainmast from the blow, he took up the slack in his line and began hauling, blinded by the glare of the sun on the water but keeping the line taut as his fish ran curving and back and curving until they could see it just below surface, the white underbelly uppermost, a yard from the boat.

Two sharks came in to attack the wounded blue before they could lift it clear with the winch and El Angelo began cursing them in a long withering bellow of hate because this was what he could not stand – their cannibalism, their blind voracious urge to eat one another alive even while they fought to the death with their common enemy, man.

Rayner, braced against the side of the boat with sweat stinging his eyes and the glare blinding them, already understood how it was that the man could curse the fish: there was a personal tie between man and fish that had nothing to do with the rope that joined them as the issue was fought out on the desert sea. Twice he almost gave in and let the line run slack; but an odd thing stopped him: the feeling that he would shame himself in the eyes of the enemy – not El Angelo's nor the boy's but in the eyes of the beast who fought him back with a strength he had never imagined.

He hauled in another yard of line and then his right foot slipped on the slime in the bottom of the boat and he went pitching across one of the mast-stays, grazing his head on the cable as El Angelo's arm came swinging to clamp round his chest and stop him. The boy was shouting something and leaping to the foredeck with a gaff, keeping clear of the jaws of El Angelo's shark because a shark is not dead until it stinks – and Puyo could tell you that, Puyo the one-arm.

Rayner could not see what was happening but he could feel the force of the taut line, and when it went slack he hauled in again, falling to the bottom of the boat as El Angelo left him to grab a harpoon. They were shouting together, he and the boy, and there was a rattle of the winchblock, and the line went slack for the last time.

El Angelo called to him, telling him to keep clear, as the shark swung over the side with its tail sending up a fan of water that fell across the boat as if it had struck a wave. The fish landed athwart the foredeck alongside the first, and Hiamo was clubbing it with a frenzied rain of blows born of fear. El Angelo drew him away. "You will spoil the skin!" He used the gaff, twice, strongly, and came to look at Rayner. "Now we will go home," he said.

Blood was already stiffening in the direct heat of the sun on his temple, where he had grazed against the mast-stay; and his arm was crimson along its whole length.

El Angelo fetched a bottle of cognac and held his hand so that he could not move his arm, and shook the bottle so that a gold cascade drenched the wound; and somehow he managed not to cry out.

"The skin of the shark is like a rasp," the Spaniard said, "but it is clean. It is not like a bite. Now we will go home."

Now that the spirit was stinging less, Rayner could say: "With only two fish? We're staying out here."

El Angelo called to the boy to start the engine, and began hauling in the loose rope of the lure.

"There is no need for us to go," Rayner said. "I am just beginning to enjoy myself!"

"We go."

"I have paid one hundred pesos for the day and we have another four hours before sundown!"

El Angelo was freeing the helm. "There will be no fee."

"I shall insist on paying!"

"I shall not accept."

The boat was already under way, and the pack of shark dispersed, to close in again as the wake spread across the water.

"If we go home now, El Angelo, I will not come out in your boat to-morrow!"

"You will not come out in any boat for three days, to fish for shark. In the morning you will remember my words."

Rayner was angry, because the hundred pesos would make a hole in the funds he had brought with him for his expenses; and the company would not send him more, now that he had been recalled. For these hundred pesos he should be able to fight with another shark and handle it more cleanly; and he would have longer time to talk with El Angelo, in the hope of steering the conversation into useful channels.

"I am very angry," he said in emphatic Spanish.

"It is because you are in pain." The boat had been given her course and was running through the glassy surface at three-quarter speed.

"I am not in pain!"

"Then you are not human."

Rayner was about to prolong the argument when his stomach reacted to the struggle with the shark-line in the open sun and to the burning agony of the brandy splashing his wound. He moved aft in awkward lunges and managed to reach the stern where they could not see him.

In an hour the shoreline became visible as a strip of ochre and white. He sat now under the awning, consoling himself by thinking of the piece of string in his pocket.

It was the measure of the day's progress. Soon after dawn, when the three of them had gone down the beach to the boat, he had told El Angelo that he had left his cigarette-lighter in his jacket, which he had deliberately left in the shack. Hurrying back for it, he was alone there for long enough to take a crude measurement from the chart on the wall. The harbour of Puerto Fuego was marked, also the jetty that broke the coastline just this side of Casano, a fishing village to the south.

Now the string had three knots in it: one for Puerto, one for Casano, and one for the small vertical cross. He could find the exact distance of the jetty from the harbour on any map and deduce the scale of the chart. The bearing of the cross from Puerto Fuego was west by roughly ten degrees south.

He had been angry just now with El Angelo because of his conscience. He had not liked deceiving his absent host in his own house, with the piece of string.

The doctor had a small adobe house to the south of the town between the beach and a patch of swampland; the place was buried in a mass of vegetation, completely shaded by the silken light-green leaves of banana palms; and Rayner thought that whoever had built the house must have hewn his way to the site with a hatchet.

El Angelo had done a clever thing: he had sent Hiamo to direct the Englishman to the doctor's house, and when Rayner was alone with the boy he had immediately offered him ten pesos to forget the whole thing; but Hiamo had simply said that *el capitán* would beat him if he found out that he had not obeyed him; so Rayner had been obliged to go.

Van Keerls was a thin and quietly-moving man with the longest fingers he had ever seen: his hands opened and shut like a pair of pale fans as he talked. His light blue eyes had pain in them, perhaps the memory of other people's. The room where he treated the arm was tiny and immaculate, a hygienic oasis in the midst of the partly rotting vegetation that writhed even against the windows and gave a pale green tinge to the white walls and enamel cabinets.

The doctor had seemingly been at work when Rayner had arrived, for he wore a white cotton smock buttoned at the neck.

"Who was the boy that brought you?" His English had no trace of an accent; it was drawling, and his hands moved quicker than his tongue.

"His name's Hiamo."

"El Angelo's boy?"

"Yes."

"What did this? Shark?"

A lot of the boracic spilled on to the floor and he plugged in a miniature vacuum-cleaner, swishing it about their feet as they talked above the whirring noise. Rayner was astonished to see no sweat on the man's face when he straightened up. He moved quietly but with deftness and controlled energy, and the tiny clinic was like a bakehouse.

"I find El Angelo too obstinate to get along with," he told van Keerls. "I wanted to stay out there fishing, and there was certainly no need to come here wasting your time, but the boy said he'd get beaten if he didn't deliver me."

Perhaps the doctor would talk about El Angelo. It would be a beginning.

"Lower your slacks and keep still," van Keerls told him. He was squirting a jet of liquid out of a hypodermic syringe into a basin, trying to clear an air bubble.

45

"What's that for?"

"The priming-dose. You'll have three more, daily. Slacks, please."

The needle was sharp and Rayner hardly felt it. "I'm sure this is quite – "

"Quiet please. Keep still."

When the doctor took away the syringe, he pulled up his trousers. "Look, if half a day's shark-fishing means – "

"It's to stop bugs getting in. Your arm's a fairground for them. This isn't England, you know." He began wrapping sterile lint round and round the arm, which now looked like strawberry jam covered in icing sugar. Then he dressed the wound on the temple. Obviously he wasn't going to talk about El Angelo. "I won't put a bandage right round the head, though I ought to. You'd only rip it off the minute you've left here."

He gave him a small round box of powder. "Cover the graze with this stuff last thing to-night. You sleep under a net?"

"Yes."

"Make sure there are no holes in it." He wrote something on a sheet of headed paper. "Take this to the chemist in the Plaza Pasteza – his name's Lucillo – to-morrow morning. It's for the next shot. Don't go anywhere else – the needles in this town are so blunt they have to take a run at you, but Lucillo's all right."

"How did you know my name?" It was on the prescription.

"You told me when you came in – "

"I don't remember – "

"You were groggier than you think." His smile was clean and gentle. It was one man's word against another's and he had taken the initiative with a direct lie, and knew it.

"How much do I owe you, Dr. van Keerls?" But it didn't work – van Keerls would know that it could only have been El Angelo who had told him his name when he had sent him here.

They went through into the shadowy hall of the house, where small banana palms had invaded the place, in flower-pots. What did the man have – agoraphobia?

The question about the fee had been ignored, and Rayner repeated it.

"Talk about that later," the doctor said, holding the door open.

"But if I'm getting the rest of the shots from the chemist – "

"Oh, you'll be back here." Van Keerls gazed blandly into

46

his private jungle. "But if you weren't just as obstinate as El Angelo I'd give you a word of advice."

Rayner went down to the cool fibrous pathway, for a moment enjoying the pleasure of ignoring the offer. But it might be useful: he was out for any crumb of information he could get.

"I'm sure it would be well meant," he said as politely as he could.

"Oh yes. The hot season in Puerto is most unhealthy for a European." The gentle smile was on the mouth but the eyes were serious. "Look after that arm, now." He shut the door quietly.

CHAPTER EIGHT

THE map that Willis had been looking at on the wall of the hotel was accurate enough in detail to give Rayner a fix. Using the piece of string with its three knots he arrived at a rough position fifty miles from the coastline, ten degrees south of west. Longitude 83° by Latitude 2°.

He sat down at the writing-desk in the lounge. All day he had toyed with the problem of what to put in his letter to Transocean. A plea of sand-fly fever was no good because it would have put him to bed if not into a hospital, and Willis would spoil that story because Rayner had seen the man once in the town and it was a fair bet that Willis had seen him too. He was taller. Simply to report "progress" would not satisfy Gates.

There was only one way of impressing him: by writing what he believed to be the truth; so he composed a respectful letter around the one sentence that mattered:

The sunken aircraft has been discovered at a depth of 65 fathoms.

He gave the approximate position and bearing. It was accurate enough to warrant sending divers down.

Over his first Pernod of the day he watched the light turning gold against the walls of the houses along the curve of the Avenida. The scene, if you could close your ears to the rising hum of the mosquitoes and ignore the constant creep of sweat under your clothes, was beautiful. The dying away of the day among the avenues of trees and the elegant Spanish-colonial buildings brought the sense of something passing for ever, more significant than just another day.

Perhaps it was that the events of this day, as they concerned him personally and so many other people, had shadows even longer than those of the trees down there. He had met a complete stranger who knew his name and had warned him to leave the town, and had written a letter that would arrive in the beautifully-appointed office of T.O.A.'s chairman with the force of a bomb.

Five minutes later when he finished his drink it was dark outside and the hotel lights had come on.

It took him half an hour to shower and dry himself, one-handed, and by that time he was sweating again. There was a warm tingling sensation along his arm, not unpleasant; but his head throbbed unless he moved slowly. About eight o'clock when the town was in full swing he walked the length of the Avenida, slowly in the cooling air below the trees, and tried to answer some of the questions.

The matter of Dr. van Keerls was straightforward. As a doctor, he would have the confidence of everybody who went there for treatment; and casualties in the fishing quarter of the town were frequent. The fact that the Englishman had booked a trip with El Angelo yesterday would have been common knowledge within hours. The fact that he had shown his hand to Ventura (and regretted it ever since) had marked him down. Ventura – Puyo – El Angelo – and now van Keerls: the grape-vine was endless. If El Angelo knew where the Skyliner lay and was interested enough to keep it secret, he probably knew where Lindstrom was, and meant to keep that secret too.

Any one of a dozen people could have told van Keerls: "We don't want that *Inglés* here. Before anything happens to him, maybe you could warn him, so that he goes."

Better than a shot from the dark; he was grateful to them for that much. But their patience would not last, once they saw that he was staying.

The question of why anyone should want to draw this veil over the missing aircraft was less easy.

The one clue was his random shot that had been right on target, when he had told Giselle Vidal: "I'm leaving this country soon." She had asked: "How?"

If she were trapped here, so might Lindstrom be.

Nor was the mystery confined to the survivors. Ventura would not talk. El Angelo had found the wreck of the plane and had carefully made a vertical cross – the shape of an air-craft – instead of an inked ring. Van Keerls had told Rayner to leave the country.

The exclusive club had extended its membership; it was not limited to survivors only.

A group of Spanish students passed him, hurrying and

laughing under the lights with the night and the town and the whole world before them; and as one of them bumped against his left arm he felt the sweat break in beads from his face, and he remembered El Angelo's words: "You will not come out in any boat for three days." Even walking along a pavement looked like proving painful.

He was making slowly for the La Ronda, not in any hope of seeing the woman there (she might never go there again, just as Lindstrom had probably never gone to Ventura's after Marsh had recognised him), but to question the waiters. One of them had shrugged when he had asked him her name, but their price might be lower than Ventura's.

He did not, for a moment, think twice about the ivory-white station-wagon parked under the trees a few yards this side of the restaurant. When its colour touched off his memory he looked at the registration plate. The car was empty.

He crossed the pavement. The La Ronda was as softly-lighted as before; the avenue outside was brighter. A boy dressed as a *novillero* was playing a guitar, picking unhurriedly and accurately at de Mudarra's "Romanesca" as if he loved it. The flamenco would come later when the people were less engrossed in the food. The place was more than half full but there was a lot of space between the tables. He drank a Pernod at the bar, keeping in the deep shadow between two of the enormous wine-casks that were part of the décor; from there he began searching the room, and it was two or three minutes before he saw her, at a table against the far wall under one of the amber lamps.

He did not recognise the man with her. They must have been here some time, because there was a piled pannier of fruit on the table. All he could see from here was that the man was Spanish or white South American. Her face looked pale and she had done her hair into a chignon.

He waited until a party of people came in and passed across the room; then he followed, so that he would have longer to study the two at the table before they singled him out. Even a few words to them might give him some new clues, and he would make the excuse of mistaken identity in the dim lighting.

He was at the table before the man looked up and saw him. To Rayner he was a complete stranger; nor did it seem that the man had ever seen him before. He looked at the girl and saw a chain-reaction of expression in her wide amethyst eyes: recognition, fear, then shock. Her head had moved slightly and she was now looking past him, at something behind. It was this that had shocked her.

He heard a voice, addressing him in Spanish. At the same time a hand touched his arm. He turned.

"You are visiting this country, señor?"

There were three of them: a major of police and two lieutenants, in full uniform with holstered revolvers.

"Yes," Rayner said.

"We are checking passports."

"My passport is at my hotel, *Comandante*."

"We have to see it, señor."

Rayner disliked the sight of policemen with guns; it was a sign of weak law. "Very well. It's not far. The Miraflores."

The major led the way between the tables. The two *lugartenientes* brought up the rear. A hush had come upon the room again and the guitar seemed out of tune.

Rayner was worried on three counts. He had lost the chance of learning more of the woman. He was being summarily taken in charge during what was pretended to be a routine check. Routine passport checks were not carried out by a police party wholly of officer-status: unless they were looking for someone special. And the question nagged: who had followed him here?

He got into the police car and the doors were slammed.

CHAPTER NINE

FIVE minutes after reaching the hotel, Rayner knew that he was in a trap.

In the foyer the major had asked for his room number and given it to the secretary, who handed over the key. Rayner and the three-man escort had then climbed the one flight of stairs to the room. Before the door had been unlocked and opened, the manager of the hotel joined them, for a reason he did not explain.

"There is no difficulty, I hope, Señor Rayner?" He was a tiny, darting man whose eyes were always looking for something awkward round the corner. Perhaps he had been obliged to usher too many tight-lipped husbands into too many single rooms despite a generous tip beforehand from *la señora*.

"None at all."

"We are merely checking passports," said the *comandante*. They went into the room, the manager too.

Under the intent surveillance of the four of them, Rayner unlocked the smaller of his cases with the distinct feeling that

50

the passport was no longer there. His careful search of the other two cases was conducted in brooding silence.

The copy of *Newsweek* was nicely evident on top of the contents of the third case. The cover picture showed President José Maria Ycaza making one of his more forceful speeches in the Plaza Grande of San Domingo, with a phantom photograph of Adolph Hitler behind him. No caption was really necessary.

"Your passport is not here, señor?"

"No." Rayner straightened up. "It has been stolen." He looked at the manager, whose expression of innocence was perfect, so practised had it become in the presence of tight-lipped husbands. Rayner said to the major of police: "Perhaps you would be good enough to take down the particulars of the theft."

"It should be reported at the bureau in Calle Charco."

Rayner would have been less difficult if only the major had had the decency to pretend he was as innocent as the little manager; but his bland, even bored expression made it obvious that he was carrying out a planned operation and would be glad when it was over so that he could do something more interesting.

"*Comandante*, you are an officer of police on duty, and a crime has been discovered in your presence. It is required of you to record the details and make your report."

So indifferently as to be inoffensive, the major ignored this and took the copy of *Newsweek* from the third case and spent the requisite number of seconds studying the cover picture as if he had never seen it before.

"Is this your magazine, señor?"

"No."

"What is it doing among your luggage?"

"It was put there."

"When?"

"When the passport was taken out."

"I regret, but we must now search these cases."

"Have you a warrant?"

"No. That would take a little time. Perhaps hours." He looked almost sympathetically at the Englishman. Patent though the whole deception was, they had taken care that the major was not to produce a search-warrant on the spot. The copy of *Newsweek* was to be seen "by accident." The major was even using his own initiative: he could probably obtain a warrant from the bureau round the corner within fifteen minutes; but the night was warm and they were all getting bored.

He could see that the Englishman was not so stupid a stickler as to opt for a wait of "hours" under guard in a small hotel room.

"You may go ahead, *Comandante*." He lit a cigarette without offering the packet round. He had no friends here.

Perhaps to make a belated show that he was not party to any conspiracy, the *comandante* took the white silk gloves from his shoulder-strap, put them on, and searched the two smaller cases before bringing out the revolver from the big one. Rayner had felt its shape when he had looked for the passport just now, and had left the thing where it was in the hope that they would miss it. A thin hope: they would not be likely to miss what they had put there themselves.

"Is this your revolver, señor?"

"No." (How did the formula go?)

"What is it doing among your luggage?" (That's right.) "It was put there." To save the farcical repetition he added: "When the passport was taken out."

The major was checking the gun. The chamber was empty.

"Have you a licence for this firearm, señor?"

"Don't be bloody silly," Rayner began in English without thinking.

"Señor?"

"Since it is not my firearm," he answered in elegant Spanish, "it is hardly likely that I would possess a licence for it." They were really taking a lot of trouble now: pretending to expect that the Englishman might be tricked into saying: "Yes, it must have been taken together with the passport."

"Unless there's anything more, *Comandante*, I will now telephone my consul." He did not think there would be anything more: no passport, the anti-Ycaza picture and the gun would be enough for their purposes.

"You will please accompany me, señor."

The attitude of the two lieutenants had become more correct and the major put his gloves back perfunctorily. They all wanted to go. The little manager, who should have been looking scandalised that one of his guests had turned out to be the underground agent of subversive elements against the State, was looking relieved. Rayner had an urge to lift him up and sit him on top of the wardrobe but one of the *lugartenientes* would be bound to take him down again. The major was in any case saying to him: "Please make out the señor's bill. He is now leaving."

They were half an hour in the lounge because there had been three items in the bill that Rayner had challenged on principle: a bottle of champagne, a box of Sumatran cigars, and a telephone call to New York. Imported French wine was prohibitive in price and the Aguadorean "champagne" was generally thought to be produced by cats; Sumatra cigars were easily mistaken for the product of the horse; and from this hotel it would take longer to telephone New York than Rayner had been at the place so far.

During this delay he was disappointed: Willis did not put in an appearance. Rayner kept watch for him while the manager sent for those members of the staff responsible for the errors. The police escort, now that they had their man, seemed quite prepared to sit beneath the ceiling-fans and wait; it was cooler here than in the street. But Willis did not show up.

If the police themselves had not been ordered to remove the passport and insert the copy of *Newsweek* and the revolver, then it could have been Willis acting either on his own initiative or under instructions from T.O.A. in London. Willis was a security man, versed in the tricks of those in the opposing team: dope-runners, arms-smugglers, bullion-thieves and stateless stowaways. Drastic though these means of getting rid of an unwanted party might seem by normal standards, to a man like Willis it would be no more than leaving a drawing-pin on someone's chair.

Gates might well have cabled: *Return P.R. to London immediately*. By this Willis would know that an ordinary recall sent direct to Paul Rayner was not expected to work, and that action on the spot was urgent with no holds barred.

Rayner disliked fighting with shadows. One can fight better if one can see the enemy. It could, in this case, be the police, or Willis, or any of the others: Ventura, Puyo, El Angelo, Dr. van Keerls, even Giselle Vidal. An anonymous word to the police from any of them would do the trick: *Englishman, Room 12 Hotel Miraflores, suspected political agent, should search luggage.*

Yet they had picked him up at the La   a. Yet again, it was not a routine passport check they   een making in there. They had known where to find him   it was a classic example of the tip-off.

The hotel bill was correct now and he paid it.

"What about my bags?"

The police major said his effects would be forwarded to the first-precinct bureau, which was where they were now taking him. Paul drove with them, thinking that this was how

a murderer must feel: the first bright chat with the polite
police; a second and more useful talk, the next day, with the
odd exhibit on view – and suddenly you were in their black
car with the doors shut, and you knew that they knew; and
the ride was short, and there was more comfort, as a last reminder of civilised living, in the seats of this mobile cell than
there would be in the one they were taking you to, with its
stone floor and small high window and the smell of the cage
about it.

It wasn't his *Newsweek* and it wasn't his gun. That made no
difference. This was a police state. This was their uniform:
white silk gloves and a holster at the hip.

They put him in a room at the first-precinct bureau with
a couple of young captains whose moustaches were beautifully
trimmed and whose dark hair was beautifully brushed. They
interrogated him with sickening courtesy, taking it in turns,
making little rushes at him like a pair of schoolgirls with their
first golden hamster, half delighted and half afraid. Then
Emmerson, the British consul, came in. They must have telephoned him.

"Rayner? Sorry to find you here. See what we can do. Have
a cigarette? These chaps been on at you? Ever known it so
bloody hot?" He added in peremptory Spanish to the two
nice captains – "Where is there a room with a fan?"

After a short delay, Rayner and the consul were ushered
into a bigger room with papers clipped in sheaves to the green
walls and furniture smelling of polish. One of the captains
stationed himself just inside the door with an expression of
sugar-plum apology and Emmerson said:

"I shall talk to Her Britannic Majesty's subject in private
at this stage." The captain went out, "*what* a rude man!"
written in every wobble before he could bear to shut the
door.

Rayner felt more cheerful. The British Consul in Puerto
Fuego obviously knew his stuff. Emmerson was a dead-faced
man with no time for the niceties and his only concession to
sentimentality was a frayed Stowe tie.

"There's nothing you want to tell me in private, Rayner?
If so, do it now. They'll be back in a minute. I took a chance on
that little flower not knowing the rules."

Rayner said rapidly; "I'm down here investigating something that some people want to keep dark. The police were
tipped-off to pick me up and search my things. My passport
was missing and someone had planted some anti-Ycaza mat-
erial and a small-bore revolver in one of the cases. Through-

out, I've had the impression that this is a planned operation to fix me right through the thorax with a pin."

The door opened and Emmerson did not even turn round. It was one of the lieutenants who had been part of the escort before they had arrived at the bureau. He took up his post by the door.

Rayner added in very fast slurred English with a strong cockney accent – "F'r'instance this cove 'ere was in the mob as what copped me at th' diner so if that was a common o' garden routine check they was on at, looks like I stopped it, don' it?"

"Right in the gob," said the consul. He looked at the single buff sheet of paper he had brought with him, frowning in the bad light over an indistinct paragraph; then he spun it round so that Rayner could read it. "This is a copy of the report just made out by Major Pareira. How's your Spanish?"

"Not bad."

The whole report was nothing more than a precise record of events from the moment when the major had addressed the "foreign subject" in the restaurant to the moment when they had driven him into the courtyard of the first-precinct bureau. The interrogation by the two young captains was not referred to: evidently he had been thrown to them for practice while the consul was sent for. No conversation between the major and himself was recorded; they would realise that he could easily contest every word, since no notes had been taken at the time. There was nothing loaded against the "subject" – no reference to "unco-operative attitudes" or "offers of resistance" or anything of that kind. They were relying on the simple mechanics of the matter: no passport; the Ycaza picture; the gun.

"Well?" Emmerson asked him.

"Yes, that's pretty much the picture. When do you want me to start my defence?"

"There is no defence." Emmerson took the report, folded it and put it back into his brief-case. His intelligent mud-brown eyes became fixed on Rayner's. "Now listen carefully, Rayner. I've checked your file at the consulate already. First thing I did when they phoned me. Nothing previously against you: good relations with the authorities here during your tour of duty in the capital: all that. How's your French?"

"*Pas mauvais. Mais doucement, je vous en prie.*"

"*Bon. Écoutez-moi.*" He went on slowly, as requested. "You can fight them, but you won't win. I am not a man who likes to say that. But you were right when you said you were a dead moth. Yes, this is a planned operation. I can pass you on to our ambassador in San Domingo right away, but he will tell you the same thing. It is your choice whether you see him or not. You have the right, of course, by international law. You – through him – can try to fight this all along the line, but you won't win, because it would go on for months and months, during which time you would of course be kept in detention. All quite comfortable: prison grub's not bad, reasonable facilities – letters in, letters out, ration of cigarettes, all that. Eventually we'd get you clear, because they can't *prove* it was your gun and your *Newsweek*, any more than you can prove they were planted in your luggage. But by the time you were cleared, they would have won; because your freedom would have been suspended in the meantime. That's all you'd be fighting them for, and you'd lose it piecemeal, day by day. Beginning from now. Don't interrupt and don't get angry. I know these things and you can repeat what I'm saying to the ambassador: I'll stand by every word. My personal duty is to help you to the utmost of my abilities and power. So I'm giving you my opinion of your situation. Now you'd better talk back before you break a vein. But keep it in French."

Rayner waited a moment, because a word said in anger might be regretted. Looking at Emmerson, he believed it was true: Emmerson wasn't a man who willingly dodged a fight. He could easily have turned on the suave reassuring routine expected of a consul, and passed the "subject" on to ambassadorial levels, together with the buck. In the middle of a corrupt situation it was good to talk to an honest man.

"You suggest I plead guilty?" was his first question.

"Yes."

"Then what?" In the words of some journalist, the firing-squad had been rattling for months in the courtyard of the Casa Roja, the barracks in San Domingo, after Ycaza's seizure of power. The president was holding his position only by continued terror methods more than two years later, and Rayner was under arrest at this minute by the same token. "Do they put me against the wall?"

Emmerson looked impatient. "If they had wanted you shot they would either have put a man behind a tree for you, or they would have put the gun in your baggage *plus* a dozen rounds *plus* a copy of some underground political pamphlet and maybe even a map of the country showing details like military camps and ammunition dumps. You are not as important as that. All they want is to stop your game, whatever that is – you say you're 'investigating' something. They can stop your game in two ways, short of murder. By keeping you in gaol, or by kicking you out of the country."

"If I plead guilty, they'll summarily deport me?"

"They would call it repatriation. These are the double-think boys."

"What's the exact charge?"

"Being in the country without passport or visa, possessing a firearm not registered with the aliens department, and being in possession of literature tending to incite opinions or acts against the security of the state: all that."

"What are they hoping I shall do?"

"They don't hope anything, Rayner. This little battle's already over without a shot fired. You start putting up a big defence case, and they put you quietly away while the show's running. You plead guilty, and they put you on a plane for London. London, mark you, not just anywhere over the frontier. Repatriation, not deportation." He got up suddenly and spoke in English. "That's it, then, in a nutshell. Please convey my respectful greetings to Bill Cosford when you see him."

Rayner stood up too. "Who's he?"

"Her Majesty's Ambassador in Aguador." In Spanish he said to the lieutenant by the door: "Just between ourselves, *Lugarteniente*, what are you going to do next with Señor Rayner?"

"I am not able to say, Señor Consul, but personal escort transport has been ordered for San Domingo."

"Oh well, if you can't tell me, you can't."

Emmerson turned back to Rayner, dead-faced. "Always remember that the people are human. It's only the little short-arses in fancy-dress jackboots who shake their fat clenched fists at us in the newspapers that we should beware of." His mud-brown eyes glanced across to the portrait on the wall; then he looked at Rayner as if he were suddenly surprised at what he was going to say; and Rayner felt he would have said it in good English in front of anyone at all – a lieutenant of the Aguador police, the Pope of Rome, a German ex-general, or a president-elect of the United States; because this was the whole sum of his philosophy and the findings of his long years of experience as a political public servant and as a man. "Because they're dangerous. They're put there to satisfy our need of violence. They are our toys, and nothing will ever stop us winding them up." He jerked the zip of his brief-case shut

57

and moved to the door. "But let's not go into all that."

The lieutenant was opening the door for him and then Emmerson was swinging round again to Rayner, his eyes bright and his mood riding him: "You know the one essential feature of a toy? It's small. And we bring out our smallest toys for our most exciting games. Never a first-class war that doesn't have a small man running it for us – the Kaiser, Lloyd George, Hitler, Mussolini, Churchill, each of 'em adored in his own doll's-house while the big clumsy children go blundering about the nursery winding 'em up until the whole bloody house is on fire. Only one hope for our generation's children, Rayner: the toys are taller this year in London, Paris and Washington. An extra few inches in Moscow and the whole of humanity might have a chance to grow up."

He went out of the room and the lieutenant motioned Rayner to follow. In the passage Emmerson turned again and the dead-face was back like a mask. "One thing I don't need to point out to you, Rayner. In a country as remote as this, communications are vital, and an airline like Transocean has a great deal of pull. So if you decide to fight your case, you'll have the full weight of T.O.A. behind you."

He shook hands and continued along the passage, getting a salute from the guard at the doors.

"You will please wait in here." Rayner was directed into a smaller room with bars at the window and bolts on the outside of the door. He was left alone. Someone outside was calling an order, something about "escort and duty-driver."

For a minute or two he thought about Emmerson. The man was too honest and he talked too much about his convictions. That must be why, approaching fifty, he was still only a consul in a remote republic. Nearly six feet and with good shoulders, he was much too big, and nobody wanted to wind him up.

It was when Rayner heard another shouted order – this time with the word "prisoner" among those audible – that he began thinking fast about his own situation. Emmerson had been right: his reaction to the warning that he could never win was an immediate resolve to fight, and it had shown in his eyes as he had listened. His sub-conscious had already changed the meaning of the imminent journey to the capital: he was going there to see the British ambassador, and Major Pareira was affording him transport.

Now he knew that it was no go. Emmerson had made the point for him, in ignorance. Even if he chose to fight them – and cool his heels in gaol for months while the Skyliner in-

58

vestigation went on without him – he would not have the support of T.O.A. Informed of the facts they would cable: *Please expedite deportation of our representative.*

The enemy was all about him.

"There is no defence."

Feet tramped in the passage.

And no choice. The fight was already over, to the bang of bolts instead of bullets. Their win.

Outside the building an engine had started up. Something was being slung into a vehicle. His baggage.

"They are our toys." And we are the toys of toys.

So he was to leave, with nothing finished. A shadow at sixty-five fathoms, marked with a cross on a chart. A face from a photograph, with a beautiful name.

They came for him and took him outside into the glare of the lamps and the smell of exhaust gas. Somewhere beyond the lights there must be the flame of the great peak in the dark, that he now knew to be beautiful.

It was not their fault because they did not know about his bad arm, but one of them grasped it to help him into the high-built military van, and he slumped on to the seat with the sweat pouring from his skin and his head fluttering with an acid-white and intermittent light.

He sat fighting off the nausea of pain and despair, his body rocking to the movement of the vehicle, his eyes shut against the sight of the khaki tunics and the polished red-leather holsters and the peaked caps that made a face less human and more like a high-beaked bird of prey; and he repeated a strange gibberish word to himself, the name of the only thing that meant anything to him now.

Catachunga ... Catachunga ...

CHAPTER TEN

By midnight the closed military truck had left the smooth paved highway out of Puerto Fuego and was ploughing along the wet-weather road through the rice-fields. The mottled rain-pattern left by the last deluge had been baked by the sun, and now the wheels broke it up and sent the dust billowing out in the wake of their going, thicker than the smoke of a train and black in the starlight.

Sometimes Rayner had opened his eyes and noted their position. Now he saw the silhouettes of the split-cane houses on their stilts outlined against the pale spread of swampland water. The shrill rasping of the cicadas was louder than the engine, and once a snake-owl had raised its whooping cry from somewhere beyond a clump of pampas. An hour later they entered the drought-belt and began climbing the foothills.

He sat with his left arm held across his lap. The unhealed skin had started oozing blood again where the man had grasped it, and the sleeve was sticking to it. His head had cleared enough to let him think. He was thinking of home.

It was necessary for him to decide. After these weeks of constant daily activity in the hot season on the Equator he thought of the chill sleet of London as a desert nomad thinks of an oasis. Even to be free of the flies would be a relief; the flies and the day-long clangour of the dredger and the stink of the shark-factories. But that was all London would mean to him: it would be cold and it would be civilised.

Here was his chance to go home; but he did not want it. His job at London Airport was of constant interest to him: it was the most difficult and therefore the most rewarding he had ever held down. But he would not happily return to it while this inquiry was going on, round the far curve of the world.

With every mile he knew he was reaching the decision he had already made anyway. He would not leave Aguador.

There was a night-flight at three a.m. They would probably try to put him on that.

Away to the right he saw the faint glow of a salt-pan, blue-white under the stars. Then they were through the intermontane basin and climbing again. He smoked a cigarette to relax his nerves and then said: "If you wouldn't mind pulling up, I'd like to relieve myself."

The escort who was sitting in the back with him leaned towards him, asking him what he had said. Rayner told him again, and the man – he was no older than twenty or so – called to the major, who was sitting next to the driver. A lot of shouting back and forth went on, because the truck was in low gear and the road was bumpy. After ten minutes they pulled up and Rayner jumped down before anyone could help him.

The engine had been switched off and the peace was heady. The stars were huge and blue and low, seeming to float among the peaks of the foothills; and there was the dry smell in the air that was only to be found in a real drought-belt: the smell of baked and beaten and shrivelled rock where there has been no water and therefore no plant or animal life for centuries.

60

The desert had this smell, the true smell of lifelessness worse even than the smell of death, which at least gave sign that something had once lived.

He walked back a few yards along the rubble of the road. The police escort was getting out of the truck and he heard them but could not look round. The thing that irked him was that he did indeed want to empty his bladder, and this gave him a problem. The other men were taking their opportunity, and this was the moment when he stood his greatest chance: one is instinctively reluctant to break off the act of urination in order to chase someone at full pelt. There would be a few seconds' delay. But if he began his run, and had to stop, they would bundle him back into the truck with a full bladder; and he could not ask for a second halt.

There was no hope of judging his chances of complete escape. The stars gave light, but there was immediate cover on each side of the road: the expansion of the rock by day and its contraction by night had broken it up until there was a landscape of tumbled boulders. Once off the road he would have running-cover for miles.

But they had a pivoting lamp on the roof of the truck; and if that did not pick him up they would wait for daylight, two of them marking the position and the third taking the truck to the nearest communication point. By noon tomorrow there would be a small army here, with dogs.

He would have no water.

One of the men called a word – not, he thought, to him. A match flared near the truck.

He emptied his bladder as fast as he could and then moved along the roadway, his feet silent in the dust; and when he was twenty-five yards from the truck he felt his spine tingling. There was silence from the truck and it was too obvious. Turning to look at the far shape of the truck he could see the bulge on its outline. A man was crouched on top of the driving-cabin, ready with the lamp. Another match flared and lit up the decoy; the second man was standing with his back turned to Rayner, lighting a cigarette. It would be the third one – probably the major – who would open fire.

It would save them the trouble of making the second half of the journey. They were from Puerto Fuego; they didn't want to go all the way to San Domingo in the dark. And the credit would be theirs: the prisoner had tried to escape but they'd been too quick for him.

He had prepared his nerves for flight. Now he had to face the strain of going back and getting there alive.

It seemed a long way. He might have been the only living thing in this dead world: the truck's dark shape was just another boulder. His foot kicked a stone and he almost cursed as if he were creeping up on the unseen enemy; but there was no need for stealth.

He heard something that might have been the click of a breech, and walked on slowly, moving his feet so that if a stone were in his path he would kick it; and all the time he kept the shape on the top of the truck in sight, because he wanted to know for sure.

The great blue stars floated at the edge of his field of vision; and now metal on the truck was gleaming in their light. If they decided to do it now, in cold blood, it would be clean through the heart with a ten-yard range. That was his only hope. Evidence would require the bullet in the back, to fit the report of deliberate escape.

The man on the roof of the truck began climbing down but Rayner had seen him, and was sure. There was the hollow sound of the gun going back into the holster, and the snap of the clip.

"I feel much relieved," he told them, and climbed into the truck sweating like a sponge.

They said nothing to him. The engine was started and the tyres span on the soft dust. The headlights stabbed among the rocks and they gathered speed.

*

The bureau was in the notorious Casa Roja, the barracks of the secret police. The man who interviewed Rayner was not in uniform and was never addressed by whatever was his rank, but simply as "Señor." The room was very orderly and the fittings almost luxurious. Even the bars at the window were painted a delicate grey. There were echoes here: one was aware that this room was one small cell of an immense building. From distant rooms voices carried thinly; the slam of a door was like a gunshot.

The man was older than his years. His face had caved in long ago, becoming a map of the country of his mind where the going had been rough. It was the face of a man who must climb the mountain with the knowledge that he would never reach the top. But the effort had left him tired unto death, rather than embittered.

His red eyes looked out from grey-white pouches at the Englishman. His voice was feeble from shouting into some wilderness of his own.

62

"I have read the report from Puerto Fuego. Do you know why you have been sent here?"

"To answer a charge."

Rayner had spent most of the journey thinking practically, and his answers were going to be short and calculated. There were two things he did not intend to do. He was not leaving Aguador. He was not going to submit to prison. And there was only one chance of succeeding. If it came he would take it. If it did not, he would try whatever else offered at the time.

"There is a charge," the beaten-looking man said, "against your name. Yes. But you are not obliged, at the moment, to answer it. Did your consul tell you that?"

"No." Emmerson had been too busy philosophising.

"Then I will tell you now. You understand Spanish well?"

"Perfectly."

The man folded his worn-skinned hands on the beautiful desk, and his hooded eyes seemed hardly able to keep open.

"This country is under martial law. In various ways this affects the treatment of foreign nationals who are subject to these laws while in the Republic. In your case you are called upon to answer the charge against you only if you resist summary repatriation by putting forward a defence."

Rayner took a moment to think this out. The man sat as still as a sleeping bird.

"I would like to get this correctly. If I let you deport me straight away, the charge doesn't come into it. If I defend the charge, you can't deport me unless my defence fails in a trial."

"Correct."

Emmerson had said: "But you won't win, because it would go on for months and months and months."

Prison had always worried Rayner. He preferred battle in the open to captivity. In the war he had experienced both. In open fight a man remains a man with something he can still call a soul; but in a barred and bolted cell he becomes an animal, however he keeps his dignity, however he keeps his faith. One cannot spend fifteen days in a solitary-confinement cell with dysentery and a brute guard without losing the respect of the self; and with that gone, all is gone. It is not the guard, but the bug, that wins. It leaves the smell of the animal cage in a man's mind, for ever.

He had been broken by those fifteen days, to the point when he had asked for a glass of water. To complete his humiliation, he had been given it.

Emmerson had said: "All quite comfortable; prison grub's not bad."

63

They could stuff it.

"In that case I agree to leave the country."

The sleeping bird opened a red eye and the claws unfolded. "You will offer no resistance?"

"Not unless there's any man-handling. I shall require a civil escort to the frontier."

The man was obviously so relieved that the interview was over already that he attempted lightness. "In this case the frontier lies one centimetre above the runway of the airport in San Domingo. I trust your journey will be comfortable." He got up wearily, easing his head back to wake himself up, or perhaps to look again at the unattainable peak that would tower through all his to-morrows.

The guard had the door open and the red-eyed man was calling orders, giving the escort a paper from the desk, asking for Comandante Pareira, saying to Rayner: "Your remark about a 'civil escort' . . . You have no complaints concerning your journey here from the coast?"

"None at all." They hadn't even murdered him.

He was taken out to the echoing passage and the full escort fell in, Major Pareira leading. Obviously the Englishman was his particular pigeon, even as far as the frontier; and this alone gave the lie to the "routine passport-check" story.

In a large airy room near the main guard-post he was invited to check his baggage. He declined. If anything else had been taken from the cases he would never get it back. He read and signed two papers, one confirming the personal details he had already given, the other confirming that he understood fully and clearly that if he made any attempt to re-enter the country within five years of having left it he would be turned back at the frontier or be allowed in under police escort and obliged to defend those charges now standing against him.

It was just two o'clock. The airport was some twenty minutes' drive through the Parque Aogusto Gomez and across the factory area. Instead of the military truck they used a modern Plymouth sedan, all-black and with no number-plate. The driver was a new man. Pareira and one of the original *lugartenientes* sat in the back with Rayner, one on each side of him.

The airport had the usual skeleton staff on duty and a bored group of thirty-odd people were watching the vision-strip news on the panel high in the wall.

Crossing the main hall, the major and his lieutenant kept so close to him that they sometimes bumped together. He wondered what punishment Pareira would receive if his prisoner got away. Severe, to judge by his caution.

"I'd like to put some overnight things in a zip-bag," Rayner told him when they had checked in with the airline.

"Your baggage will be with you on board." He had dropped the "señor" long ago.

"No, it will be in the luggage compartment."

"Then you must take one case with you."

"They are all fairly large, and it's strictly forbidden."

"Where is the zip-bag?"

"The airline will give me one."

Pareira looked about him. There was no crowd here for the prisoner to get lost in; the group of passengers were still staring at the vision-strip.

"Very well," he said. He was getting edgy now, with fifteen minutes to take-off. Instead of walking beside Rayner, he and the lieutenant fell in behind as they went back to the T.O.A. bureau. The officer on duty was new to Rayner; he had never seen him even in London. He was given a T.O.A. zip-bag.

"There's nothing else I can do for you, Mr. Rayner?"

"Pot of vanishing-cream would come in handy."

"I'm sorry!"

"Doesn't matter. We take off dead on the minute?"

"So far as I know, sir."

Rayner lit a cigarette. "You like it out here?"

"I'm hoping to get used to the heat."

"They certainly turn it on, don't they?"

When he turned round he saw that two sergeants of the airport police had joined Pareira and the lieutenant. It looked as though the major had called them over from the departure point. The duty officer in the Transocean bureau was looking surprised.

Rayner could not believe that his deportation was so vital that it took a major, a lieutenant and two sergeants to put him into an aircraft. If his nuisance-value was so great, surely they would have "put a man behind a tree" for him, as the consul had phrased it, long before now. Or the major would have been given definite orders to let him "escape" on the road from the coast and then shoot him down.

It didn't matter. There was no time to work this one out. He had twelve more minutes. The escort of four armed police trailed him carefully to the weighing-in counter and watched him closely as he took a few personal things from the cases and put them into the zip-bag. But even if he had had a gun among the baggage he would only have got a couple of quick shots in before they riddled him and dropped him.

Perhaps the red-eyed man had been more alert than he had looked, and more intuitive. He might have told Pareira: "I have a feeling the prisoner is taking his deportation too easily. Don't let him out of your sight."

The group of passengers were flowing towards the departure bay and the first ones were going through.

"Follow me," said the major suddenly. The airport sergeants showed him the way through to the assembly-point via the staff quarters. They reached the tarmac ahead of the main group of passengers.

Rayner kept in step, not turning his head but moving his eyes to left and right. The tarmac was well lighted by tall standards and the Skyliner 12 stood less than fifty yards from the main building. The fuel-bowsers were already crawling away from the plane and the starter-truck was in position, with the twin cables plugged in below the fuselage. The baggage truck was coming away and the T.O.A. ground-crew were securing the baggage-compartment doors. The position-indicator lights on the aircraft were already winking. It was five minutes to take-off.

There wasn't a chance. He was in the middle of the armed guard and there was no immediate cover. They would break his run with a fusillade.

They reached the steps. The two sergeants took up their position one on each side of them. The lieutenant held back, his hand resting idly on his gun-holster. The major came with the prisoner as far as the bottom step. Rayner turned and looked at the white-lit tarmac between the steps and the airport building. The duty officer of T.O.A. had not come out to see him off; and that was his luck.

"You will board the aircraft, please."

"But of course, *Comandante*."

Going up the steps he saw that most of the passengers had cleared the assembly-point. A stewardess was leading the first of them across to the plane.

As Rayner reached the cabin he heard the radio-man's voice through the open doorway of the flight-deck, checking his set with the airport control.

The mobile steps forward, which Rayner had used, were being drawn away.

The police contingent stepped back a dozen paces, strung out a little for better observation. A steward shut the door and the security-locks were slapped home.

Within three or four minutes the quadruple jets began blowing, and a ground-crew officer took up his position at the

66

port wing-tip. He thumbed-up for all engines running and then gave the clearance signal. As the aircraft began rolling, he saluted, turning away to clear the slipstream.

Major Pareira dismissed the two sergeants and walked with his lieutenant back to the airport building.

CHAPTER ELEVEN

HIAWATHA Moses ran the new hemp through the mesh with the long curved needle and the surf lapped at his feet. El Angelo had taken the boat not long after noon, which was a strange time. Señor Puyo had gone with him. They had taken tackle and a basket of *empanadas* and two bottles of wine but he knew they had not gone to fish because they had taken no lure or bait.

He mended the big net as best he could, though there was blood already on his fingers. It must be finished before dark, because El Angelo had told him. It would be unthinkable that the net would not be finished, because the words had come from the mouth of El Angelo. When he was a child, Hiamo had believed people who said that at sundown, if El Angelo stood here on the sand and looked towards the west and lifted his great arms and called to the sun that it should not go down into the sea, the sun would stay there for ever on the horizon, so that it would never be night.

Hiamo was not sure that he didn't still believe it. El Angelo was not like other men; sometimes his face with its beard would be as calm as the face on the cross in the church of San Domingo that he had once seen, the time when the beam of the sun had slanted across the shrine and he had cried with the beauty.

He never asked questions of *el capitán*, except of course about the handling of the boat and such things. To-day he had wanted badly to ask a question but had dared not. To-day the man had walked on the shore again, as he had done a month ago: the man with the beard and the wide straw hat. There were many men in Puerto with beards, and some of the fishermen wore big straw hats against the sun; but this man was not a fisherman.

He had walked slowly along the shore and when he came to a group of fishermen they stopped talking and he looked at their faces but said nothing, and passed on, and came upon others, who drew back a little, some of them smiling and making way for him. He had spoken only to one man, and that was El Angelo, standing with him for a moment and looking across the ocean. Hiamo had overheard a little of what they were saying.

Did the fishing go well?

It went well. There were a thousand fish in the ocean.

And many boats, to catch them with?

There were fifty boats. More than fifty.

Hiamo could not hear everything, nor did he understand what he had heard. Everyone along the shore said that he was too young to understand things. He had been with Pepito and the others, that time, in the business of the *ferrocarril*; but they said he was too young to know anything. Maybe they were right; he was bad at guessing and sums and could not read. But he would like to know who the man was, who came to walk on the shore. Sometimes he thought he might be Jesus. Jesus had a beard but not a wide straw hat. People said that Jesus was coming again. Hiamo believed a lot of things like this since he had been warned by the sign of the cross in the sea.

When El Angelo brought his boat to the shore it was nearly sundown; and all the time the boy helped to winch up the boat and settle it on the timbers he wanted to ask El Angelo who the man was with the eyes that glinted in the shadow of the big straw hat. But he knew that El Angelo would not tell him.

They had not been out to catch fish, though there were a thousand fish in the ocean. The lines were still coiled.

Luis Puyo walked alone from the shore and spoke to no one, though men called to him as he passed them. A crowd had formed at the bottom of the flights of steps that led up to Ventura's Bar, but he did not stop until he saw the ambulance trying to get through the crowd; then he went back and made his way between the people and saw the man who sat propped against the bottom step. His face was still recognisable because his head had fallen back against the stones and not forward over the terrible wound of the throat. Someone had thrown sawdust over the long trail of blood where the flies were buzzing. Luis Puyo looked at him once and moved away. He was Montaya, the seller of lottery tickets. The board was propped beside him but all the tickets had gone. Yet Puyo knew that the killing had not been made for theft. You do not have to cut a man's throat in order to snatch his board of tickets. The tickets had vanished afterwards because there were some who wished to profit even from the dead.

Luis Puyo made his way to a room in a narrow street at the end of the waterfront drive. He would tell them that his son looked thin and pale but otherwise well; and he would mention having seen the remains of the lottery-ticket seller. They might even know who had done that; but it did not matter. It mattered only that it was done.

CHAPTER TWELVE

TRANSOCEAN'S chairman had been waiting an hour at the Hotel Miraflores before Willis came in.

During that hour he had asked two different porters where Mr. Rayner was; they said merely that he had left without any forwarding address. Gates assumed he had got on a plane for London as instructed; and he was believed. He had sensed trouble from Rayner, without quite knowing why. His request to remain here in Puerto Fuego had seemed a little odd, but hardly amounted to defiance; and now he was on his way home.

Gates, who had the kind of energy that needed throwing off, had already studied the map of the town on the wall and paced the length of the lounge with its arches and palms and Spanish leatherwork, to look at the map again and pace again until the sweat was soaking into his clothes and he had to shout for a litre of *naranjilla* with ice and sit down. Sitting was worse than pacing because the inaction bothered him and made him irritable. He continued to sweat.

He thought of Willis, as, waiting, one thinks about the person one is to meet. He had admired Willis over some ten years for his cool control. Willis never hurried yet was never late. He never looked at his watch yet always knew what time it was. With the unearthly energy of a snake he would slip smoothly from place to place and arrive ahead of the people with pounding feet – of whom Gates was one. Had Willis known that the chairman of T.O.A. was here, he would of course have been waiting to greet him, five minutes early. Gates had told no one here that he was coming. Only one traffic officer – to his credit – had recognised him on the way through the San Domingo airport. He wanted neither Willis nor Rayner to expect him. Much of Gates's success had derived from his habit of lightning swoops. His father, a Birmingham brassworker, had told him: "Whenever you can, surprise people, son. It gets 'em all caught up – an' then you're in."

He supposed there was more than one way of surprising people: his own direct method and Willis's method of "getting 'em all caught up" by finding their weakness from a distance and then prodding it. Willis was primarily an observer, which was why he was good at his job; but he could observe things and people only from over the kind of wall he had built about himself, above which the small clear eyes set high in the head were not noticed.

Gates had learned to surprise people, and having come to see the advantage he was uneasy with men like Willis who could ably surprise him back. But he still admired him for what he was often called by members of the board: a cool one.

Willis came into the hotel not long before sundown, neat and light of step in a linen suit and canvas shoes as if just in the town for an hour from a cruising liner.

"Well if it isn't Mr. Gates . . ." But the tone of surprise was put on, as though he had seen his chairman through the window in passing and wasn't going to say so. Perhaps he had.

"Hallo, Willis. Hoping you'd turn up. Have a drink?"

"Willingly. The rum here is very good."

"Rum? Doesn't it make you hot?" A fool question: nothing short of hellfire would make Willis hot. Even there the wall would keep most of the heat off.

"I like the flavour," said Willis with his lop-sided smile. A waiter was already coming, apparently in response to some telepathic order. When Gates had wanted his litre of orange-juice he had been obliged to shout down the lift-shaft before anyone would come.

"Do these chaps understand English, Willis?"

"Possibly, sir."

"Then we'll go somewhere quiet when we're ready to talk turkey. To start off, do you know for sure if Rayner's gone back to London?"

"I rather think so. He was deported."

"He was *what*?"

"I've talked to the consul about it. Mr. Rayner was seen on to a plane at three o'clock yesterday morning by police officers."

"Why?"

"Incriminating articles were put into his luggage and the police were then advised to check on him. Deportation seems to be the correct procedure in this case."

"How do you know this?"

"I noticed that he had left the hotel two nights ago and I asked why—"

"Didn't you know I'd cabled him to return?"

"Yes, Mr. Gates, but he seemed reluctant." He observed the indignation with mild interest. "They told me here that he had been arrested."

"They told you? Who?"

"One of the porters here."

Gates's annoyance increased. The porters had told him simply that Mr. Rayner had "left".

"Arrested."

"Yes. So I popped round to the consul the next morning to see if there were anything I could do to help. By that time Mr. Rayner's flight was already six hours airborne. The consul had already telephoned San Domingo to see what had happened to him." He took a calculated sip of his white rum, watching Gates over the rim of the glass.

Gates said: "But they can't handle T.O.A. people like that! Why didn't you cable me?" He looked up in irritation.

"Señor Gates?" the porter asked.

"Well?"

He opened the telegram. *Rayner deported 3 a.m. to-day. Stop. Alleges he was falsely compromised. Willis.* The time and date was 09.00 yesterday.

"Your cable's been turned round in London for me." He slipped it across the table to Willis. He was too annoyed by this rabbit-from-the-hat aptitude of Willis's to apologise for his quick question. "Why did they want to run him out of the country?"

Willis moved his long narrow head slowly like a radar-finder. The porter was out of sight. "I think it became known that Mr. Rayner was interesting himself in the subject of my own inquiry here. It is not popular with the local people. I have special locks on my baggage. The climate suits me here." The corners of his small clear eyes crinkled in wintry amusement.

"By God, I'm taking it up with the ambassador, then!" He found the quiet gaze sobering. "After the inquiry's all over, of course."

"Yes. Publicity at this stage might be unwise, Mr. Gates. In any case, you did want Mr. Rayner to return, didn't you?"

Gates gave him a very straight look and asked: "You've no idea who fixed him, have you?"

"Oh no."

"None at all?" This direct gaze had forced out many a confession in the boardroom.

"It wasn't, I feel sure, a fellow-countryman."

"I didn't suggest you did it, Willis." Though of course he had suggested it.

"I was thinking of Lindstrom," said Willis blandly.

Gates took a long swig at his drink. "Have you seen Lindstrom?"

"Not yet."

"You think he's here?"

"Oh yes."

"Look here, isn't there somewhere we can talk?"

"The open air is very good for that, and we could watch the sun go down."

"To hell with the sunset." They finished their drinks and Willis led them along the Avenida del Mar with his short deliberate steps. The sun was nearing the ocean but its heat lingered and the paving was hot underfoot. People were beginning to come out of the buildings as if drugged by the day.

"A beautiful avenue," murmured Willis.

"Very nice. Now what have you found out, Willis?"

As if preparing a speech for the falsifying of the company's accounts, the security man said carefully: "There is an atmosphere of tension in this town, Mr. Gates. Tension and expectancy. Precisely the same atmosphere I noticed in Bangkok last year, just prior to the current revolution. We see small signs everywhere. This Ycaza person is not popular. People won't tell you but they will show it if they can. Watch them in the post office and other places, putting the stamps on the envelopes with their fists. Notice in the bars how liquor has accidentally been splashed across the excellent portraits of the president. Only yesterday I saw a group of talking men broken up by the police – only five men who might have been discussing the bullfight news or the girl in red at the corner: but the police sent them packing. Only this afternoon a lottery-ticket seller was left in the street with his throat slit, where normally one would await the dark and dump the body in the sea at the disposal of the sharks. Again it was the same in Bangkok: a talker would be left silenced as an example to others. But it is not the same in San Domingo, where I was this morning – "

"You don't mean the police are cutting people's – "

"Oh no! The man was killed because he seemed about to talk *to* the police." He stopped walking to peer about him, still as a stork; then he moved again and caught up with the chairman. "Something is on, Mr. Gates. Something is *on*."

"How does this involve the Skyliner 10?"

"I can't say, yet. I hesitate to air suppositions – "

"Let's have them good an' aired, Willis."

"There seems a strong disinclination among the local people to talk about the missing aircraft, even to remember it. They are all dumb, suddenly, until one passes on to the bullfight news or the girl in green at the bar. Nor are what we might call official circles ready to discuss it either. *Nobody wants to know.* This is highly interesting, of course. An inquiry into something that is being hushed up is obviously the more worth pursuing. The only real pointer is a brief item of news, now two years old, I noticed in the files of *La Nación*, a daily paper in San Domingo. I made a copy of the report."

He pulled out his slim neat wallet and took from it a sheet of paper, giving it to Gates. They stopped walking and while Gates read, the thin perfectly-formed writing Willis gazed across the avenue at the man who stood in the doorway. He must be a police detective. The world over, these chaps were never taught to stand in the open where one was less easily noticed. Surely the whole idea of a frame was to focus the attention on the picture.

Gates was mumbling the words as he read. *During a fracas at the Peón Bar not far from the Army Barracks, two officers attempting to restore order received knife wounds from which they died immediately. They were Capitán "Gusto" Rimiz, of La Valler, aged 30, and Lugarteniente José Torres, aged 33, of San Domingo. The most rigorous investigations are being pursued.*

When Gates had finished mumbling Willis said: "That is the approximate translation. Visiting the Peón Bar, I made a quiet but rigorous investigation of my own. The two officers were pilots based at the seaplane unit at Lago Azul."

Gates had more sense than to pretend he saw something when he didn't. "Well?"

"We notice the date, Mr. Gates. Fourth March, 1961. The day the Skyliner 10 was last heard of."

"Remarkable, I suppose." He stood uncomfortably in his sweat-sodden clothes and decided that one fine day he would up and tell Willis: "I don't bloody well pay you to keep me guessing – I want the *goods*."

"I think so, yes. The seaplanes operate across the ocean, of course: it is convenient to base them on the lake so near the capital. Perhaps these two pilots were patrolling the area when the Skyliner ditched, and knew something about it, and were silenced. The man at the Peón Bar told me that no one else in the fracas died of wounds, nor was even wounded. As you say, remarkable. I am of course following it up, but

73

it will take time. There are few people as willing to talk as my friend at the Peón."

They reached some little iron tables and chairs, and sat down to have a drink. Gates did not think much of this news report. He knew a coincidence when he saw one. Willis had been here only a few days and it was quite natural for him to dig up bits and pieces that seemed significant at first.

"You haven't seen Lindstrom, then."

"Not yet."

"Or any survivors?"

"No."

"I had a cable from Rayner two days ago. He said he felt an urge to follow through. I suppose he had *something* to follow through? What was it?"

Willis composed another short speech. "Nothing definite, perhaps; but he was most helpful in telling me the lines he was working on. They were the same as my own, and for an amateur I consider he did well."

"So well that they kicked him out."

"Not 'so' well, but 'too' well. One has to cover one's spoor and he lacked experience. But he seemed certain that Lindstrom is being hidden and protected by local people. He also told me he recognised a surviving passenger –"

"A *passenger!*"

"A Mademoiselle Vidal, an actress of serious reputation but little international fame, working with the Comédie Française." A pause, while he considered. "I may say that I felt he told me rather less of this person than he could have, Mr. Gates."

"You're not serious. Rayner doesn't look at women, and if he did, he wouldn't start any malarky in the middle of an inquiry as important as this!"

"Malarky, Mr. Gates, crops up at the most unlikely moments. If we remember, Caesar was frightfully busy when he ran into Cleopatra."

"But we're talking about Paul Rayner!" He was disappointed in Willis. A romanticist makes a poor security officer. He said with emphasis: "The thing is that if there were any survivors other than Lindstrom, the whole case becomes more complex and more dangerous. Competition among the world airlines is extremely hot. You know that. An airline is hit hardest by the publicity following a crash – and that's why we've had such a storm to weather, with the Skyliner 10s. But now we're back in the public's confidence. Apart from the odd tyre-burst and a case of a jammed undercarriage at Shannon,

74

there hasn't been an accident with the Skyliner 12s. since we put them into service. So T.O.A. doesn't want to rake up bad publicity all over again. In *spite* of this I called an urgent meeting of the board the minute I had this report from the steward that he'd seen Lindstrom alive. Nobody can say I was ready to hush the thing up – you know that. You were at two of those special meetings yourself."

"I was indeed."

Gates looked round, but did not drop his voice. It was a habit he disliked in others. If you had something to say, then spit it out straight.

"On the other hand, Willis, there's this. Technical failure, outside the matter of negligent maintenance, is the fault of the manufacturer who made the plane. Pilot or crew failure counts directly against the airline itself. That's why I took immediate action on Marsh's report. This inquiry has got to be made, Willis, but it's got to be made with good sense and discretion. Until we are *certain* that Lindstrom is alive, we don't want any publicity. We don't want to rake up details of a two-year-old disaster for nothing. You understand?"

"Oh, yes. That's why you sent me out here to replace Mr. Rayner. He might –"

"I trust Rayner," said Gates emphatically, "as much as I trust you. And that's one hundred per cent."

"Oh, quite – and thank you. It has nothing to do with his reliability, but his appreciation of the position we're in. That is what I assume."

"Then you're right. But you're here chiefly because you're an experienced investigator and he isn't. He also has a damn' good job of work to do in London, and that's why I recalled him in no uncertain terms."

Willis nodded his long narrow head, reading between the lines of Gates's off-the-cuff speech, holding the result to a mirror, checking for contradictions, rereading it in the light of his knowledge of men and particularly of Gates, and making a free translation, which read: *For the time being we want to keep this whole thing just as quiet as everyone else. Rayner's a danger to us if he stays out here, and that's why I called him in.*

"If," Gates went on, "there are survivors other than the pilot – this woman Rayner says he's recognised, for instance – then we'll have someone to check Lindstrom's story. What beats me is why the woman hasn't come into the open."

"Perhaps for the same reason as Lindstrom's."

"What's that?"

"I don't know."

"Then find out."

Willis allowed the corners of his eyes to crinkle. From Gates, whose character he knew, it wasn't a peremptory order to an employee, but a statement of confidence. He knew that if anyone could find out, then Willis could.

"When will you be going back, Mr. Gates?" Because Gates had undertaken a round trip of ten thousand miles to tell Willis one thing; and he had told him: that this must remain a secret inquiry unless it looked impossible to avoid handing it to the Air Ministry and the public.

"To-morrow, unless you dig up anything big. I won't say I was hoping you'd have Lindstrom winkled out for me to talk to, because you've not had long at the job; but that was the idea at the back of my mind that sent me out here."

"Of course. Who knows, I might be lucky enough to oblige, between now and the time you leave. So much can happen in twenty-four hours." He was watching the man who was coming across the avenue, wondering if he had seen them sitting at the little iron table.

"Well I'm not sticking in this god-forsaken furnace for the sake of doing nothing, Willis. I'll think over what you've told me and then we'll have another session. There'll be an idea or two buzzing in my head by then."

"I'm sure there will, Mr. Gates." He saw that the man had indeed recognised them: that was why he had crossed the road. He was coming to speak to them.

"I don't mind admitting, Willis, that I'm extremely relieved that Rayner's out of this country, even though the measures used were drastic."

"Ye-es," murmured Willis mildly. "But I rather think your relief is premature, Mr. Gates, because here comes Mr. Rayner now."

CHAPTER THIRTEEN

WILLIS rose smoothly to his feet. Gates saw Rayner and got up in exasperation.

"They said you'd been deported, Rayner!"

Rayner looked around and said quietly: "Careful, sir."

Willis was studying him with an eye as fast as a camera-shutter. Rayner looked dead-beat and in some kind of pain. He hung his left arm oddly. Stubble was on his lean drawn face. The linen suit was badly crumpled. So he was very serious about sticking tight in Puerto Fuego. He didn't look as if he'd slipped the police without a running fight.

"Sit down, Rayner," said Gates in a lower tone. "Sit down." He reached out and swung another little chair across for Rayner. They all sat down and for a moment no one spoke. Gates was worried. Willis was observing. Rayner was thinking: Lucky to be here.

He had just posted the promised letter to Edwards, care of Transocean Airlines, London. Bless Edwards, and luck.

Captain Edwards had been busy with his last-minute checks before take-off and had not seen that the T.O.A. London Airport chief was escorted to the plane by police. Rayner had taken a seat right forward and by a window so that Major Pareira could see him there until the aircraft turned out of the bay. He could still not believe how slow-thinking a police organisation could be, even here on the Equator where life had to be lived at half-pace.

They knew he worked with T.O.A. and had some authority in all the airline's ports of call. They must have known — or hadn't it occurred to them? — that the 3 a.m. San Domingo-London flight was on the T.O.A. schedules. At every stage of the short journey from the Casa Roja barracks to the very door of the aircraft he had expected them to see the red light. They hadn't.

When the plane turned from the bay the period of waiting began. The next three minutes would decide whether or not he was going to cross that one-centimetre frontier. It would take roughly two minutes for the plane to reach the start of Runway 9. After the first minute had passed he went forward and through into the control cabin, flapping his staff-pass at the stewardess. The crew were at their busiest but he couldn't help that.

"Captain Edwards ... ."

"Hallo, sir! Didn't know you were on board."

The radio operator was still checking his set with the tower. The navigator was preparing his chart-sheet. The line of blue marker lights went flicking past the windows. The machine rose and fell on its hydraulics. The jets whined faintly, outboard.

"Look, Edwards, I've left a case at my hotel with a batch of urgent papers in it. No need to stop now, but let me off when you meet the runway. Won't delay you."

Edwards looked up with an expressionless face. "Bit irregular, sir. We're rolling."

"That's all right. I'll send a message to London in your

name, so you'll have something official to show." He watched the marker lights losing their jumbled pattern and swing into perspective as the Skyliner 12 turned into the runway.

"Your other baggage on board, Mr. Rayner?"

"Yes, but I'll pick it up in London. I shall be on the next flight out."

Edwards checked instruments and said: "Well, sir, I really don't know."

The Station Superintendent London Airport became impatient.

"Look, if you want to turn and go all the way back to the bay and have your passengers wondering what's wrong with the aircraft that's up to you. You're the captain."

That was the last word he would say. More would make the pilot suspicious. It must rest on that.

They would be watching the plane, Pareira and the junior officer and the two sergeants, making sure it was not going to turn back with any technical trouble. But they were half a mile away. All they could see was the vague shape of the plane with its high tail-unit lying darkly among the galaxy of lights. The tower was also watching the plane. Clearance had already been given by radio, and now Edwards saw the green light being beamed to him from Control.

Rayner made a quiet fuss with his zip-bag to show that he was confident about getting off. He thought that the mention of the passengers might win the day for him. Here was a station chief reminding a subordinate that the welfare of the passengers came first. This principle had been drummed into the poor devils at every stage of their training as pilots.

There was just one other point. Give a good pilot a long clean runway and every instrument on the panel set for take-off and he hates having to turn back. He is not, by nature, a groundling.

"Okay, sir. If you'll send that message."

"I will."

The navigator swung the door open for him and unclipped the emergency ladder.

"Don't worry, I'll jump. Thank you, gentlemen – have a good trip."

It was a six-foot drop and it shook his arm up, but it didn't matter. This was the right side of the frontier. He waved from the wing-tip and the jets were gunned up and the brakes came off. As the machine began rolling he backed away, shielding his eyes from the dust and the hot stinking wind of the fuel-oil. The Skyliner lifted and the sound shook the ground, and in another minute there was nothing to be seen of her but the red and white winking lights against the black volcano range. Then the dust settled as she swung into her outward-bound circuit.

He checked the zip of the bag and began walking towards the boundary lamps and the road back into San Domingo. All he could hear now was a faint whispering rush among the stars. *Catachunga*.

The Pan-Aguador car-hire bureau did not open until eight o'clock in the morning; by the time he arrived there he had slept for two hours on a patch of waste ground littered with confetti and spent firework cartridges. His electric shaver was no use to him but he washed in the starlight with the water from the overflow of a reservoir and had a drink at the first bar to open to get rid of the taste of the chlorine.

He went to the Pan-Aguador people because they knew him personally. T.O.A. used them exclusively for their passengers. It was a risk because he didn't want to be seen in the country now; but he had no passport to show to any of the other firms. He chose a small Dyna-Compact, as grey as the rocks along the mountain road that he would be taking. He did not stop to buy any food for the trip, but took three bottles of mineral source water and some cigarettes.

There would be police blocks on the wet-weather road to the coast. He drove ten miles from the capital through the factory area and the great waste of volcanic lava the colour of an elephant's hide and unrelieved by a single grass-blade; then the zigzag track led downwards to boulder terrain a thousand feet below.

In this October-May season nobody used the dry-weather road because it became impassable for some days after tropic rainfall. Farther towards the coast there would be mud but he would just have to get through it. The first obstacle was a scattering of rocks from a cleft in the escarpment and it took three hours to shift a path for the little car. The noon sun struck down on to the land with a blinding glare and his head was throbbing, partly because of the terrain: after some time the never-ending shapes of the fallen boulders confused the eye.

The next halt was twenty miles from the coast and with less than one hour's daylight left. The road simply ended in a wall of heaped rocks. It looked man-made; but there was nothing man-made in this stretch of land, except the road; and that was gone. By midnight he had worked for five hours and rested for two, at short intervals. An intermontane Indian shepherd helped him for a while, speaking no Spanish but making gestures of doom and despair and pointing southwards many times, where Rayner knew the wet-weather road lay.

In the early hours of the morning the tremor came. He was sitting in the car to rest the pain in his left arm when it began, as a gentle shiver among the boulders. He knew what it was, and got out.

There was a jagged line of rock running north-south some two miles above this stretch of the track; from it these fallen rocks had originally come. The car would give him as much protection as an egg-shell. The shuddering came in rhythmic waves and the little Dyna-Compact began rocking on its springs. He was clambering over the remainder of the road-blockage when the movement grew very strong, and rocks began clattering on the higher slopes, their brittle sound loudening as they neared.

Standing on the lee side of the obstacle he prepared himself to wait. There was nothing he could do. In the starlight some of the boulders reared twenty feet high, but their shelter would be treacherous. Black, massive, solid, their very tonnage made them dangerous: they had rolled here from the higher land; one day they would roll again. Above their sculpted shapes the stars lighted a low sky. Surely some of this rising sound was echoed back from the lowest of those stars. They trembled in the void. Rocks ran now from ledge to ledge and clacked one on another as they hit and bounced and tumbled lower, sometimes flying high into the noisy air and splitting as they struck ground, thin slivers fluting as they razored the dark. Somewhere a big one was on the move. Rayner listened to it, to that one among them all.

He could not see it. Somewhere to the east and running south in the dark, running wild, cast out suddenly after a hundred or a thousand or a million years and set moving, it shook the ground with trembling spasms that could be felt only between the greater vibrations of the earthquake.

He hit the ground on his left side and bit off a shout of agony. He lay still. The ground had become like a goods truck running fast across points: one could no longer stand, and there was nothing to grab on to. Everything was red, now: the stars, the dark, the shivering rocks. He could not see the little car; by now it might have been buried. There must be blood in his eyes, with everything so red; or his nerves were bleeding. Something was making him shout. Not a word, just a long deliberate vibration in his throat. Not a call for help: no one could help him now. A shout perhaps to reaffirm his own exist-

80

ence among this multitude of thundering stones, a shout of protest against obliteration.

The red stars pulsed in the red sky. His arm was aflame. The land was on the march.

He was afraid. An earthquake is worse than a storm at sea or a storm hazarding an aircraft because there is the ship to shelter in or there is timber to cling to if the ship is gone, and there is hope of another ship, or making land; there is the hope of the aircraft dodging the heart of the storm, of staying airborne long enough to reach a landing-ground – it is the land that counts, that will sustain the man once he has gained its safety.

But here the land moved and shook and threw the man down; there was nowhere to run for safety. Nowhere.

He could hear now what he was shouting. Now it was a word. *Stop! Stop! Stop!*

The big rock rolled in the red dark, crashing against the others and sending them on the move, God at a snooker game down the dark hill. Dust rose from the fissured lava and hung in the air. The rocks ran through it. Splinters of chipped stone flew and made mad music above the drumming of the land. *Stop! Stop! Stop!* Stillness was the only shelter now and nothing was still. The dead land was alive. The red stars wheeled in the shaking sky, colliding.

*

It was still dark when he opened his eyes. His body shook in a fit of coughing because his face had been buried in the dust. When he moved, his arm flared and he passed out again.

He must have slept, eased by the knowledge that the earth was still. Sitting up, he moved his right hand across his face and wiped away the dust. Something like joy awoke in him. The earth was still. The sky was clear. He listened. There was no sound anywhere. He stood up and staggered, half-falling and cursing and straightening, angry. In the blue light of the stars he looked at his watch but the glass was smashed and the hands curled among the splinters like dark hairs.

He found the little car. It was slung flank-on against the obstacle in the track, the metal body flattened and gouged. He began walking away and remembered the zip-bag. It was jammed in the gap where the windscreen had been. He freed it and saw a gleam of bright glass. The last bottle of mineral water was unbroken. He drank it from the bottle and took the bag in his right hand, climbing over the heap of rocks and going on down the track.

81

An hour after the sun had come on like a sudden lamp, mounting the volcano range high against the east rim of the earth, two basin-dwellers, Indians, helped him on board their mule-cart. They were taking their wares down to the market in Puerto Fuego – carpets, moccasins and leather belts, baskets and pottery, the work of several families and many weeks.

They talked all the time between themselves, now and then speaking to Rayner. The word *aludi* was often repeated, something near the Spanish word for "avalanche." It would be the talk of the market to-day. The track was clear for most of the distance, for it turned south through the scattering of gold-mines away from the path of the landslide. By noon they were into the swamplands and skirting the rain-forest. An hour later they reached the seaport and the Indians went out of their way to leave him outside the hospital. They pointed their brown arms at the building with urgency and he nodded yes, he would go in there. He offered them money but they shook their heads and drove away.

He waited until they could no longer see him and then walked away from the hospital and through the mass of narrow streets running down to the waterfront drive and a mile beyond, to the little adobe house buried in its vegetation at the edge of the swamp.

Dr. van Keerls opened the door and looked at him and said: "What a mess. Come in."

In the main room of the house was a man whom Rayner recognised instantly. Van Keerls was opening the door to his immaculate little clinic, asking: "Why didn't you go to the hospital?" But he couldn't have known about the mule-cart. The hospital was the natural place to go.

Rayner was standing still, looking at the other man. Fate being devious, it had needed an arrest, deportation and an avalanche in order that he should come here with his pain, and see this man. To van Keerls he said: "I don't like hospitals. Besides, you said I'd be back here, didn't you?"

The doctor was waiting for him in the doorway. "Come in here, will you?"

Rayner ignored him. His anger rose as he looked at the man. Someone was going to tell him. He would make *someone* tell him.

He half realised he was swaying on his feet and that his voice was rising to a shout. "What happened?" he asked the man. "What happened to the plane? You survived it – you should know! *What happened?*"

CHAPTER FOURTEEN

HE was a short compact man, light on his feet and with quick eyes. He looked pure Spanish.

The energy drained out of Rayner. He stood waiting for an answer. In the doorway van Keerls watched him. Sometimes a man in this condition would go straight down before you could catch him. The Spaniard didn't speak. He darted his glances from Rayner to van Keerls and back. At last he said to the doctor:

"He is ill."

In Spanish Rayner said: "My head's all right. You are Colonel Juan Ibarra."

"Yes."

"If you admit that, you admit everything –"

"I have never been ashamed of my name –"

"So you were on that plane. And when it crashed you survived."

Ibarra stood perfectly still in the middle of the room with his eyes down, listening to every syllable.

Rayner stood with his feet apart. He knew the doctor was expecting him to fall over. "You came out of that crash, Ibarra. So did the pilot. So did the woman. How many others? Tell me their names. Tell me why you have to hide out like a pack of animals. Tell me why you're scared stiff, the lot of you. I won't pass it on. I've got to hide out myself, now. That puts us on the same side, doesn't it? *Why don't you tell me what happened?*"

He was shouting again.

Ibarra said to van Keerls: "He is ill. You must help him. If you will excuse me." He moved for the door.

"Don't just go," Rayner said wearily. "It's all you people can think of – running away the moment you're recognised. Lindstrom, the woman, and now you." He shut his eyes as he heard the door opening and then closing. There was nothing he could do. He wasn't fit enough to grab Ibarra and drag him back and make him talk, even if he had any right.

"Come on, Sunshine," said the doctor; and Rayner followed him into the clinic like a somnambulist.

"Did you get your injection yesterday, from Lucillo?"

"What?" Everything was too bright in here. The leaves and tendrils writhed at the windows. "Who's Lucillo?" He couldn't remember having seen the name on the backs of any of the forty-two photographs. Colonel Juan Ibarra, yes. Not Lucillo.

"The chemist I told you to go to. Plaza Pasteza."

He was trying to get Rayner's jacket off but the sleeve was stuck with blood.

"No. Hadn't time. Listen, what was he doing here? Ibarra? What's he doing *alive*?"

"Keep still." He had the jacket off except for the left sleeve. He began rolling the sleeve down inside-out, using long scissors to snip the lining clear of the bloodied lint.

"I'm not trying to do anyone any harm," Rayner said, talking more to himself or to *them* than to the doctor. "I'm trying to find out what happened to the plane. She was one of mine, due in at San Domingo. It's my job to find out!"

The sleeve came away and van Keerls put the jacket across a tall chrome-legged stool. "How did you get into this mess, Rayner?"

"I tell you she was one of mine. T.O.A. sent me out here to —"

"No, I mean *this* mess." He began work on the clotted lint.

"Avalanche. Listen, I've got a certain amount of faith in you." His voice sounded slurred as if he were drunk. "I've decided to trust you, just so far. You've —"

"How much sleep have you had since you left here two days ago?"

"What? Not much. Trust you. That's why I came here — walked in the sun for two bloody miles. If you won't tell me about Ibarra, you might consider telling me where I can put up in this town. I'm on the run now, can't show myself." His laugh sounded dreadful. "I'm joining the Survivors' Club. Honora — hon-ry member!" He was silent for a long time, trying to think out what he had been saying. Odd images kept floating across his mind. The little Dyna-Compact, crushed like a tin toy. Captain Edwards's face. *I don't really know, sir.* The mad red roller-coaster stars in the drumming dark.

Van Keerls had tied a square of gauze round his mouth and he examined the flesh of the arm. "What happened to your hands?"

"Shifting boulders. Listen —"

"Shut up and keep still."

Rayner closed his eyes again. Instruments clinked against porcelain; the tap gushed. His arm was being smothered in something cool, and the relief made him light-headed.

"There's three of 'em now, Doc. Three alive. Be funny if I found ninety-nine ... the whole lot. Where's th'other ninety-

84

six, d'you know? I bet you know. If I give you my word not to –"

There was a jab in his arm and the shock opened his eyes and he stared at the doctor's face. "What's that stuff? By God if you're giving me –"

"You'll snap this needle if you don't keep still."

Low on his breath Rayner said: "If that's dope you're giving me I'll murder you, my son."

"You wouldn't have much chance, would you?" The needle came out smoothly and the skin crept as the ether pad touched it. He shivered suddenly, as one does in a fever.

"Right. In here, now."

It was a room as small as the clinic, with just a low couch. A sheet and pillow, everything clean and white, the most soporific sight in the world when a man is tired.

"Lie down." He was pulling Rayner's shoes off.

"So it was dope." He held on to van Keerls and to consciousness, his left arm a riot of pain as the muscles tensed.

"The only dope you've got inside you is fatigue. First we get rid of that."

"I trust you."

"You've no option, old boy. But you're in luck. I'm a doctor, not some prize character out of Edgar Wallace. Now lie still and relax –"

"Listen, if you –"

"Oh, shut up. Relax."

Rayner stared up at the thin Nordic face with its calm blue eyes, and suddenly it seemed to spread out in waves of water that slowly grew dark.

He was alone in the small room when he awoke. For some minutes he lay thinking, until suddenly he realised that there was no pain in his arm. Whosever side van Keerls was on, he was a good doctor. He found him working at a microscope in the clinic, still in his white tunic. He did not look up.

"Feel better?"

"Much."

"Come and have a look." He stood up and made room. Rayner's eyes were heavy from his sleep but he concentrated at the microscope. Within an irregular pool on the slide there moved a mass of hook-shaped forms.

"What are they?"

"The name takes rather longer to spit out than those Welsh railway stations, but the thing is you're free of them. I took a swab from your arm. You were pretty beleaguered. If you don't have another injection to-morrow they'll gang up on you

85

all over again, so don't say I didn't warn you."

"Lucillo, Plaza Pasteza."

"That sleep has given you some sense." He drew the slide out and put a yellow drop of liquid on it and went to wash his hands. In a perfect mimicry of the tame family doctor he went on: "Well, Mr. Rayner, I think that's all we need do for you at the moment. Keep the arm as motionless as you can – no golf for another week, I fear, and we'll have to deny ourselves that nice glass of sherry before dinner for a few days. No alcohol, m'm?" He dried his hands and his tone dropped the mincing timbre. "And in case I haven't made my point I'll add that you don't find this bug in Gorgonzola. It's a killer."

"I'm grateful to you." He realised they were probably the first civil words he had said to this man. "I'd like to know your fee. Two visits."

"Let's say fifty pesos."

Rayner took his jacket from the stool and found his wallet, but van Keerls stopped him with a quick lift of his hand.

"In the other room, please." He led the way on his quiet gliding feet. "If you put a five-peso note under that microscope you'd see the entire six volumes of *Equatorial Indigenous Malevolent Bacilli*." He accepted the money and put it into a drawer. "Thank you." He helped Rayner into his jacket. "Sorry, but I had to cut the lining out."

The Transocean Airline zip-bag was where he had left it, near the door. "Dr. van Keerls," he said, trying to make up for his previous outburst of wild speech, "I need your good advice."

"I gave it to you once but you wouldn't take it."

"I can't leave Aguador."

"Then that's that." He leaned his long body against the bureau, studying Rayner with the same kind of gaze that he used at his microscope.

"If you knew anywhere safe I could put up for a few days, would you tell me? And would you not tell anyone else that I was there?"

Van Keerls went on studying him for a few seconds and then folded his arms and looked at the leaf-filled window.

"You put me in a tricky position, Rayner. Nothing like as tricky as yours, I grant you."

Rayner said: "How much do you *know*?"

"I know one thing. If you stay in this country you're going to get killed, sooner or later. You're between two fires, you see – the police on one side, and certain people on the other. And *neither* party wants you to succeed in what you've been

86

sent here to do, which is to find out what happened to that plane."

Rayner asked: "Did you know I'd been deported?"

"News gets about."

"Then you know I must have made an effort to stay put. So you know it's no use telling me to go home."

Van Keerls turned from the window. "Yes."

"I can steer clear of the police all right. You'd better warn me who the other 'certain people' are."

"I'd 'better'? Why should I? Yours isn't the only life that's in the melting-pot. As far as anyone in Puerto is concerned, Rayner, you are expendable." His light eyes had the look of pain in them again, the memory of other people's, and perhaps the awareness of pain to come. "You see, if I tell you where to find shelter, you'll go on with your investigations, and I'd be letting down more than one of my friends. So it's no go." He opened the door to the green-filtered dazzle of the sun. "If you're lucky, and only get hurt, you know where to find me and I shall always be at your service, just as I'm at any man's who comes to this door."

Paul took the zip-bag in his right hand and walked to the road through the tunnel of leaves. In the heat of the afternoon sun he turned towards the town.

In every seaport of the world there is a Lloyd's agent. The one in Puerto Fuego said yes, the bag could be left in his office for a few hours, owner's responsibility, of course. It was a relief to be without it because he had not been able to change it to his left hand.

He decided against reporting the loss of the Dyna-Compact to the Pan-Aguador office in the town. He would in any case lose his 100 peso deposit and the insurance company would see to the rest. He had paid in advance for three days, which now gave him that period free of the manhunt that would be raised when Pan-Aguador told the police that the car hadn't checked in and that the driver's name was Rayner. With luck a shepherd or a mule-driver would find the wreckage before long, and the police might assume that the driver had jumped out of the car to avoid being trapped in it and had been caught by a rock and buried.

He saw Willis by chance, and recognised Gates with him at the table outside the bar. He needed to see Gates, badly; so he crossed the road. He noticed that he had already formed the habit of watching for uniforms.

When the three of them had sat down there was the moment

of silence before Gates asked: "What happened to you, Rayner?"

Rayner knew both men were studying him. The stubble and the crumpled suit were a help: Gates had hardly recognised him just now. Nor would the police in three days' time.

"I ran foul of an avalanche."

Willis murmured gently: "You should have taken the wet-weather road." He couldn't resist telling you how much he knew. The landslide hadn't affected that road to the south.

"There were police-blocks."

"Ah."

Gates lost patience: "Look here, Rayner, we can't have our people on the run from the police, even in this place! What d'you think the publicity's going to do to the airline?"

Rayner looked at him for a moment. He didn't think he was going to remain one of T.O.A.'s "people" very long. He was about to tell Gates several things that would get him fired.

"I was glad to see you here, sir. Didn't know you were coming."

"By God I'm glad I did! I'll tell you one thing, Rayner – I'm going back to-morrow and you'll be with me on board!"

"I don't think you could manage that, sir. I'm not meant to be in the country and I've no passport or exit visa. I'd be an embarrassment to you at the departure check, and –"

"You're an embarrassment already – I suppose you know that?"

"Not my fault, I'm afraid. My deportation was fixed."

"If you'd come back to London when I told you, it wouldn't have happened."

Rayner thought that for a normally shrewd man the chairman was taking a clod-brained line, so he said: "Mr. Gates, my job in London's responsible and exacting. You took me off it and sent me here after what must have been careful thought. You can't just cable my recall and necessarily expect to find me on the next plane. I'm not a marionette."

There went the job. No matter.

After a moment Gates said evenly: "I can get you out of this country. They want you out, don't they? You don't really think they'd hold you up at the departure check. So when d'you intend leaving, Rayner?"

"I hadn't thought much about the actual date, sir. I'd say I shall feel ready to leave when I've seen the wreck of the plane brought to the surface." He found his battered pack of cigarettes and lit one.

"Why *then*, Rayner?" Gates was speaking quietly, for him.

"I can't explain. Once I see that aircraft on the surface. I suppose I'll be satisfied that all this fog of secrecy is finished with. I don't trust it. I don't trust anyone."

"You trust me, Rayner?" The question was casual.

"No, sir."

Perhaps B.O.A.C. or Empire Airways would take him on. He knew most of their people, and four years' service with T.O.A. was a good reference, even if they'd slung him out.

"Why not?"

Rayner dragged on his black Sumatran cigarette. "Nothing personal, of course. I'll put it this way. I don't think it's possible for you – the head of a huge concern still working to clear a twenty-million-pound deficit – to see this thing quite so clearly as I do, as an individual employee free of any company problems. An organisation as big as T.O.A. has been built like all the others, as much by subtle shifts and expediencies as by progressive vision and hard work. I wouldn't *expect* you to save my neck if it meant jeopardising the well-being of the company. And so you can't expect me to put my trust where I ask no quarter."

For fully a minute Gates watched the spread of his fingers against the top of the table. Willis had switched his very interested gaze from Rayner's face to a point some fifty yards beyond him along the pavement. Rayner waited for Gates to speak, but it was Willis who said:

"Rayner, forgive my butting in, but there are two police officers coming this way and looking at every face they pass. You have about half a minute to get up slowly and go, if you feel you should do that." He continued to peer over his invisible wall at the two uniformed men in the distance.

Gates's thought-train was broken and he looked first along the pavement and then at Rayner. The sun was lowering to the ocean and the great avenue of trees was turning rhubarb-red. The lights of the bar had come on minutes ago.

Rayner looked at Willis's eyes and tried to read what was in them; but there was nothing in them; they were as bland as a pair of pearls. His spine began creeping. He did not know why Willis was doing this. There might not be any police in sight at all: it could be a simple way of getting rid of the embarrassing Mr. Rayner so that Willis could have a word in private to Gates. If there were police coming, they might not be "looking at every face" but merely patrolling the street; and any one of a dozen intentions might have made Willis warn him: to get rid of him; to remind him of his weak position; to remind Gates of the same point; even to get him rearrested by making him call attention to himself just as the patrol came up. It would be dangerous to believe that Willis was simply trying to help him.

He tapped ash from his cigarette, glancing across the façade of the bar; but there was no glass door at an angle that would serve as a mirror. He could not turn round. Reason began its tussle with animal instinct: unless by sheer chance the San Domingo police had heard that a Señor Rayner had hired a car from Pan-Aguador, they didn't know that he was still in the country. He had three days' leeway that would now end technically at eight a.m. the day after to-morrow. There hadn't been a general search started yet. But there was a slight chance that one of these police officers was Major Pareira or one of the lieutenants; and they would recognise him even with the stubble on his face. Reason here was on the side of instinct: *get clear*.

With the half-minute already down to some fifteen seconds he realised that it was neither reason nor instinct that kept him in this chair, but an emotion: pride. He was damned if he would leave Willis and Gates here sipping their drinks while he scuttled away like a hunted animal.

He refused even to lean his elbows on the table and cup his face in his hands, casually. Gates and Willis were watching him. He began listening to the footsteps of the people who went by. It was a long fifteen seconds. If he were caught again they wouldn't send him on a T.O.A. plane, and there'd be an escort with him as far as Panama, and Catachunga would be lost for good.

He watched Willis, particularly his hands. If Willis made any sign to the patrol there'd be good red blood on Rayner's knuckles as they put the handcuffs on.

"We'll go on talking," said Gates and Rayner nearly laughed. Gates was more worried than he was himself. Bad publicity and all that. "You've got it off your chest, and I'm going to be as straight with you, Rayner. Willis here tells me you've recognised a passenger. A woman. Is *that* why you're so determined to stay out here?"

Willis's hands were still, one dangling from the wrist with his arm hooked over the back of the chair, the other holding his glass. Unworried ease.

Rayner had heard Gates's question but it would take a few seconds to think out the answer. It wasn't simply, "No." He could see her face now as if she were sitting at this table. How much his efforts to stay in Puerto Fuego had been due to that beautiful face he would never know. But she had built Cata-

90

chunga for him, out of a heap of burning rock. That was probably the only real answer, impossible to give Gates: "I'm staying here because of Catachunga."

The footsteps of the people passed along the paving stones; their shadows moved along the wall in a strange slow dance among the shadows of the trees.

About deadline now.

Suddenly Willis was talking in rapid Spanish: "I simply don't understand how anyone can possibly say that Turano's cape-work is better than El Volete's if you watch them in the same ring on the same afternoon and with a run of bulls equally brave. His sword-work – yes! Turano can kill at the first thrust and make poetry out of all his stuttering with the cape –"

From the edge of Rayner's field of vision he saw the dun colour of the uniforms and the flash of the white pipe-cord. Corruption in toy drum-major's clothing.

"– But I can tell you I once saw him do a *media-Veronica* with a three-year-old bull that looked like a butterfly in a fit! Show him a four-year-old and he'll be over the *barrera* with the bull wiping its nose on the cape – and that's his trouble. Hands, feet, a straight eye and an instinct for a hooking horn, but no guts. No *cajones*!"

Rayner glanced along the pavement. Yes, they were looking into people's faces. They hadn't bothered much with the three men at the table: you don't spend your time discussing the bullfight if you're trying to keep clear of the police.

He felt badly about Willis. He did not like suspecting the innocent.

"I'm most grateful to you, Willis."

"A pleasure. But I suppose you'll still go on saying Turano's better with the cape."

Gates said to Willis: "How near was that?"

"It's hard to say, Mr. Gates. There's so much going *on* in this town that one loses track."

"To answer your question," Rayner told Gates, "I'm staying out here because I want to know what happened to the *Glamis Castle*. I'm in touch with that crash now as if it had been yesterday. You gave me a ball of string to untangle and now I'm half-way there."

Willis said with a faint smile, "There's something rather engaging, isn't there, about undoing knots. . . ."

"That's all very pretty," Gates began.

"No, sir. It stinks. Close on a hundred people lost their lives and a thousand felt the grief. I was at San Domingo that day and I had to lie to the people who were waiting there for the husbands and mothers and sons who were never going to arrive. One man tried suicide and I saw him at the clinic afterwards. He looked alive but he was dead, inside. Wouldn't *you* want to –"

"Now steady, Rayner. You've got yourself knocked about in an avalanche but we need to think straight. Willis has been sent out here to take over from you and he's a top professional. Won't it satisfy you to read the reports of this case when it all comes up again?"

Rayner looked at the square reasonable face. "*Will* it all come up again?"

"It'll have to, man! Didn't I start this new inquiry myself?"

Rayner began losing touch with reality, by a degree. Except during the seeming end of the world when the boulders had thundered down the mountain he had flogged his mind along a score of different tracks that could lead him somewhere. Perhaps he had over-thought. Brain-fag. It had almost shocked him to realise just now that Willis was a friend and not an enemy. He had been wrong. He might be wrong about Gates too. A few hours ago he had been shouting at a stranger in a stranger's house – *what happened to that plane?* And the doctor had said: *If you stay in this country you're going to get killed.* Soon after eight a.m. the day after to-morrow there'd be a manhunt up for him. What else could he hope to learn if his only thought was how to stop being caught? Why not just let Willis take over and quietly find the answer?

So even part of his own mind had turned against him.

"Listen, Mr. Gates." He knew the fatigue was coming back: he needed more than the two hours' sleep he had taken at van Keerls' house. He didn't really know what he was going to tell Gates; it was all in his mind but he would have to listen to his own voice before he understood. "It's hot along this coast and I've lost a bit of sleep, but there are some facts I'm going to give you. To-day I saw a man who was on board that aircraft and I spoke to him and he admitted his name –"

"A man?"

"Colonel Juan Ibarra. A survivor."

Gates asked heavily: "You're certain, Rayner?" He was worried by Rayner's mood and by the wild note in his voice that he was trying to keep quiet. Something had got a grip of the man.

"Certain. I recognised him the moment I saw him and I asked him what had happened to the plane. I told him I knew his name – because it's on the back of the photograph I found in the files of a local paper. He was a survivor."

"And the woman?"

"I recognised her too, even by the light of a street-lamp, on this pavement not far from here. Mademoiselle Giselle Vidal." He leaned over the little iron table, staring into Gates's stone-wall face. "I knew her car – a white open Mercedes – and for three days I kept watch for it with field-glasses before I saw it again – for three days in this heat, you don't know what it's like, maybe you do – and then I followed her into a restaurant and watched her for an hour before I talked to her and listened to her. The night before last I met her again in the same place – she was so close to me that I could have touched her! She –"

"That's enough, Rayner!"

"Enough?"

The two men were watching him gravely and neither spoke. He realised he was leaning across the table. Had he been shouting at Gates? He leaned back, his eyes picking on Gates's wrist-watch, on Willis's dangling hand, on the half-empty glass of Pernod in front of him, avoiding their watching faces. His own voice was asking without heat: "Isn't that what I was sent here to get? Proof?"

They said nothing. He knew he had been talking a lot about the woman. Too much. Now it wouldn't matter what he told them: they wouldn't believe him. He closed his eyes. He must see it from Gates's point of view. Here was Rayner looking like a tramp, wanted by the police, telling his chairman that he didn't trust him, asking to be sacked. How did Gates know he hadn't gone round the bend after a month in this deadly heat? Got mixed up in some wild anti-Ycaza movement because of the woman he talked so much about? What proof was there of his sanity?

Ask the consul, Emmerson – he'll tell you how I was fixed. But it was he who had told Emmerson.

Ask Dr. van Keerls – he'll tell you I saw Colonel Ibarra. But would he? Van Keerls had friends he mustn't let down.

Ask Ventura – he'll tell you I tried to bribe him to give me Lindstrom's address. Ventura was dumb. They would all be dumb. Puyo. El Angelo. All.

He had no proof for Gates. After five weeks, Lindstrom was still a skeleton in the sea.

The trump card was no good, now. He had just torn it up. It would sound absurd: a cross seen by chance on a map.

He opened his eyes. Sweat ran into them, stinging. His voice was weary. "Listen. I know where the plane is lying. I sent you a letter. I know its depth and position. Will you arrange to send down a diver?"

After a long time Gates said quietly: "Can you tell me what proof you've got?"

An inked cross. "No."

Gates looked away from him.

Rayner got up, scraping the iron chair on the paving. The lights were pale along the shops and bars in contrast to the sweep of bright gold along the horizon. The lights confused him. Like a man who knows he is half-drunk he took great care with his feet.

He said: "When are you going back?"

"To-morrow," Gates said.

"I'll try to get something before you go. Some kind of proof."

He left them at the table.

CHAPTER FIFTEEN

HE supposed they were still watching him, from the table. Gates had looked embarrassed – an expression Rayner had never seen on that square and unimaginative face before. One of his top station supers had gone barmy and he didn't know how to handle it.

The dun-brown colour came again among the pretty dresses and the tropical suits. The same two were coming back; or it was a different patrol. He took the first street, keeping his slow pace. The tall houses trapped the heat of the day, and its waves flowed against his face. How did the lungs find anything in this air to give to the blood?

The street was narrow but a car had just turned into it from the Avenida. It was going slowly. Normally when a car straightens after a corner it accelerates.

The street smelt of oranges and flowers and drains and marijuana; the little shops were doing more trade in this hour than during the whole day. The sun was down and the strip of sky above the eaves was already indigo and pricked with stars. The sharp smell of the exhaust-gas was spreading through the street. The car was crawling in first gear. He kept his pace and did not look round.

He needed a new watch because the avalanche had broken his old one. He would go into the first jeweller's. In Puerto there was one jeweller's to every bar, because of the small-time gold and emerald and diamond concessions scattered throughout the mountains. One man and his son would scratch for a year, and find one stone, and live on it for a year.

Normally a car would clear the way with its horn and you were lucky if there were a doorway to jump to. He no longer thought it was a police mobile patrol: one of them would have got out by now to catch up with him on foot. He had been waiting for the dying of the engine and the click of the door, but the car was still moving. It might belong to the other side: van Keerls's "certain people." There weren't many strollers like himself in this street, but groups stood in shop-doorways. A shot would be too risky here: there was no fast run for the car afterwards.

A neon sign, shaped like a dangling fob-watch, hung not far away. As he neared the shop he saw that it had a narrow mirror at an angle in the doorway, like many jewellers had. First he saw himself reflected in it, a tall, thin, shabby out-of-work white, hardly recognisable. Then the low flat radiator of the ivory Mercedes.

He kept in the middle of the roadway so that it had to pull up as he turned. He moved round close to the front wing, but she wasn't trying to get past him. She held the door open, so he got in and she drove off again, reaching the little square where a couple of checker-bodied taxis were standing. She made a round of the plaza and then took a street that would lead down to the harbour, as if suddenly deciding where they must go.

The web seat-fitting was cool against his back. From here among the narrow streets he could not see it, but he knew that now the sun had gone down, the beautiful crown of the volcano would be glowing. He wanted to sleep.

"I was in the La Ronda," she said with her slight Parisian accent. "I saw you walk past."

He realised now that he had walked away from the little iron table without seeing anything, and had passed the place that was so important to him.

"Where are we going?" he asked. The smell of the water was brackish on the stifling air; the smell of wet rope, pitch, diesel fuel and rotting fish.

"A place where they do not know me. What is your name?"

"Paul Rayner. *Enchanté, Mademoiselle Vidal.*"

The one gold ring gleamed as her hand moved on the rim of the wheel.

The port was quiet; the dredger was not working. Fishermen, boatmen, travel-touts and waterfront bums were moving into the open, looking at the sky because they had not seen it since dawn.

She ran the Mercedes between two stacks of raw white pine that a timber-ship had dumped, and got out of the car the moment the engine was off. Rayner followed her across the cobbled jetty to a shack of a bar where some men were drinking. The place had just been sprayed with insecticide and the mosquito screens were already across the windows.

They sat at a table in a back corner. She was less tense, underneath the show of calm, than she had been when they had sat together like this at the La Ronda. For the first time he saw her smile to him.

"It is not very chic, M'sieur Rayner."

"If they don't know you at this place, how do you know it?"

"I have seen it from across the water, from the peninsular road, often. Nobody would think I would come here."

"Would they have champagne here?"

"I do not like to drink champagne." He wondered at the distaste in her eyes.

"Would you rather we spoke in French?"

"My English is so bad?"

"It's perfect but I thought you might have missed your mother-tongue after two years." He noticed that she wore no jewellery, only the plain ring and a cheap wrist-watch. The corn-coloured hair ran down to a simple white dress; her arms were brown and slender. She said: "I have exactly one hour left."

A creole reeking of marijuana was near them and Rayner asked her: "What will you drink?"

"Anything."

He ordered Pernod for them both. There was no distaste this time when she heard him give the order. He had been watching for it. She was a Frenchwoman who disliked champagne, and she hadn't commented about missing her mother-tongue. He wondered if she hadn't returned to France because for some reason she hated her own country.

"There is so much to say, mademoiselle."

"Yes. But we have an hour."

"That isn't long. You begin."

She held her hands together on the rough-wood table but did not clench them, as she had before.

"Who are you?"

He said: "I don't want to scare you away, like last time."

96

"I know more about you, now."

"How?"

"I was there when you were arrested." The look of fright passed again across her eyes.

"That makes me acceptable?" he asked gently.

"Yes. What did they do to you?"

"Tried to deport me."

Her mouth quivered in surprise. "*Expulser?*" She had to make sure she understood.

"Yes. I slipped them –"

"*Comment?*"

"Escaped from my guard." He knew they were fast returning to her original question, which he'd been trying to dodge. The answer to "Who are you?" involved the missing plane; and he was afraid the mention of it would scare her off again. Then she said:

"So you were not on that airplane."

"No." He didn't ask how she knew. She and the other survivors were prisoners in some way, and deportation would be their one dream. So he could not be a member of their exclusive club.

"I believed you were on that airplane," she said.

"I know. I wanted you to think that. I'm sorry." He tried to hope that within the next few seconds he would know the answer to everything, that after these jading weeks they would all take their place in the pattern; Ventura, Puyo, Ibarra, the cross on the chart. It seemed too much to ask, but here was a survivor. He hadn't meant to put this one major question so soon. "What happened to the plane?"

She held his eyes for as long as she could, and when she looked down he knew it was no good. She said: "We crashed on the sea –"

"I know –"

"Well that is all."

"Was the plane on fire?"

"No –"

"There was engine trouble?"

"No –"

"Why did you crash?"

Her quiet hands were clenched, the fingers bloodless under the brown skin.

"Was it a case of pilot error?" he asked more calmly.

"*Comment?*"

"A mistake by the pilot. Were you off course?"

97

"I do not know. I was only a passenger." It pained her eyes and her voice and her hands to have to talk about it.

"Do you know what made the plane hit the sea?" He hated himself for insisting.

She looked at him in silence. He said: "Then if you know, why can't you tell me?"

In a moment she said: "It would be dangerous for you, to know. Dangerous for me to tell you." She said again: "Who are you?"

The creole brought their drinks and a jug of iced water. Rayner told her: "For me, this is a day for celebration."

"Yes?"

"Yes. I hope that by this time next year you will have reason to celebrate this day's anniversary." He raised his glass.

"You are celebrating that they did not deport you successfully," she said.

"No. But that deserved a small cheer too. As to who I am, I work for T.O.A. and I am here to find out what happened to the Skyliner 10."

"I see." She had the odd trick of looking at him so directly that he became half lost in the blue regard and couldn't think clearly. "But it was over two years ago."

"The pilot has just been seen alive. In this town." He didn't feel tired any more; he felt so alert again that his very face must surely look different, losing what poor old Gates would call a wild, mad look.

"The pilot," she said. "Yes."

"Do you see him often?"

"I have not seen him since we escaped."

"Escaped?"

"From the airplane. It sank very quickly."

"How many of you survived?"

"I am not sure. Perhaps six or seven of us."

"Yourself, Captain Lindstrom, Colonel Ibarra. Who else?"

She had withdrawn a little. He placed his hand lightly across hers on the table. "Mademoiselle, I've no right to question you, but you see the position: I'm here to find out about that crash, and you can tell me so much, out of simple kindness."

Her eyes mistrusted him. He took away his hand. This girl was full of wounds, some recently healed. If one were clumsy one would break the skin again.

"Why did they arrest you?" she asked. What trust she had in him depended on that arrest. She feared the police – she

98

had been frightened when she had seen them coming to the table in the La Ronda. If they were an enemy, the Englishman must be a friend.

"A lot of people want to leave that plane where it is, at the bottom of the sea. I want to raise it. They know that. So they compromised me, and I became officially an undesirable."

Nervously she said: "I thought they were going to take you away to be shot."

"For what?"

"For being —" she broke off and sipped her drink.

It could be only one thing: for being a member of the exclusive club. For being a survivor.

"On that plane?" he said casually but it was no good. Her eyes were lowered. She said:

"You told me: it is all so dangerous."

By little degrees it was coming out. They were not only prisoners but in fear of their lives. If they could find them the police would arrest this girl, and Lindstrom, and Ibarra. And have them shot. "For being . . ." For *knowing*. For knowing what had made the Skyliner ditch.

She had said just now, "Perhaps six or seven of us."

"Who are the others?" he asked. "Who else survived? You can trust me, because —"

She was standing up suddenly. "No. I cannot trust you or anyone."

He stood up slowly. In Puerto Fuego there was a jeweller's shop to every bar; but trust was beyond anyone's price. She was walking towards the door and he found some money for the drinks.

He paid and went out. She was standing by the Mercedes. The stacks of white pine hid the car from the peninsular road.

"*Je regrette, M'sieur Rayner.*"

"I understand." He managed a grunt of amusement, "I'm wanted by the police now, like you and the others, because I couldn't trust anyone either. I thought that you and I might be able to help each other." Light came from the screened windows of the shack, but the piles of timber made a shadow. In the starlight he could not see her face clearly. "Tell me," he said quietly, "what doubts you still have."

She leaned against the car, closing her eyes, perhaps the better to think. "How did you know my name? Why did you follow me to the La Ronda, twice?"

"I have photographs of some of the missing passengers

99

and their names are on the back. I recognised you. How else can I find out what happened? You were there."

She walked a few paces towards the harbour wall; he did not follow. She wanted to think. He mustn't lose her now. Against the dark water she stood like a slim candle, indistinct in the gloom of the room into which he had wandered uninvited.

He lit and smoked a cigarette, waiting. There was so much that he couldn't fit into the pattern. No jewellery; a cheap chrome wrist-watch; but a beautiful white Mercedes. A *white* Mercedes; the only one in the town. Easily seen. *I have exactly one hour left*.

She was coming back. He threw the cigarette away and said in a low voice: "You will be bitten by the mosquitoes if you stay here."

Looking away she said: "I must go now, anyway."

"Or you'll break your parole."

"*Comment?*"

"*On ne doit pas manquer à sa parole.*" No jewellery that she could sell to pay her fare to anywhere; a cheap watch by which to know the time; a car, easy to trace, at her brief disposal. White slave. The idea sickened him. It couldn't be true.

"I will tell you why I must go," she said, "and why I cannot trust you. You want to find out what happened to the airplane. When that is known, I will have to die." She pulled open the driving-door and got in. Her hands held the steering-wheel rigidly and she turned her face up to him, sitting so still that in the pale light she was like a doll in a pretty toy car.

He hadn't meant to tell her, because it would sound like bribery; but now it might help her to know, if she believed it. "Once the wreck of the plane is raised, I shall be going home to London. I would be able to put you on board a plane at San Domingo, and no one would recognise you or stop you. I can arrange it."

Her eyes were no more than blue shadows in the darkness of her tilted face; but he sensed that she was seeing for a moment the boulevards of Paris. When she answered, her voice as sad as a child's, Paris was as far away as Paradise.

"You would have no time to help me. It would be too late. If you raise the airplane, you will be going home alone."

She started the engine and he leaned close to her so that she would hear him clearly. "*Écoutez*. I will come to this bar every day, hoping there will be a word from you. Leave it in the name of Señor French – it's easy for you to remember."

He stood back from the car and watched her turn. Then the sound of it died away.

For the first time in this town he had put his trust in some-one; yet she had only to tell them: "He will be there every day." And he would find them waiting for him; and the wreck of the plane would never be raised; and she would not have to die.

CHAPTER SIXTEEN

COOGIE MERCER sat with his legs out straight on the top of the cabin and his back to the mast. In the dim light of the stars he looked like part of the boat, a stowed canvas.

He was watching the ebb and flow of the phosphorescent surf. The fishing-boats had put to sea a couple of hours ago and where some oil had leaked there were small rainbows swirling on the water. Far over the ocean he could see the new moon, so fragile, so pure in the night that he wanted to reach up and bring it to his boat for safety till it had time to grow. In latitude 0° you didn't often see anything so cool and delicate prettying the sky.

"A fortune," Sam Stowe had been telling him. He had listened to Sam for almost an hour. Now he had gone, and he could sit on the cabin and look at the blue-green shimmer of the surf and the rainbows and the virgin moon.

Sam was like most men. They never thought about what was going on right now, this minute; they could only ever think about to-morrow and next year when they'd do this and do that — then they'd strike it real rich and be happy the rest of their life. Looking and scratching for the damn' stuff all over, so exercised about it that it took all the living out of their life. They never got to look at the surf or the moon or their own soul.

"A fortune," Sam had told him. He'd been telling Mercer about it for six months now, ever since Mercer had sailed his *Sea Queen* into Puerto Fuego, dropped anchor and opened for business. But that kind of business was crazy. Sam had the notion there was a safe full of uncut emeralds in the skipper's cabin of the *Dorea*, a thirty-ton ketch that had foundered on coral off this coast some five years before.

"I seen the paper, Coogie. That skip was takin' stones down to Lima when his boat went down with all hands. A man in Acariquaz told me it was true what the papers in the port-office said — nothin' illegal or anythin'. A fortune. You go find it an' we split. That's fair. You're the on'y man I've

101

told, about where that ship's lyin'. Less'n a hundred fathoms."

"In a spot so thick with shark they look like sardines with the tin off."

"You ain't scared o' shark, Coogie, hell, man!"

"Not scared of automobiles either, but I don't go walk under their wheels."

Sam had spat into the sea. "You c'n go down in a cage, man!"

"Once saw a guy go down in a cage, Sam. Never saw him come back up though. Got fouled in the wreck."

Sam had gone off good and frustrated like always, saying the same thing before he went. "No man knows where that ship is, Coogie, 'cep' you'n me. Don't you ever forget that. You go tellin' people an' it amounts to piracy on the high seas!"

"Okay, Sinbad, it's our own secret fortune, and safer down there than in any bank you could name."

Mercer watched the long roll of the surf with the starlight glinting on its million emeralds, along where the oily rainbows ran, topaz and sapphire, opal, ruby, pearl. Far up there, a diadem in the sky. Wherever you looked.

He thought it was Sam Stowe coming back, but the voice was English. "Is that Mr. Mercer?"

He turned his head against the mast. "That's me, Jack."

"Can I come aboard?"

"Watch the plank, it's just scrubbed, still wet." When the man came closer he saw it was the Limey who came along the shore sometimes. Right now he could use a shave.

"You're a diver."

"Yep."

"Brissing gave me your name. The Lloyd's man."

"Oh, sure." He got up. It looked like trade. "Got some Scotch below."

Before lighting the lamp he fixed the mosquito-screens. There wasn't a hole in them anywhere, and the lamp's copper bowl was brilliant.

"You run a good boat, Mr. Mercer."

"She's tidy, Jack."

The Limey hadn't said his name yet. A lot of people in Puerto didn't. He poured some whisky.

Brissing, the Lloyd's man, had told Rayner there was only one diver in the town any good. Mercer wasn't pricy but hard to get. He had to be interested in a job to take it on. Rayner had not told Brissing what the job was. He had just taken his zip-bag and left it at the *pensión*, which was a broken-down mansion – the Castillo Marco – right at the end of the water-front drive where the road started along the peninsula. The Mercedes would pass the place every time it went into the town.

He had put down a fifty-peso note for the concierge instead of a passport, as the tout had recommended. The remainder of his expenses was running low, but there might be enough for Mr. Mercer.

"Have you got a submarine camera?" he asked him.

"Guess I haven't."

Rayner was having to decide in these first few minutes how much he would trust Mercer. If any of the "certain people" heard that a diver was looking for the *Glamis Castle*, he wouldn't live long. This must be pointed out to him, and it meant telling him one or two things.

He liked the face. It was practically flat and the colour of brick. The nose had been thrown on from a distance as an afterthought, and it stuck out off-centre between quiet Saxon eyes. The mouth went all shapes when he talked; when he was silent it was zipped shut in a dead-straight line above the big square chin. His voice had a rough wheeze to it; like many divers he had been down too deep too often.

They sat on a bulkhead bench of exquisitely-grained Siamese yang, beneath a carved wood panel. The cabin-brass was polished until some of the slots were worn away from the screwheads. These details, too, were part of the face of Mercer, part of his character.

"The operation," Rayner said, "has to be kept private."

Mercer looked merry. "Never known one that hasn't, Jack. Hope it isn't emeralds. Already got a guy with emeralds."

"There's nothing of any value on board."

"Well *that's* new!" He looked in admiration at the stubble-faced Limey.

"Not saleable value, I mean. First of all, how much do you charge for a day's work?"

Mercer took a careful swig of whisky. "Can't say. Depends how far out I go and how far down. What set of gear I have to use, insurance, so on. Insure myself every time I dive, and there's a rate for the depth. Deep dive needs a deep pocket."

Rayner hadn't expected him to commit himself at this stage. Mercer was waiting to hear just how "private" the job was. Privacy too would have a price.

"Although I don't want anyone to know about this job, it isn't crooked. But a lot of people here in the town don't want it to be done. People along the shore here, probably friends of yours."

He paused, but all he received was: "Speak to me, Jack."

"The government of Aguador is, I think, against the idea."

"Me, I'm an American citizen."

"Would it therefore be possible for your boat to go out some fifty miles from this coast and do a day's work unnoticed?"

"Nope. Ask any of these friends of mine along the shore where a particular boat is at a particular time and they'll sniff the wind and tell you." He watched the Englishman, trying to size him up. There was nothing out there, fifty miles off this coast; nothing he'd ever heard of.

"Then how would you operate?" He put Mercer down as a born ways-and-means man.

"Well, we'd go out at night, same time as the fishing boats, keep on going when they stop, find the position and wait for dawn. Nothing to say somebody won't come up on us, because the Pacific Ocean's a kiddie-pond for all God's chillun t' play in."

"Can we hire an under-water camera?"

"Guess we can. Don't know where. Is that all you want – just pictures?"

"For the moment."

"Uh-huh." He topped up their whisky, looking more non-committal than ever. "To show the salvage company the way she's lying?"

"Partly. Mainly to prove that she's there." The Scotch was warming him towards Mercer. The man seemed puzzled by the whole idea. "A lot of people don't believe that she's there."

"They don't?" He looked in sympathy at the Limey.

"Colonel Ibarra believes it, though."

"He does?"

"Of course. So do the others."

"Sure." He began thinking of the best way to get this screwball out of here and off his boat.

"Doesn't it surprise you that Ibarra knows about this wreck, Mr. Mercer?"

Mr. Mercer put down his shot-glass and held his hands flat together. "Look, Jack. Would it surprise you to know that I have never met this colonel guy?"

"You didn't say so."

"I didn't?" He rubbed his hands together, thinking about

104

it. That was dead right: he hadn't said so. He'd just let the guy talk on, because there was an odd tilt to this whole thing, the Limey coming here with that look in his eyes like he had a fever on him, saying how the Aguadorean Government was against the idea, and how a lot of people didn't believe the wreck was there, so on. Something didn't gel, and from the great green deeps the mermaids were calling to him – *You want no part of this, Coogie, no part of this....*

"I'll tell you a little more," the Limey was saying. "This isn't a difficult dive. The depth is some hundred and fifty fathoms, and the position is approximately fifty miles west by ten degrees south of Puerto Fuego. There is an undersea plateau running north–south in that area, and the wreck is lying on the plateau. That's why the depth is not very great. Now do you know the area I'm talking about?"

Coogie Mercer tilted the bottle but the Englishman put his hand over the glass, so he poured himself a final shot and drank it. The screwy thing now was that the guy was talking sense.

"I do. Around how big is the wreck, mister?"

"It's an airliner."

Mercer blinked at him, and suddenly he knew that the man was very, very serious.

"Speak to me, Jack."

"How long have you been based in Puerto?"

"Six months, bit more."

"Where were you two years ago? In March 1961?"

"Sixty-one, I was nosing around Fiji."

"You may have forgotten a news item. A Transocean Skyliner 10 ditched in the sea off this coast on its way in to San Domingo. There was the normal inquiry with open findings because there was no physical evidence. For certain reasons my company – which is Transocean – is making a new inquiry. I believe the wreck has been sighted. All we want you to do is to get a picture, or at least confirm that it's in fact in that position. Then we'll raise it."

Mercer gave himself a couple of minutes to think, staring at nothing. "Just one thing. How come so many people don't want us to go find this plane?"

"We suspect sabotage."

Mercer nodded. Rayner said: "If you've been here six months you must have friends along the shore. Some of them would want to stop this dive, if they knew."

"Sure I got friends. My work's my business, not theirs." He looked steadily at his client's face. "Take it there's also
105

people who aren't my friends who'd try to stop me, from what you say. Just how far would they go, you imagine?"

"They wouldn't stop at murder."

"Uh-huh. Makes it interesting. You be ready tomorrow, say around sundown?"

"I will."

"Call it a date, Jack."

During the night the *tramontana* rose and by morning the streets were powdered with volcanic ash that smothered the traffic as the wheels sent it clouding up. Towards late afternoon the wind died and the heat came back, and people took shelter again from the sun. The bars became crowded.

In the shade of a jetty locker outside the Bar Salidizo a pariah dog lay flat on its side, with flies crawling on the twitching fur. An old woman sat asleep, squat as a black loaf, the fishing-net draped across her lap, the needle and twine still in her loose hands.

Rayner followed a group of men into the bar, losing his identity in theirs. He ordered Pernod and looked around him as if he might see a friend here, his glance passing disinterestedly across the faces – Spanish creole, coast-strip Indian, mestizo, mulatto, the far-flung sons of the sons of the kings of Araby and the princes of Inca cast here by time and the trade-winds to pick at a longshore living. Few of them looked at him. Of these few, one was a beautiful Levantine boy.

A bunch of touts had a poker game running, with an hour to go before the next branchliner seaplane cut its white path across the harbour gulf.

The proprietor was near him, at the end of the bar, and Rayner got up, leaning across to him. "Has there been any message left here for Señor French?" The man motioned him to wait. Rayner sat down again, watching the faces idly, keeping his left arm across his lap as men pressed their way between the table and the bar to reach the room at the back where the fumes of the marijuana were thickest.

The proprietor, a massive half-breed with sagging jowls and permanently half-closed black-olive eyes, had come back to the bar and was wagging his head ponderously. No message.

Rayner hadn't expected one so soon. She would need time to think. Having thought, she might never send a message. But she must have known why he had promised to come here every day, putting his safety and perhaps even his life in her hands. It had been the only way of getting her to trust in him.

The creole brought his Pernod and a jug of iced water.

106

An argument was breaking out among the poker players, and money spilled to the floor; they began scrambling for it, squealing like monkeys. The massive half-breed lumbered through the groups of standing men and began beating the touts about the head. They protested fiercely, liberal with their blame, each innocent. Within two minutes the game was resumed and the bar fell quieter.

Rayner poured the iced water into the Pernod and was lifting the glass to his mouth before he noticed. He put the glass down and looked at it. The liquid had not clouded, as it should; it remained a clear pale yellow.

He lit a cigarette, and passed his idle glance across every face. Only one man was watching him, as idly, with his half-closed black-olive eyes. There was, after all, a message for Señor French.

CHAPTER SEVENTEEN

GOLD light stabbed through a broken slat of the shutter and made a beam of smoke across the bar; and men moved through it, their faces lit unnaturally. The smoke eddied along the beam. Everyone in the bar was talking except the poker players.

Rayner looked down at the clear yellow drink in his glass. A few weeks ago he would have thought merely that the barman had brought Jacinta-quina in mistake for Pernod, or that the Pernod was stale; a few weeks ago it would have seemed melodramatic to suspect that the chemical change in this drink was probably lethal. He was now a few weeks older. Whatever had been dropped into the glass was, by chance, a catalyst that prohibited clouding on the addition of water. They did not know this, whoever they were.

The big half-breed proprietor had turned away and was watching someone else through his half-closed eyes. It meant nothing, that sleepy-toad look. Rayner curled his hand round the glass so that no one should see the colour, and then looked again at every face. Every face was strange to him except the creole's and the proprietor's; he had seen them in here yesterday. In ten minutes he had drawn blank except for one point: the beautiful Levantine was no longer here. It meant nothing. Two men had come in, and one had left; it was natural in a bar.

It was possible that they would let him go alive, and try again later. First noting the position of the proprietor and

107

the creole barman, he got up, and began moving through the crowd of men, taking the drink with him. If they were going to try again immediately, this was their chance. It would be so easy to slip a knife into him below the ribs and turn away as he staggered and be gone by the time he fell.

He ran the slow gauntlet, not looking at their faces but their hands as he pressed between them... "*Perdón* ..." keeping his drink as steady as he could, feeling the heat of their packed bodies, breathing the fumes of the Sumatra weed and the marijuana and the sweat and the light volatility of alcohol ... "*Perdón* ..." raising his eyes sometimes for a quick check to locate the proprietor and the creole and to make sure the Levantine had not come back, keeping his left arm shielding the heart ..."*Perdón* ..." as they made way for him, swaying and shuffling, indifferent to him, absorbed in their talk of the big fish, the tax on diesel fuel, the girls in the brothels, until he neared the door and the rising heat of the sun outside and the brightening glare.

He passed through the linked-cane curtain, moving sideways in case someone were waiting for him outside. The sunshine was blinding and he had to pause before he could see details: the long ochre train of the fishing-net, the old sleeping woman, the pariah dog in the shade of the jetty locker that he had remembered. There was no sign of movement anywhere.

He walked slowly, cupping the glass in his hand to conceal what he could of it: then he crouched in the shade of the locker and held the glass near the muzzle of the dog, speaking to it gently until it was roused and got to its feet with a lurch, too weak to run, its eyes wild in fright.

"*Tomé, guapo ... tomé ...*"

No dog could resist the smell of aniseed, and he disliked suspecting the innocent even when they were unknown. "*Tomé, perrito ...*" The lolling tongue found the source of the smell. When the dog had drunk, he straightened up and dropped the glass over the jetty wall, standing in the half-shade and waiting, watching the door of the Bar Salidizo and the gap between the timber stacks where the Mercedes had been last night. *You want to find out what happened to the airplane. When that is known, I will have to die.*

No one came through the linked-cane screen. From the middle of the harbour came the rattle of the dredger's chain, filling the sky with musical thunder.

When the dreadful shivering began in the dog he moved away and looked back only once from a distance to make sure, hating himself for having taken even that poor life in the defence of his own.

The boats put out soon after sundown, their dark shapes cutting through the phosphorescent surf and wallowing until their engines were started and the screws gave them headway. There were some twenty or thirty of them out from the crescent beach south of the harbour, and the *Sea Queen* slipped past the green beacon to join them. The dark sea was striped with the white wakes, and as the first boats reached the fishing-ground the hurricane lamps began shining, bobbing on their floats among the troughs of a short sea.

Voices came across the water, and the splash of the lines and lures. Already there were the comet trails below surface as shark moved in, and the first lantern dipped and went down as a hook was taken.

The *Sea Queen* kept going at half-speed, and Mercer gave the wheel to one of his three-man crew. Within minutes the last of the lamps winked out, eastwards towards the land.

"Did anyone see us?"

"Hard to tell, Jack. Nobody hollered out."

They had already discussed the fee for the dive and settled for a hundred and fifty pesos as a basis. "Haven't located a camera yet. Any case you don't want the expense of hiring one until we've seen pree-cisely where she lies. Could've shifted around, see, in the deep currents – there's water that slops up across the edge of that plateau and goes sweeping over the flat, though it can't be too strong because I've seen ropeweed there." He shouted to his technician: "Gotta eat, ain't we?"

The man whose name was Ibituba threw out a light line astern and began waiting for a bite. Rayner told Mercer he was going to turn in.

"Okay, Jack. Take a blanket, goin' to be cool." He fell into one of his reveries, watching the moon's reflected crescent flying through the troughs and crests, faithful as a seagull.

They woke Rayner an hour before dawn at just gone five o'clock. Working-lights were burning on the maindeck and the gear was being prepared. The small wind had died and the sea was hard glass dotted with stars as bright as those in the sky.

"We're over the spot, Jack. Dead over. 'Less she's shifted."

It suddenly seemed to Rayner that a cross on a chart was little enough to go on. The ocean, unbounded in the starlight by any visible horizon, had worsened his mood: if currents ran strong enough on the ocean bed they could have shifted the plane right off the plateau and into depths where no diver could go. He did not know how long the cross had been there, or what currents had run since El Angelo had marked the position.

"Keep smiling, Jack. Black as hell right now, but when the sun's up you can almost see the ground, this area."

He went on checking his equipment, talking sometimes to the three Indians in a mixture of American, Spanish and coast-strip patois, while Rayner watched the east sky. Within twenty minutes the light came spreading and spilling across the spine of the Andes to flood land and ocean and sky. Heat touched the skin; the eyes narrowed for the day.

They were spraying Mercer's hands and face with a matt black stain from an aerosol canister; his scuba-suit was all-black, even to the strap-buckles and mask-rim and the air-valves on the twin cylinders behind him. He gave a white-toothed golliwog grin to Rayner. "You'll feel more optee-mistic now, Jack. Half-hour before dawn and the hope goes like air out of a balloon. Look down there."

The surface was already becoming transparent as the angle of the light increased, and small fish moved in a mass like flowing hair. Perhaps it would go all right, this urgent day, with Coogie Mercer's confidence and the strong light of the sun and a bit of luck thrown in.

"Ain't using the pressure-suit yet, till I get me a fix. Can go down near enough half-way for a look around. From there I can see the top of the plateau, and the Skyliner's a big enough bird if she's all in one piece." He threw Rayner the crossed-fingers sign and let them put the lightweight helmet over the anti-condensation mask.

To the technician Rayner said: "Will there be shark in this area?"

"Perhaps, but they seldom attack anything black below the surface. The boss is not worried." His quick smile faded. "But, señor, do not throw anything overboard, however small, even a cigarette end."

Mercer eased the nylon harness and gave a nod. They helped him over the side and set the winch to drag-check. He went down slowly to leave a chain of bubbles rising; with-in two minutes he was lost from their sight in green water.

The *Sea Queen* had returned in mid-afternoon, making a detour northwards and rounding the peninsula into harbour, because her passage would be noted from the shore. For an hour Rayner lay on the bed in his room in the Castillo Marco, thinking himself out of the black mood that had come upon him since Mercer had said: "Okay, we just go on trying, Jack."

Mercer had made six dives, moving the boat each time he surfaced, and once he had gone down in the pressure-suit because he had seen the rough shape of a cross; but it was a freak rock-formation in the wall of the plateau. Rayner's doubts, always persisting deep in his mind, had surged up to overwhelm him, until he was certain that El Angelo, sighting the freak rock-formation below clear water from his ship, had been merely puzzled by it and had marked it on his chart, meaning later to investigate and find out if it were the mast and cross-spars of a wrecked vessel.

With the reserve of his company expenses Rayner could afford Mercer for two more days. It might need a month before they found the *Glamis Castle*, and then only if she had not been dragged from the plateau into the depths by a strong current.

At nine to-morrow morning the Pan-Aguador Dyna-Compact would be reported missing, and by nightfall the Puerto police would be hunting him. Already he was irked by the need for constant caution in the streets and even here in the *pensión*. Whoever had laced his Pernod knew he had not died; for their pride's sake they would make sure next time.

Lying in the moist heat and listening to the buzz of flies, he tried – as he had tried all day – to beat the blackest doubt of all, but it nagged him without pause until he could think of nothing else. To deal with it he would have to go there again, as he had promised, every day.

He reached the jetty before sundown and saw that the body of the dog had gone. It would already be a skeleton among the debris of the harbour bottom. The old woman was not sleeping; her hooked fingers fretted at the net and she moaned as she worked.

Six men were in the Bar Salidizo. The proprietor was dozing in a huge cane chair long since altered by his weight into a basket. The creole was behind the counter. The Levantine was not here. Rayner recognised three faces of the day before; the others he had never seen, here or anywhere. He greeted them with a patois word used by fishermen; one of them answered. They had been talking when he had come in; now they were silent.

Above their heads an electric fan rotated, one of its blades
111

missing; with each turn there sounded the click of a cracked bearing-ball. There was no draught from the fan. Just the noise, the kind a needle makes on a finished record.

He stood where he could see the movement if the linked-cane curtain parted.

"You drink, señor?"

"No."

The bearing-ball clicked, clicked.

The huge half-breed began snoring in his basket.

One of the six men went out and the cane links jingled as the curtain closed.

He went over to the proprietor and shook him. It was like shaking a boulder. The sleepy-toad eyes came open. Sweat had run from the temples to gather and drip from the jowls.

"*Que hay?*"

"*Tiene Usted uno mensaje para Señor French?*"

The dark gold eyes regarded him unblinking; the breath was dragged in and out of the enormous lungs; the sweat dripped.

Rayner had his back to the door but he would hear the sound of the canes.

"*Momento.*"

The man eased his bulk from the chair and lumbered behind the bar, nudging the creole aside; but the creole did not go anywhere.

Talk had started among the five men, of the most primitive and disarming kind.

"The sea is good now."

"There will be fish to-night."

"Last night I saw the manta ray."

"This is a fine story!"

They knew he could understand Spanish. He moved towards the door. The man who had left here had been gone a few minutes now. The proprietor would take his time. He must wait.

The lop-sided fan clicked, clicked.

Mingled with the smell of the marijuana was that of frying octopus, from the doorway behind the bar. The five men went on talking stupidly, none looking at him.

"*Si!*"

The man's mouth was stretched in a semblance of pleasure. Rayner took the envelope. "*Gracias.*" He parted the curtain – "*Saludji, señores!*" One of them answered.

He found some shade outside, with a wall behind him and a clear run available. The note read: *I will be where we*

112

talked. Not in the bar. To-day at the sunset.

Not even initialled. An hour from now. Between the stacks of white pine, over there.

At five minutes to sundown a man could be seen clearly if he walked into the narrow alley between the stacks, and five minutes after sundown it would be totally dark. Two men, one at each end of the alley, could close in and there wouldn't be a chance.

There was of course no question of not turning up.

CHAPTER EIGHTEEN

HE did not leave the wall when he had read the message, because he could see the doorway of the bar from here and he wanted to know why that one man had gone out.

The old woman had gone to sleep over her needle. He wondered why she sat in the full sun and wore black. He wondered who she was. It was now very important to know who everyone was.

In the distance across the flat sun-bright stones of the quay-side the touts were gathered. The seaplane would be due in fifteen minutes. Two figures were coming through the glare and walking steadily, not with the slow-motion gait of the hot season. They did not see him in the shade of the wall, but went straight into the Bar Salidizo. One of them was the Levantine. In less than half a minute he came out alone and stood looking about him. He was in a white silk shirt more like a blouse, and skin-tight jeans, with rope-soles against the heat of the stones.

Rayner moved and the boy saw him and started towards him, slowly, with the grace of a stalking cat; and Rayner went to meet him. Except for the flowing train of the fishing-net that had the colour of dried blood, the area was deserted, a small no-man's-land of sun and stone. They met roughly in the middle, and stopped, facing each other under the circling sky.

With a casual turn of his beautiful head the Levantine looked to see if they were alone. There was no one. The old woman was a piece of quayside furniture like the jetty locker. The boy drew the knife. It was a pretty one with an ivory hilt and a short narrow blade chased with a serpentine design; the boy would not carry one of the crude Indian things with a stained wood hilt that the fishermen used.

Rayner asked in Spanish: "Who sent you?"

113

The Levantine smiled with his thick pretty lips and did not answer.

"Colonel Ibarra?"

The smile.

"Puyo?"

But everyone in Puerto Fuego had been struck dumb when the plane had ditched.

Rayner took a step towards him because he was angry and the only way to close with the boy was by provoking an attack. He moved his feet into the stance for a spring and Rayner stopped, winding his handkerchief round his left hand for a shield. He thought it astonishing that even here in a town where much of the law was in any man's hands this boy should be prepared to kill in the open and by daylight. Perhaps he wanted to perform for the men who would now be watching from the windows of the bar; it would be irresistible to an exhibitionist.

Rayner closed to within arm's-length and did not take his eyes from the bright blade; the boy was almost a bystander now; the knife alone was the enemy. Once that was dealt with, the boy would run whimpering: that much had been in his soft grey eyes. But he knew how to work. The blade was held point upwards, as one holds a burning torch. More strength was needed this way, because most manual work with the right hand conditions the muscles for downward blows, as in hammering; but an inverted blade is terrible to look at: its implicit aim is for the soft areas of the groin, belly and stomach instead of the hard shoulders and ribs. You can hope to get in below a raised knife before its swing gains strength; with the blade pointing upwards you can't get in above it: you will run on to it. There is great danger in making an attack because the solar plexus is exposed, and knows it. The plexus does nearly as much thinking in a crisis as the brain.

The boy must know all this; he had been taught well. He was waiting for the folly of an attack. Rayner moved again on a slow foot, turning his body to present the hip instead of the groin, watching the knife, noting how steady it was, knowing that he must bring his hand down not on the knife-wrist but where it would be when he moved – darting up in an attempt to slip in below the ribs on the heart side. A left-handed man would have been better off, able to present his right flank instead of his left.

Rayner moved by centimetres, obliging the hand to tighten its grip harder on the hilt and the arm-muscles to maintain

114

their tension at thrusting-pitch. They would be using oxygen by now at a high rate and generating heat, and they would fatigue quickly, however supple. The strength of the coming thrust was already being tapped. Perhaps the boy knew this too, but he waited, his lips curving back across the teeth and his grey eyes narrowed; he breathed at the top of his lungs, keeping them filled; there would be hardly time for a last-instant inhalation; there would be no reserve of the oxygen he needed so badly: the arm-muscles were drawing it fast from the bloodstream and the blood was being starved.

The sun made colours on the steel, a haze of orange and blue. Rayner knew the serpentine design by heart now; he had lived with the thing for ten intimate seconds. Among the colours was the light shifting pattern of his own reflection. The blade was shivering a little because of the muscle contraction. The boy's arm must be burning; sweat was running at the wrist.

The heat from the sky hit their bodies and washed across the stones, the enemy of both. The light pricked sparks from the granite and the glare splintered against the eyes. From the harbour rang the mad bells of the dredger and from the walls their echo came. The blade shivered in the heat.

When Rayner moved his right arm by another degree the boy's breath jerked in a sob and the knife came up in a leaping spark and a foot stamped as the balance was shifted and they brought their hands to the business of thrust and parry with the man's shirt ripped and blood springing while the boy drew back and thrust again and again, twisting the blade and trying to find a way in with it as Rayner closed with him in a half-crouch to use his ribs and thighs as cover for the groin and abdomen while he broke each thrust with his wrist and pressed forward to bring his left foot between the rope-soles and work for a trip if the chance came: but the knife was up now and swinging down hilt first in a carving motion past the face with its edge whining close and leaving a red gash across the shoulder, and Rayner caught the wrist for the first time, lost it and caught it again, squeezing the sweat from the skin.

His left foot was ready and he brought his weight against the boy, bearing on the wrist until the arm doubled and the head rocked back and the balance went. Pitching to his knees the Levantine was already twisting for a run but the wrist was caught and he hung with his legs splayed and his whole face shut with pain. Neither of them moved; it was a question of waiting. The fingers of the trapped hand were swelling as the artery pumped the blood in too fast for the veins to drain it. The knife hung loose in the crook of the thumb. Rayner knocked it away and it clattered on to the paving where the blood-spots were drying as they fell.

"Who sent you?"

The face had lost its beauty; it had become any man's face in pain. The fingers were thick and purple, sprouting in a growth from Rayner's hand like some hideous fruit. He did not ease the grip because the boy was waiting to run, and once gone he would answer nothing. To save time he put a lock on the arm and began applying pressure. "Who sent you?"

"*Ayy-iii . . .*"

Pressure. Question. The face agonised.

"Who?"

"Can not speak. Pain."

"This is nothing yet. Who sent you?"

He was afraid the wrist would snap. Then the boy would faint and could tell him nothing.

Pressure.

"*Who?*"

"*Ibarra!*"

He loosened the grip and the beautiful face collapsed and the head lolled.

"Pick up the knife."

The hand moved quickly enough, the fingers skating across the stones.

"Give it to me."

The boy held the knife by the hilt, the point of the blade towards Rayner. If he wanted it, he must try to take it, the boy's eyes said; so Rayner snapped his wrist and knocked him cold, flinging the knife into the harbour and dragging him by the shirt as far as the bar. It was too hot to leave him outside. He pulled him upright and pitched him through the linked-cane curtain.

There was a row of waterside tenements that stood like rotting teeth in the harbour's mouth; he stopped at the first door that was out of sight of the Bar Salidizo, and beat on it until a woman came and looked at him in fright. They were light wounds but the blood had soaked his shirt. Above him the brass sky was spinning, catching the heights of the tenement and whirling them with it.

His speech was thick but he kept his voice steady to calm the woman: she looked like slamming the door on him. "*Agua, señora – agua fresco – un poco de agua fresco, por favore.*"

116

"*Pobre chico – pobre, pobre...*" The tone of the mother, wherein would lie the sole safety the world would ever know. She took his hands and led him inside.

A couple of girls, one of them beautiful, a gipsy, looked in at the door while the madame was bathing the cuts and sprinkling spirit on them. She sent them away: "Later!"

"Fine girls," he said, out of gratitude.

"They are clean and they are fiery," the woman told him in her crooning mother's tone. "How did you know my house, *chico mio?*"

"It has a good reputation, *madre*." When she had stopped the last of the bleeding he asked if by chance her good husband had a shirt he would sell; and she fetched him a blue cotton fisherman's blouse that was pressed and smelt of soap. She asked the price of a dozen new ones and he paid her willingly. He would have been picked up for certain on the way to the nearest shop: with his left arm smothered in van Keerls's bandages and knife-wounds on his torso he would have looked like a runaway stretcher case.

The time by the enamelled Toledo clock was twenty minutes past five, incredibly. Sundown was at six. The woman helped him ease the sleeve over the left arm; not once had she asked what had happened to him. Discretion was her business.

"You should not go yet, *chico* You are still weak."

"Perhaps I will come back."

"You will never have seen such a choice!"

"I am sure."

He thanked her and asked the way to the back of the tenement. It was ten minutes to the Plaza Pasteza and Lucillo the pharmacist gave him a shot according to van Keerls's prescription. Next door was a barber's. Clean-shaven and with a quick trim, he was able to let a little of the elation come in. He knew the name of at least one enemy. Ibarra. And the Levantine was out of the running for two months: it had been the right wrist.

He waited at the place he had chosen, between the legs of a fixed crane, that reared above the white pine stacks into the darkening sky. She would come only from one direction with the car, and only from one other on foot. In the distance he could see the Bar Salidizo; in the foreground the timber was flank-on, and he could see anyone going in there from either end.

The dredger had stopped work and the lighter sounds of

gulf traffic drifted across the water. The sun dipped beyond the peninsular road. For a minute the whole waterfront ran with red light and then there was nothing left but the pale squares of windows and the thin chain of lamps strung along the bay. Seconds later the quayside lights came on, marking the timber and the mouths of the two streets that he must watch. In his pocket he fingered the folded sheet of paper, as if it needed physical contact to keep his faith in it.

CHAPTER NINETEEN

THE Castillo Marco was down for demolition; before long it would collapse in any case. Rayner's room had the air of a long-disused set on a Hollywood back-lot: there was even a four-poster with twisting pilasters, and dusty angels were transfixed in flight across the enormous ceiling. The mosquitoes, humming at the window screens, might have been the echoes of the violins that had once played on the minstrel gallery outside.

He did not quite believe that she was here. They sat with the lights off to discourage the insects that were already in the room; the crescent glow of the Avenida del Mar flooded the walls and he could see her in every detail. Her scent was in the room.

She had left the Mercedes some distance from the jetty soon after six; he had seen her before she had reached the timber stacks and they had walked back to the Avenida, taking a taxi, and he bought a rose-orchid for her at the door of the Castillo. It might have been an evening in Kensington.

"I am sorry that I was late," she said.

"I thought you wouldn't come."

"There was . . . difficulty in leaving the house."

"Why did you come?"

"Why?" She looked at the lights of the Avenida.

"All right: you expect you will tell me. And I expect you won't."

"I can trust you, now," she said.

"Why?"

"You said the police were looking for you, and you said you would go to that place every day. I knew your name."

He asked: "Did you tell anyone where I could be found? I don't mean the police – anyone else, a friend? Ibarra?"

"I do not have friends. That is why I came. Now I have told you."

"Now you have a friend."

"I think so." She tried to smile.

"You know where I live, now. I am in your hands." How Gates would have laughed. To hell with Gates.

"Why do you ask me if I told anyone where to find you?"

"Someone knew I was there. It doesn't matter. I've probably been followed for days. But please don't tell anyone I'm staying here, even if you trust them."

"I can not trust anyone –"

"Me."

"Yes." She really smiled. When had she last smiled like this? He put out his hand in the half-light and she took it.

He said: "I'm going to do all I can to raise the wreck of the plane, but I'm going to make sure that you won't be hurt."

"It does not matter. Some time it must finish. Two years is long enough."

"Tell me what happened." He got up and leaned at the window because there might be things she would not like saying, because of the cheap watch and no jewellery and the car. Her voice came to him half-muted by the acoustics of the cluttered room.

"I do not know what you want to know."

"As much as you feel like telling me."

In a moment she said, distressed, "If I help you to know what happened, it means –"

"No, it doesn't, Giselle. Give you my word."

She said bleakly: "I came to Aguador about a piece of land my husband had left to me in his will. It is not very big but I wanted to see it. I have not seen it yet." Her voice faltered. "I do not know what else I must tell you."

"Let me help, Giselle. You said there were possibly seven other survivors. How often do you see them?"

"You will not know if I am lying to you, Paul."

"You won't lie because we trust each other and we can help each other. We are the only friends we have in this town."

Almost a minute passed. She began very slowly and lapsed sometimes into French because the effort of telling him at all was taxing her.

"The airplane stayed floating for about two hours. When it was dark we left the airplane on two of the rafts which the captain inflated. There were about fifteen of us, some in one raft and some in the other. The captain worked very hard although he was injured. I do not know his name. We had to cover the rafts with oil. There were some torches so that we could see. We drifted away from the airplane; some of the people were singing in the dark. Three of them were very badly hurt. Then we lost sight of the other raft. We drifted for three days, about seven of us. In the heat of the sun. There was no water for us but we had some food tablets. Every day there were sharks. One person went mad and jumped into the water. It was –"

There was silence. She wasn't even crying. He left the window and found her standing up, and held her while she dug her small face into him and clung to him with her body shuddering.

"It's all I need to know, Giselle."

"No. I will tell you it all now." She spoke into his shoulder. "I do not know what happened to me, very well. When we came near the shore I wanted peace and so I jumped into the water, like the person. It was night. They called to me. I did not mean to swim, but I swam for a time. I do not remember any more of the night. When it was morning they found me on the rocks near the harbour. That is all."

He went on stroking her hair and waited a long time before he asked gently: "Why did you have to cover the rafts with oil?"

She shook her head against him, perhaps not wanting to lie even by saying she didn't know.

"Who were the others in your raft?"

"The captain. An officer of the Aguador Army –"

"Colonel Ibarra?"

"I did not know their names. He spoke to us, telling us what to do."

"And what had you to do?"

"It was very dangerous," was all she said.

He decided not to ask her anything more. When the wreck was salvaged, every question would be answered, and no one hurt. She must have half lost her mind in those three days of heat and thirst, following the shock of the ditching. She had been lucky, swimming near the shore. The fishing-fleet would have been out, attracting the brutes.

"I was badly ill for a long time," she said quietly into his shoulder. "It was a man called Garcia del Rio who found me, on the private beach, where there are the rocks. He took me into his house. He made me pretend I was his wife. Sometimes I tried to escape. I am allowed to use the car every day for two hours, but I must go back punctually or they will send the police to find me and then I would be shot. Sometimes I drive for an hour, away from the town; but I can not

120

make myself cross over the *mi-chemin* – when it will take –

"The point of no return –"

"Yes. I have lost my courage. It makes me angry that I have lost it, but anger is not courage –"

"Your nerves took a beating out there. You were lucky to get through." He stroked her living hair.

"Once I tried to take the seaplane flight into San Domingo. I had saved up the money for the ticket after the first year. But I saw the airplane moving on the water, and I came away, feeling very bad. I do not like to see airplanes on the water. I have no passport or exit visa and my money and my traveller's cheques were lost in the airplane that time. I lost my courage, Paul –"

"It will come back. Takes time."

"It is difficult, when a person is alone."

"Now it's going to be easy."

"I can not believe this." She turned her face, watching the lights at the window. "I have not helped you, but I wanted to try."

"Oh yes, you've helped me." The plane had remained afloat for two hours, because the cabin was pressurised and the fuel-tanks would have been three-quarters empty coming in to San Domingo from Panama. Therefore there had been no bomb, no explosion, and no fire. They had covered the rafts with oil. For one reason only: to conceal themselves from the air when dawn came. And Ibarra had given orders.

What could have been on board the *Glamis Castle* that could not be flown straight into San Domingo, that had to be concealed, that had to be safeguarded even at the cost of ninety-nine lives? The members of the exclusive club were the only people who knew. He was not one of them.

"You must have written many letters to Paris," he said, tracing the cool whorls of her ear with his thumb as he moved his fingers in her hair

"Yes. I nearly posted one of them. But it would have started an immediate inquiry."

"Like this one, that I'm making –"

"Yes. And I do not want to die, even now."

"Especially now."

"Yes. Especially now." He felt her smile.

She was trying to look at her watch.

"It's all right," he said. "Another hour. What would happen if you didn't go back, Giselle?"

She freed herself and stared at the bright window.

"He would make a telephone call. Then I would be taken

121

by the secret police. And shot."

She was obviously repeating the warning that had been drummed into her with regular and hypnotic insistence until it was in her soul.

"Why?" he asked, his tone no more than pertinent.

She turned away and the light fell across her slender neck and cast shadows in her hair. "Because I am exclusive to him and when he is finished with me there must be no other man." She moved deeper into the shadowed room, wanting to tell Rayner but finding it difficult because he was the first. Coming out of prison one is frightened by the distance of things. "I have become indispensable to Garcia in some way. I do not know why. Perhaps he does not know." She saw Garcia's face as she spoke, his face exposed for a moment when he did not think she was watching him. His eyes full of phantoms. His toy within reach whenever he needed to clutch at it for comfort. A brute child afraid of whatever dark it was that she alone could keep away.

She turned to look at the Englishman. His silhouette was against the bright window and his face was dark. This was the dark of which Garcia had learned to be afraid. Another man – any other man. The invader. Reaching this town from the far side of Garcia's unremembered infancy. The nemesis.

How did Garcia tolerate her few hours of freedom? Often he would send the chauffeur to look for the Mercedes in the town and take her back. In an hour from now the feverish world of Garcia del Rio would crack and turn mad about him, if she did not return; and he would take her with him into the vortex.

How clean and sane the silhouette looked. How strong. But Garcia was stronger. His gold-fingered hand on the telephone, and they would come for her, the police. And she would have to die.

Paul, watching her stilled face in the glow from the Avenida, thought: "Indispensable" ... The greatest need of womankind: to be needed. It was the nexus of motherhood itself. A role acceptable to an actress, above all others.

"Giselle –" but it would be pointless.

"Yes, Paul?"

He said the first thing in his mind. "We should be going. The traffic's heavy down there, at this time of the evening. We have to find the Mercedes."

She came towards him.

"It was not what you were going to say to me."

"No. It wasn't. But we must go."

She stood for a long time watching his dark face. "Will I be able to see you again, Paul?"

She had begun shivering in the warm air.

"Whenever you need to." He became matter-of-fact and moved past her, finding a pencil and a scrap of paper from the escritoire that the last tenant had left in a litter. "Keep this number somewhere safe and telephone me if you want me urgently. Better still, commit it to memory. If I'm not here, leave a message with the concierge for Señor French. The concierge is all right – I pay him well. But don't take chances."

She was worried by his change of mood. His voice was very precise and English and cold.

"You are angry," she said.

"Very." He fetched a sweater from the zip-bag.

"Why?" she asked.

"There's no time to tell you. I have to get busy on a few things, and some of them are to do with you, and I'm not sure I've got any right to do them. When do I hope to see you again, Giselle?"

"I will be in your way. It is the airplane you want."

"Yes. I think she's lost, though, gone too deep now."

He stood in front of her, restless with his decisions. "I should be here after mid-afternoon to-morrow. Will you come?"

"I will try."

"Remember: I'm with you, all the way. *Cent pour cent.*"

They took one of the state-owned checker-bodied taxis to where she had parked the Mercedes. He had stopped the cab short, but they could see that someone was sitting at the wheel of her car.

"It is Garcia," she said.

"Why?"

"He is waiting for me."

In the garish lights of the street her face looked pinched and hopeless.

"Did you know he'd be waiting for you?"

She must have seen the thought in his eyes. "No." Her fingers dug into his hand. "If we do not stay friends, all is finished for me. You have to trust me, too." She left him and he waited at the edge of the wide pavement, facing the roadway, until the Mercedes had turned and came sliding past. He kept his sun-glasses on and didn't move his head as the car went by. She didn't see him, and could not have imagined he would still be there.

When he reached the *Sea Queen*, Mercer said: "Never thought you were going to show, Jack."

"I'm sorry. Got held up."

The brass gleamed in the light of the cabin lamp.

"Been in a fight?"

Spots of dried blood on the trousers. Mercer was one of those who observed details while gazing mildly into the middle distance.

"Yes."

"How's it with the other guy?"

"Worse. We ready to sail?"

"Guess there's no rush, Jack, but we'll light out if you want." He looked into the middle distance. The Limey was all mainsheets and top-gallant to-night, some reason. "Missed the fishing-fleet, went out at sundown. We can steer wide, though." He shouted an order in coast-Spanish and got an answer from the deck.

Within fifteen minutes the *Sea Queen* slipped between the harbour lights and swung due north, running as if for Esmeraldas for longer than an hour; then she turned west by south with the Puerto fishing-fleet below the horizon. Before midnight she was set on her course into deep ocean. Above her a plane on the Panama run lowered towards the coast. Below her the sea was black.

CHAPTER TWENTY

AT twenty fathoms the sea was pale jade. The sun, now climbing towards noon, made a brassy pool on the surface above. The boat was a black pod floating near the rim of the sun's pool. The stream of bubbles rose, pearl-coloured in the undersea light, from the expulsion-valve. A group of dorao were standing off, interested, like a flock of green darts gilded by the sun's screened light.

Mercer had made three dives in the black short-depth suit, free-swimming with cylinders and frog-feet and webbed gloves, making a square-search that took him half a mile from the boat and back. The boat had moved at each interval, increasing the number of the squares; but they never left the eastern edge of the undersea plateau.

The water was almost at peak-clarity. The rope-weed that fringed the plateau was not decayed, and gave out very little "dust" to cloud the vision. Plankton in this season was thinned by the off-reef current that came up past the coast shallows of Zacapu and ran northwards well beyond Esmeraldas.

It was an almost perfect diving-sea: bland, predictable and stable. It was a shame to take the Limey's money.

The group of dorao followed him, moving parallel and swinging at ninety degrees to watch him every time he stopped. He would like them to get out of here, but here was a big place. Small fish attract big fish. There'd only been one lone blue that had come to take a look at him on his second dive, a twenty-footer on the stray. It had made a couple of slow turns and then sheered off. He'd hardly bothered with it.

He crossed the edge of the plateau again, making back towards the boat, enjoying himself, the pressure at some thirty-seven pounds and the water almost too warm for comfort. Below, the plateau was marked with the pull of the current that fanned out the rope-weed until it showed the white of its roots. A cloud of squint-fish went down across the escarpment, new-born and racing off nowhere and back for the hell of it, and the dorao followed it to pick and choose from the tail-end out of mere greed.

He had been below for twenty minutes and the gauge was down into the fifth sector, with ten minutes to go. He didn't see the three hammerheads until they were close, because they'd come up from west almost behind him. It was the long beams of their shadows through the water that he saw first. He took a look round and brought his arms and legs together, standing still and doing nothing, casual-like.

They were full-grown males, twenty-five feet and pale sand-colour in the jade light. They circled him, simply because they didn't have any air-bladders to keep them afloat without moving. Their wide T-shaped heads made them look like high-altitude jets as they turned, their shadows playing through the deeper water like dark searchlight beams. One of them came in slowly, and Coogie Mercer began calling it names, because a hammerhead shark could accelerate like a Thunderbird in nought seconds when it was ready to ram. Once rammed, he'd be dead before the other two flashed in for the pickings.

There was a lot to dislike about a hammerhead. It was three hundred and fifty million years old, for a start, and looked it, with the swivelling eyes set right out at the ends of the head-vane and the shoulder-skin wrinkled like old leather. It didn't look like a fish. It looked like something that had come up out of the great deeps and couldn't get back. A haunting spirit, ugly as a nightmare but with a conventional appetite for living flesh.

"Geddout, will you now?" said Mercer into his mask. The thing was circling again, but closer than the other two; and once it sped up to take a ram at nothing, swinging out on a fifty-yard curve and coming in fast to slide past him so close that the slipstream turned him half round. The other two did the same thing. They were getting restless.

He checked the gauge; there were eight minutes left. That was okay. If these bastards didn't come in for him within sixty seconds they'd just sheer off. They weren't ones for hanging around: these were the ram-and-run boys.

A wide shadow was flowing across the escarpment below as the squint-fish came back. The shark wouldn't be interested in any squint-fish; there was no blood in them, that size. Half a dozen dorao, two or three feet long, went chasing the cloud, but the hammerheads didn't budge. Between the plateau and the dark of the deep that ran down five hundred fathoms to the ocean bed the three shark moved, keeping their distance at maybe a dozen yards, with the bronze glow of the sun tinting their sand-brown backs and sparking dully across the cluster of sucker-fish that clung to their bellies. They held their slow circle nose to tail, so that he had to twitch his webbed gloves to turn with them and keep them in sight. He began losing orientation; the sun seemed everywhere and the pattern of the plateau was changing under the cloud of squint-fish.

"Bastards. The hell out, will you, Cri'sake?"

There was no weapon he could use, even if he were forced into the final hazard of defending himself. Draw blood from one of these and the others would go frantic. He'd seen it happen, off Fiji, ninety miles out from shore where the deep-sea shark ran. A native diver raking the reef for white coral had come up for air with one leg gone and the blood leaving a plume through the water – a half-grown tiger shark had gone for him and followed him up, tearing the kid in halves before anyone on the ship could lob a heaving-line; and in less than two minutes a pack came in and the terror began – the feeding-frenzy often seen around tuna fleets when there is blood in the water. After the pack came the strays, all kinds – blue, tiger, mako, duskie, grey nurse and hammerhead: the reef ran alive with them and they cut the surface into rag with their dorsals, homing for the blood-patch and attacking whatever they saw, ripping at the guts of their own kind in their frenzy, ramming the ship's sides and knocking themselves out cold, to be ravaged by the rest while the sea turned red around them. A thirty-foot mako had even chopped at the ship's screw and was jammed by its own jaws until the pack made for it and took it away piecemeal.

126

"Get the hell now, will you now?"

With six minutes on the gauge the big one was nosing in again, starting its slow run from maybe twenty yards and looking small, head-on, just a hump of sand-brown with the head-vane sprouting on each side, the eyes steady, the dorsal fin erect, the thin curved scimitar-tail waving in slow-motion – and then the thing got bigger as it came in fast with the three main fins catapulting the half-ton dead-weight of its mass in a straight ram that spun him full circle without touching and brought the sweat out of him in a springing rush, because now he was afraid.

They were here to do business. They were going carefully at first because they had tried ramming a black drifting spar before, and remembered. Their snout was sensitive. But they remembered also that submerged timber sometimes floated among the carrion of a wrecked crew.

He was frightened, knowing now that he must frighten the enemy. They were circling closer, encouraged by the rush of the big one that had spun him round. Until it smells blood the shark is afraid of anything strange; once it smells blood it is afraid of nothing. It is the true coward, brave only in greed.

Mercer counted off sixty seconds while he waited, twitching his gloves to turn him as they turned, to watch them as they watched him; then the big one swung wide and came heading in for him in a long-range run, too impatient and maybe too hungry to stand off and sight the aim as it had before. This time it came straight for him with the eyes swivelled forward in close focus and the sucker-fish streaming from the belly in a bunch of gold as the speed rose and the shape of the thing expanded as it homed on the man to ram him.

He waited until he saw the crescent jaw come open beneath the head-vane and then he threw out his arms and legs and felt the brute's rush pass above him as it used the vane to clear the thing that had suddenly become strange in the shooting out of limbs that had not been there before; and Mercer climbed after it, dragging water with his webbed gloves and thrusting with his feet, working smoothly but working hard, losing the shark within seconds and glad to, but driving himself higher, knowing they would follow and that it was a question of time and speed and luck and where the boat was and how busy God was – but the pressure was dropping and the light growing strong and there was a chance: the one he'd taken so many times and got away with in the name of Mercer's Luck.

He took one look below and saw them rising, gold now in the dazzle of the sun. His chest was tight inside the rubber-weave of the suit every time he took a breath from the empty-ing cylinders and the sweat was gathering down his legs, but his brain was clear and he knew instantly that it was a boat-hook going down and not a harpoon that would draw blood and bring the bastards to a frenzy. The light burst against his eyes and the world turned blue and white; he could hear a man shouting but didn't know what the words were; the dark shape was to his left and he flicked in that direction and set-tled into long slow strokes, half-submerged, unable to see now whether they were sheering off or starting a run that would ram him and snap his spine. The big shape of the boat was close and through the sweat-film that stung his eyes he could see a rope-ladder snaking overboard. They'd strung it from the derrick-arm and they were hauling up the moment he grabbed it and got one leg between two rungs. His shoulder hit the side of the boat as he swung clear of the surface but the heavy rubber took the shock from the blow. The sky and the sun and the foremast swung across his masked vision and a face swerved past him, its mouth in a shout; then he pitched on to the foredeck among rope, and swallowed the knot of saliva in his mouth, and hit the release-catch of the harness to free himself of the cylinders.

The Limey was flipping the head-clips and the mask fell away. After a dive in the silence of the sea, air-sounds are very loud; it was like the Limey was hollering at him.

"You all right, Mercer?"

"Sure, Jack. Find me a cigarette."

Two of the Indians were dragging the surface with a line for the boathook that had come up and was floating.

"Who threw that thing?" asked Mercer.

One of them answered. Mercer thanked him simply and then looked at the technician, Ibituba. "Get the deep dress set up."

Rayner smoked a cigarette with the diver, squatting on the coil of rope. "I think we'll call it a day now, Mercer."

He had seen one of the hammerheads that had reached the surface within a few feet of the man. The closing of its jaws had sounded like a cricket bat hitting a six. The very length of the thing had tightened his scrotum when he saw it. One of the crew said there were three of them. Three like that.

"Got one more square to cover, Jack."

"Look, that position I gave you isn't very accurate. It was the best I could do, but it might be a mile out. It could take us months."

"Oh, sure."

"I'm not even certain this position marks the plane or some other wreck. If I'd known you were likely to meet with that kind of thing down there I wouldn't have come to you at all, with a position so vague."

"Sure."

Rayner stubbed his cigarette out and didn't throw it over the side. "I'll tell my company to send a ship out with grappling lines and an underwater television camera. They'll find it if it's there."

"Guess so, Jack." He called to his helmsman: "Okay, we take her south forty-five west, 'bout a half-mile!"

The engines were started. Ibituba was laying out the long-dive pressure suit. Rayner looked at Mercer's nigger-minstrel face and said: "I've no more funds for any more dives."

"Sure, Jack. This one's on me." He dipped the end of his cigarette into pooled water and flicked it into the scuppers; then he went aft to the cabin.

Rayner did not follow him. The man was not, anyway, going down again to look for any wreck, but simply because he had to.

Ibituba looked up as Rayner crouched beside him. "Will he be any safer in that suit?"

The Indian shrugged, his long face impassive. "He knows what he is doing. And I have fitted the repellent." He tapped the long cylinder. "It is quite good. It is made by U.S. Navy."

"What does it do, Ibituba?"

"It sends out black fluid, like ink-fish, with smell the shark does not like. It hides the man in black cloud. It has saved many lives, in U.S. Navy."

"Will he use it?"

"No."

Rayner got up and leaned at the rail, looking down into the clear water. Nothing moved there. The bow-wave fanned out, sculpting furrows on the glass sea.

The sun beat against the sea and ship. The main awning had been rigged, and the two handlers were hoisting buckets from the water and pouring it over their heads. The boat lost way and the engine died. In twenty minutes Mercer came out of the cabin and got into the deep dress after they had re-blackened his face. The helmet was much bigger, pressurised with the suit, and they lowered him from the derrick-arm with naval precision. The time was 1.40.

The ship was becalmed. Over towards the south horizon a group of flying-fish leapt and sailed, hardly disturbing the dead surface. There was only one other object breaking the horizon's circle. It had come up from the east, landwards.

"What boat is that?"

The helmsman shaded his eyes and fetched the telescope. After a while he said: "Fishing-boat, señor. From Puerto."

"Whose boat is she, do you know?"

The man studied it again and put down the glass. "No." He wasn't interested. The boat came no closer, but remained standing off perhaps three miles. Rayner watched it all the time. He could see the details of mast and superstructure, but nothing of the crew. If there had been a diver going over the side, he would see him unmistakably from this distance.

The time was 2.15. Soon afterwards there was a pull on the cable and Ibituba began running the winch, very slowly, checking the depth-reading at intervals and stopping the winch motor for ten minutes at a time. Just before 2.35 the dark helmet became visible in the water, still ten or twelve fathoms down. After one more interval of waiting to depressurise they brought Mercer to the surface and swung him on to the deck. His movements were easy and there was no sign of damage to the suit. They unlocked the helmet and he spat strongly over the side, waddling back and saying to Rayner:

"She's there, Jack. On the plateau. Still in one piece."

CHAPTER TWENTY-ONE

THE light of the late sun flooded the walls of the town, their colours aching bright against the eye. Westwards, astern of the ship, the glare bounced from the sea. There was no gulf traffic at this hour, and the *Sea Queen* rode between the harbour piers on a straight course for her berth.

Rayner had shared a rum with the diver in the shade of the awning; neither had spoken much. Before they had left the working-area the precise position had been fixed by the R.D.F. with 5-Island Beacon the main reference. Rayner's position had been a thousand yards west and fifty south in error. A piece of string is not an accurate instrument. Mercer had put him into the short-dive suit and taken him over the side and down to ten fathoms; and even from there he had seen the ghostly outline, silver-grey and shadowed against the rope-weed, the shape of a cross. Back on deck he had taken off the mask and said: "It's not the rock-formation you saw yesterday?"

"That was black, composed of fissures. Rock-pattern don't

130

have any tail-plane either. Couldn't get down to the full one-fifty fathoms but I was more'n half-way; she was so clear I could count the windows. Who cares how deep she is? If you can see her, you can salve her."

The ship ran home through the white-hot afternoon, and made harbour an hour before sundown. The clarity of the light was moving to the heart; the leaves of the Avenida were etched green and black across the white walls of the town. The only ugliness was in the dredger, sticking from the water like the skeleton of an extinct sea-beast, and in the group of uniformed men waiting by the *Sea Queen's* berth.

The ship's engines were at slow and the bow-wave was no more than a ripple. They were two hundred yards from the quayside.

"Mercer!"

"Yep?"

"You'll get the rest of your fee – take my word." He was swinging a leg over the side. "Tell them you don't know me. Tell them I wasn't on board. You went out alone –"

"Hey, listen –"

"Do what you can." He slid feet-first into the water and sand.

"You *crazy* –"

"*Capitán, he* –"

"*Shuddup!*" Because the Limey must really mean what he was doing. Out there he'd looked sick to his stomach after seeing that hammerhead, and he wouldn't go overboard for a gag. And in the harbour he had a chance. There'd be a blue shark around for sure, maybe more; but the bastards were well-fed here and might not make for a swimmer.

"*What is the gringo* –"

"*Shuddup an' listen!*" He had seen the party of police, because a skipper's eye is on the berth from the minute he enters harbour. The Limey had said: "The government of Aguador is against the idea." Mercer didn't even see that he had a decision to make, or any choice, because he was a born non-conformist. Give this man big mischief and he's with you. "Now listen, you three." He moved midships so that the helmsman could stay with the wheel. "You know me. I don't like questions. Just telling you this: we went out there alone, without that gringo. Do some work on our own, over a wreck we've found. But we couldn't find it this time. Okay?"

The water ran streaming softly past the sides. "No gringo – never heard of him." The engines beat slowly in the heart of the ship. "Went out working on our own like we 'casion'ly

131

do. You got that?" The uniforms were so clear that he could see the shine on the gun-holsters; but astern of the ship the sun was low in the sky and the sea was a glare of gold and blinding to the eye. From the quay-side they wouldn't know it if the *Sea Queen* suddenly put out all of her canvas, even. "And don't yap. Play it real dumb with the zip on. I'll handle the spiel. Now just get that."

They said nothing, but let their solemn eyes rest on his face for a moment. Then they moved to their positions with the line. Once, a long time ago, Coogie Mercer had been a U.S. Marine, and these coast-strip Indians had been in his ship six months. The only doubts in his mind were to do with the crazy Limey who was so sick-scared of shark.

The police didn't make a move until the ship was tied up and the landing-plank down on its rollers. The ordeal was short, and he remembered enough of his Spanish just to get him by without being clapped in irons for being sheer criminal illiterate.

"Where is your passenger?"

"What passenger?"

"We are going to search your ship."

"Like to see the warrant." But they'd got that fixed: a Customs man was with them. Immediate right of search.

They searched the ship.

"Where is your passenger?"

"I *got* no passenger!"

"Where did you take your ship?"

"Look for a wreck."

"Tell me about the wreck."

"I can't do that."

"Then get into the police-van."

"I can't tell you about the wreck because I have a partner, in a project. I can't let him down."

"What partner?"

"I can't give you any names."

"Then get into the police-van."

"Listen, I want your word that this remains strictly confidential. I can't let the guy down, see? You know what honour is – you're a police officer."

"What is his name?"

"I can't tell you any names. If you like we'll go talk to him."

"Take us to him."

"Okay, okay."

So they went to find Sam Stowe.

That was it, then. The Limey had got away from the bastards. Had he also got away from the bastards in the harbour water?

It was dark by the time the police left him and Sam Stowe. They sat in the waterfront bar below the fisheries refrigeration plant, with its motor that thumped like an anxious heart. They drank whisky, on Mercer. Sam's piggy eyes were bright with unholy rage.

"I gotten a feelin' you was a two-faced son of a 'Frisco whore the firs' time I clapped eyes on you, Mercer. I gotten a feelin' you was a bitten-gutted son of a –"

"Okay Sam, let's keep it short, I'm a shit. Now listen."

He told Sam about needing to put the cops off the track of a guy who'd tried to help a guy who'd run foul of a guy who ... while Sam drank a lot of expensive whisky and screwed his pig-eyes into knots to mean he wasn't going to believe one word of this, hell or high water – because it didn't matter what Mercer told him now. Mercer was hooked, checked and struck and ready for gutting.

When he had finished, Sam said: "Yup. So now the whole blame town knows 'bout my wreck, an' –"

"The cops won't go yapping –"

"They won't go *what*? Them guys'd go yap their pisser right off at th' root jus' t'get a *look* at an easy buck, *hell* man!" He screwed up his pig-eyes so tight they must have gone inwards to gaze in pity at his ravaged soul. "To think that even a two-bit mean-fisted – but I won't go callin' you names – I'm a man of charity. To think that an ex-*Marine* should stab a fellow-citizen right here –" he got his arm half-way round to his shoulder-blades but couldn't quite make it with his hand, though it looked real agonising by the way his face got pinched together – "right here in th' back when anyone'll tell you there's no more harm in Sam Stowe than you'd find in a noo-born baby's –"

"Okay, Sam, okay." There wasn't any choice, because the cops had asked him where he'd been diving and he'd given them the position of Sam Stowe's sunken dream-boat with the cofferful of uncut emeralds, in case they'd grill Sam himself to make him confirm the story of the *Dorea*. It had looked a real good idea at the time, spur of the moment.

"Whadya mean, 'okay, okay'?" demanded Sam. There was the kind of silence that gets into a church when the preacher's just asked the bride whether she will or no. Then Mercer said:

"I'll give you six dives. Six. Then if there's no emeralds,

you'll be satisfied." He looked at Sam with pity, because it would break the old man's heart.

Sam finished his whisky and looked by accident at the barman, so Mercer ordered again.

"We-ell," Sam said. "There's a fortune there. A fortune. But she's down reel deep, that ketch. Hunnerd fathom down an' that's a long way in any direction, Mercer."

"I can go a hundred, you know that."

"Yeh, but with all them shark there? Place is plagued with 'em, an' –"

"Shark don't scare me, for Cri'sake –"

"Yeh, but maybe I woul'n't git so much sleep if you was t' git your ass nipped off by one o' them blame things, on *my* account." He swigged half the whisky shot and screwed up his face again, this time in uneasiness about Mercer and his ass. "I'm a man o' charity, y' know that. An' I'm goin' to tell you reel frankly it's more'n I c'n do – it's more'n I can *do* – to let you take a risk like that on *my* account."

He went on about charity and hooman feelin' and all that for maybe another full ten minutes while Mercer checked the bar-chit and reckoned it had cost him just on fifteen bucks to pay the rent on Sam Stowe's dream.

"What's the delay by phone to London?"

The clerk looked at the clock. "Three hours, sir."

"I'll send a cable instead." He took a form from the rack and pulled the ballpoint down on its spring and wrote the address: *Transo, London*. Then he looked up sharply at the clerk, who had a clean butter-coloured face with strong white teeth and level eyes and a crew-cut. It was an all-American face.

The Englishman looked at the faces of the other men behind the counter. "Have you any Aguadoreans working here?"

"Just the messengers, sir." He thought this man might be a nut, in here with his clothes dripping water and his eyes glinting the way they did. You saw them around places like Puerto. It was the sun.

"Will this cable go through any native hands?"

"No, sir," the young clerk smiled. The Englishman still had a way of saying "native" that made you think at once of an aborigine with a spear.

"This is highly confidential and I can't code it."

"That will be all right, sir." He began gazing in some uneasiness at the red that was staining the sodden shirt across

134

the chest. The man got started with the message and then tore
up the form and made out another one, reading it three or
four times before he turned it on the counter and slipped it
towards the grille.

To: *Transo, London.* MESSAGE: *Qualified diver has sighted
and identified wreck practically undamaged and salvable* STOP
*Will await your salvage vessel so as to furnish precise details of
position* STOP *Please reply to Mercer M.V. Sea Queen Puerto
Fuego Harbour* ENDS SENDER: *Glamis.*

The clerk reversed the form. "Will you please enter your
name and address, sir?"

"Sorry." P. Glamis, 10 Calle Castillo, Puerto Fuego.

"Thank you, sir." He checked the rate. "You can pay in
pesos or U.S. dollars, whichever you wish."

The whole billfold had been under water, too, and the 25-
peso note was limp. "Sorry. My liquid funds."

The clerk smiled politely and put the note in a clip on the
wall to dry, making out a receipt-of-cable chit and watching
the man go out of the bureau. Then he stood waiting for a
mermaid to come in, or someone.

The moon was three nights old, a copper arc above the dark
eucalyptus of the peninsular road. Evening traffic filled the
avenue with a plague of glow-worms. Half a dozen windows
in the Castillo Marco were lit and he counted up and then
along in case she had asked the concierge to let her into
Señor French's room to wait for him. His windows were dark.

He had lain for half an hour in the bottom of a derelict
tender after climbing from the hideous water, slowly recov-
ering from nausea. He had never hunted lion but he knew that
he would have no more than normal fear of them – fear of
simple danger that was part of man's self-preservation mech-
anism. A lion stood four-square on its legs and made a noise.
A fish had no legs and it slipped in silence for you through the
water that would itself turn enemy if you were wounded.

When the sun went down, Mercer's ship was deserted; and
the two police-vans had gone. If they had taken him this time
it would not have meant deportation. The *Sea Queen* had
made her careful detour north towards Esmeraldas before
turning for Puerto; the ship that had moved in to watch her
in the open sea would have made straight back, and there had
been time to alert the police. El Angelo, perhaps, and using
van Keerls's telephone. The same pattern as the faking of the
evidence at the Hotel Miraflores. The diver's boat had been
directly over the cross on the chart, caught in the act. The

government of Aguador was against the idea, and this time a bullet would dispense with the embarrassment.

This morning at nine o'clock – ten hours ago – the Pan-Aguador car would have been reported missing. The hunt for him might have started at any time after that. Now it would intensify.

The concierge was not at his desk in the shadowed baroque hall. He passed no one on the staircase. The key of his room was in his pocket: he never left it on the concierge's board. Before putting on the light in his room he went to look at the street from the central window, in case anyone had followed him or was posted on watch. After a thorough check he was satisfied that there was no danger outside the building. It was from behind him in the dark room that the voice came.

CHAPTER TWENTY-TWO

IN the dim light he saw the long pale face of Willis against the dark arm-chair. He got up slowly.

"Would it be safe to put the lights on, Mr. Rayner?"

Rayner went to the switch and snapped it down. Willis peered at him with interested eyes and murmured, "I'm so sorry to barge in like this, but I didn't want to wait about in the hall and be seen." He studied his reluctant host. Even with his usual clean shave, Rayner was hardly recognisable. His clothes were so much bagwash and had blood on them to boot. The chap must be going slowly bonkers down here. The woman, of course. He said:

"I'm leaving here in the morning, having finished the case. It occurred to me that I might be of some service to you."

Rayner wondered if he had misheard. He was not going to ask him to repeat it.

"What service?"

"I thought perhaps that if you felt ready to go home, I could have a shot at taking you with me. Otherwise I don't know what you'll do, you see."

"Did you just say you'd finished this case?" asked Rayner

"Yes. The final report went to London to-day."

Rayner stared at him with reddened eyes. It seemed absurd that Willis should have got to the core of the matter so fast. He didn't even know where the plane was lying.

"Congratulations," he said. "It looks as though I've been wasting my time."

"Oh, hardly. You wouldn't have dug your heels in here so

136

resolutely without some absorbing interest. And we never waste time when we're interested, do we?"

How did people stop themselves from hitting this cool face with its observant and neutral eyes? Damned if he was going to ask how the man had "finished" his "case."

"I can't leave yet, Willis, even if you could get me out."

"Ah."

"I want to see the plane raised."

"M'm. Will that take long, I wonder?"

"As soon as we can get a salvage team working we can examine her. I took a look at her to-day but she's down too far to see details." He enjoyed the flicker of surprise that came to Willis's face.

"So you've seen her."

"Yes."

"Splendid." The small eyes were narrowed in thought. "I really am awfully glad. Physical evidence will support my findings." His tone was level and quiet. "May I ask who was with you when you saw it?"

"The diver, of course. She's a hundred and fifty fathoms down, and even he couldn't go that deep –"

"I see. I see. Perhaps you'd like me to take a message to Mr. Gates?"

"I've cabled him."

"He'll be delighted!"

"Will he? The publicity won't do the airline much good."

Willis said: "It won't hurt the airline, Mr. Rayner. No one was to blame. No one at T.O.A., I mean. I suppose I couldn't talk to this diver-person of yours? You see it all helps. The chance of examining the wreckage would make our case certain. Is your diver a local man?"

"There's nothing much he can tell you that I can't, Willis."

"No. No, that's true." He looked for his Panama hat.

Rayner said with weary amusement: "You think I've gone round the bend, don't you?"

Willis found the hat and looked at it carefully. "Oh, no."

"Right round the bloody bend . . ."

Hesitantly Willis said, moving to the door, "Mr. Gates is a hard man to convince. If I could tell him I'd seen the diver . . ."

For an odd reason Rayner felt sorry for him. Willis must be a lonely man. It showed in his face. You can spot a lonely man a mile away. They are dull. It doesn't matter how exciting their work is. They are so dull that no one wants to know them.

"I'll trust you with this, Willis. His name is Mercer and you'll find his ship berthed in the harbour: the *Sea Queen*. Don't ask him the exact position of the *Glamis Castle*, because –"

"I don't want to ruin our case, any more than you do." Willis was very serious about this. "Does this Mercer person know that he could sell that position to President Ycaza for a king's ransom?"

"It must have occurred to him. He's not interested in money."

"Two of them!"

"Sorry?"

"I met another man who wasn't interested in money, it must be ten years ago now, in the Antarctic. They're getting to be quite common."

Rayner came to the door. "He's all right. I have to trust him, don't I? Go and see him, but be friendly. As far as I know he's just done me a good turn. That makes two of *you*." He offered his hand and Willis took it, his small bright eyes probing the jaded face.

"I'm going to be personal, Mr. Rayner. I saw the lady last night, when you left here. A woman as lovely as she can break a man up faster than an iceberg sinks a ship, and I've seen it happen. You're not round the bend. But you're going. Do watch it, won't you? A man on the run travels lighter alone." He went down the great curved staircase, his Panama hat bobbing among the shadows.

Rayner closed and locked the door. He had told Willis where to find Mercer because there had been no option. They all thought he was going starkers because of a woman, and that cable would be ignored as a device for justifying his stay and extending it. It needed Willis to go in and tell them the true score: that if they didn't raise the *Glamis Castle* as soon as possible, someone else would find it and blow up the evidence. Even Mercer was a danger and was himself in danger. Until the wreck was raised, the death roll of that ditching would increase. For an hour he sat in a cane chair, trying to relax, lighting cigarette after cigarette, watching the red tinge that was coming into the blue neon glow on the ceiling as another sign lit up along the Avenida.

The problem was not how to get her away from del Rio, but away from herself, from the biggest role she had ever played in her life.

When the footsteps reached his door he got up silently. The knock was neither feeble nor urgent: it might be anyone's. He slipped the bolt out and moved back with the door as he opened it.

"*Señor French?*"

"I'm here." The concierge.

"*El teléfono, señor.*"

There was a booth in the hall and he picked up both the ear-pieces.

"Who is it?"

She spoke in rapid French. She would be on the beach path along the peninsula. He tried to make her speak more calmly but it was hopeless. He could only just recognise her voice. If she reached the Yacht Club jetty first, he told her, she must wait there for him: a rendezvous a mile long was too chancy.

He rang off and went back to his room to lock it, forcing himself not to hurry because the concierge was in the hall. In his room the whole ceiling was now lit with red, and going down the steps into the street he saw the flames rising half-way along the peninsula, tall and curling, licking at the moon.

CHAPTER TWENTY-THREE

TRAFFIC was clogging the peninsular-strip road and mobile police were trying to force a gangway for the fire-tenders that were still coming in with their sirens howling. A fire-float was crossing the harbour with its pumps ready for blowing and the land-crew standing-by to receive the hoses. The flames, now catching the tops of the eucalyptus trees, threw grotesque shadows across the water. Half the house was already gutted, taking fire with its timbers dry from the heat of the day; one of the Moorish arches had collapsed, crushing the ivory station-wagon.

Smoke lay thick on the calm air, clouding among the lofty eucalyptus and blotting out half the sky, its shadow black in the moonlight and shot through with the headlamp beams as the first tenders pressed their way in.

On the tall wrought-iron gates of the drive the orange glare brightened the shield with its device of a twisting river and three crowned otters, the arms of the House of del Rio. Atop the gate-columns the twin stone eagles held their wings half-raised, petrified in the flamelight.

As a balcony crashed, great sparks showered as far as the paved road, catching the hood of a private car, and others began trying to turn and go back, their path blocked by the same panic-manoeuvre that started in a wave and produced chaos within minutes under the dark cloud of the smoke. People left their cars as the first petrol-tank exploded; many of them ran through the avenue of trees and the grounds of other houses for the safety of the beach pathway.

Near the Yacht Club jetty the land-crew was hauling on the fire-float hose and spinning it out as the first gush from the pumps came through.

Three children ran hand-in-hand along the beach path, their excitement turning to tears. A dark snake slipped across the stones and found the water. A heron flew up from the river-mouth and turned along its course away from the blaze.

Ash floated like black snow from the fringe of the cloud, drifting as far as the Avenida del Mar where the traffic was at a standstill as people left their cars to climb the stone balustrade, a grandstand for spectators.

Others were coming along the beach path but were already turning back as the smoke lowered under the haze of water from the hoses, and he was able to see her only because a headlamp beam swung across the path from the higher road where the trees were thin.

"Giselle!"

She was standing on the jetty half in shadow, with the lights of boats passing across her face; her eyes were shut and she looked asleep; he had to say her name again before she moved her head. He had been somehow afraid to touch her, as one hesitates to touch a sleep-walker.

"Paul?" As if she could only just remember him or who he was.

"Are you hurt, Giselle?"

"No." Tears had dried on her face long ago, but she was trembling. "The house is burning down," she said, "the house is burning down."

"Come away."

She let him lead her by the hand through the drift of smoke; people moved among the trees, their faces sometimes lit by the shooting out of new flames. The tall eucalyptus was on fire, its arms writhing in a static dance above the livid wreckage of the mansion.

They reached the curve of the Avenida and pressed their way through the crowd. People stood thickly on the flight of steps outside the Castillo Marco, their faces turned to watch the fire, their backs to the cavernous entrance. He led her behind the throng, finding the hall empty. The concierge was out on the steps and had not seen them.

140

She began sobbing and the sound echoed from the well of the staircase; they climbed together and he unlocked the door of the room, holding her for a time until her body no longer shuddered; then they went in. On the ceiling the flight of dusty cherubs was washed in carmine light; a rustle of voices rose from the street to fill the windows.

She stood with her back to the windows, her hands covering her ears, her head rocking slowly between her hands. He pulled the shutters across, and their rusted hinges squealed above the crowd's voice; the ceiling grew dark and the room more quiet; he could see no more than her pale dress and the light of her hair.

It couldn't have been easy, he thought, to do that.

"Paul. Where are you?"

"Here." He did not touch her. She had said, "I have become indispensable to Garcia, in some way." She had, in a hideous sense, left a child in the flames.

"Why do you not ask me what happened, Paul?"

"Because I know."

"You know it?" She looked at him for the first time since they had met on the beach path; her eyes held the reflection of the reddened shutter-slats. Her voice was a monotone. "There were tall candles, and when I ... was alone, I moved them close to the canopy of the bed, and then I waited a little time, and then I went away from the house by the terrace where nobody saw me." She turned her head aside. "You did not know about the candles, did you?"

"No."

She said with sudden violence: "They were tall and red, and now they are nothing, they will never stand erect again. *Maintenant je suis propre. Je suis propre.*"

He found the bottle of *anis* in the glow of the red shutters and poured some out. He said nothing; she hadn't said that to him particularly; she had wanted to put into words her wish to be clean again, so that she could try to believe it.

She took the glass and they drank.

"Was del Rio in the house, Giselle?"

"Yes." She looked at the door and he said:

"You'll be all right now. No one can come in here. To-morrow I'll start things moving to get you out of the country."

"That is not possible now, Paul. They are hunting for me already. To-morrow it will be worse."

"Don't think about it. Everything's under control."

Then they stood finishing their drink in the dim light while the glow along the shutter-slats grew pale and died away to leave the cool colours of the Avenida lamps and advertisement signs. The crowd had left the street quiet and traffic was moving normally. There would be police cars down there, the crews scanning every woman's face along the pavements, going into the La Ronda and other places to question the waiters and instruct them that the moment they saw her they must telephone their information.

To-morrow, yes, would be difficult.

He went into the bathroom and put out a clean towel for her and tidied up the cabinet. When he came back she was on the Florentine couch with her legs drawn up and her hair falling across the dark velvet. He opened one shutter and sat for an hour looking across the harbour and the avenue. The moon's reflection shivered and broke to the occasional passage of a boat; along the peninsula there was still the glow of the embers, and the smell of the smoke was still on the sultry air.

When he went over to her she was sleeping, and he lay on the bed, listening to the wings of the insects and forming his plan for to-morrow. He had slept for some time before she came on her bare feet to the bed and woke him, to lie close against him, hunched like a child in his arms and falling asleep again.

"It will grow again," he said.

"Yes."

Her soft hair lay in a heap on the bed and he tried to use the scissors deftly as he had seen the barbers do, but it was much trickier than it seemed; but when she looked in the mirror she said he had done very well.

"What colour is the dye?" she asked.

"Black, I'm afraid. Spanish black." He helped her with the task, making sure there was no blond left at the roots, afterwards cleaning the hand-basin very thoroughly and putting the empty bottle with the other things that would have to be disposed of: her dress, stockings and shoes and the beautiful locks of hair.

He had spent more than an hour, going from shop to shop, bringing back a pair of denim jeans and a loose shirt that would conceal her slight breasts. The eyebrow-pencil was no good because it looked like make-up, so he got the dye-bottle again and used the last few drops. The fine down on her arms was fair, but she would wear her sleeves down to the wrist.

She cut her lashes and her nails short herself, while he left her to explore the building. On the first mezzanine there stood two gigantic Moorish vases, each in an alcove and dark with the dust of years. He dropped the bundle into one of them.

He had not told her about the newspapers but she must have known how serious things were, by the trouble he was taking to change her identity so completely. Her picture was on the front page of the three main national dailies, alongside flashlight shots of the gutted mansion. The police were mounting a widespread search for the missing woman, who would be required to answer "several grave charges" including arson and attempted murder. There was little mention of Garcia del Rio, who was said simply to be "deeply concerned" and "grieving the loss of one of the most sumptuous residences in the country."

There was no reference on any other page to the hunt for Rayner himself or to any inquiry made on board the *Sea Queen*. This wasn't surprising; if they could find him they would dispatch him in secret and the official reply to questions from London would be that Mr. Rayner was last seen boarding the 3 a.m. Transocean flight out of San Domingo on a depotation order, details of which were recorded in the files of H.M. Ambassador.

When he went back to the room he found her practising a masculine walk, with a mirror propped against the wall.

"You'll have to shuffle a bit," he said, "to stop the hip-swing."

"*Comment?*"

He said it in French and she nodded, dragging the rope-soles across the bitten parquet.

"And stoop a little, hunch the shoulders."

"Yes." She looked down at her shirt. "I will buy a thin scarf, to flatten them more."

He found a silk square among his baggage and cut it in half, pinning it for her instead of knotting it so that nothing would show at the back.

"Do the sun-glasses fit?"

She put them on, and immediately the whole disguise fell into place and she was a Spanish youth standing there, looking a little lost.

"That is good, Paul?"

"Terrible. You don't look like you any more."

She said, taking off the glasses and staring into them, "Why are you doing this for me? You have no more use for me, because you say you have found the airplane."

"We'll go out now and find somewhere to eat."

"It is a big risk for you to take, because they want to have

143

me shot and that means –"

"They're not going to find you, Giselle." He forced the picture out of his mind – of this slender thing against a wall with a squad drawn up. If it came to the push, would he give his life for her? Probably. He turned away and checked the street from the window; there were no police in sight but that meant nothing: half of them were in plain clothes, the secret branch.

"It's all clear," he said.

She didn't move. He wished he didn't have to make her go out there, but a woman came to do the room every day.

"I told you, I lost all my courage in the airplane accident." Her eyes looked hunted.

"You don't need any. You're unrecognisable. Whenever you can see one, look into a mirror, then you'll get used to the idea of being safe."

"They are looking for you, too. It would be easier for you, alone."

He said over-cheerfully: "You won't be with me for long. I'm flying you out. Put the glasses on, and we'll find some food." It was all right, with the sun-glasses on, because then she looked like any boy on the street, and he could forget the burning frustration that had kept him sleepless most of the night while she had lain against the very hardness of his body that was unassuageable, because if she let it happen it would be out of gratitude. It would take her a long time to forget the red candles in the house she had destroyed.

"I am not hungry," she said like a child.

He made her put on the sun-glasses. "You need a cigarette in your mouth."

"I do not smoke."

He lit a cigarette and put it between her lips. "Let it go out. Try it in the mirror – let it hang down a bit, like a spiv."

"*Comment!*"

"*Comme un blouson noir.*"

She obeyed him, but the result was comic. He said "You're hamming. Even a spiv doesn't look that sloppy!" Seeing him laugh, she smiled and took the cigarette out and kissed his mouth, standing away from him a little and looking at him strangely as if uncertain of what she had done; and he was unable to think of anything but her mouth that a moment ago had looked so comically sloppy and now was firm again and soft and slightly parted, Giselle's mouth, quick to kiss.

"Paul," she said.

"We've got to go."

144

She said; "I have not kissed a man since two years. I have not made love."

"I know." The house was ash, now, and there'd been no love made in it, whatever repeated rape there had been. Is that what she was trying to tell him? Had she seen an expression on his face, and misinterpreted it? More probably, she believed he hadn't made love to her in the night because a whore wasn't to his taste. *"Maintenant je suis propre."* She needed his respect, desperately – his or any man's.

"You did not want me, in the night." She must have tried hard not to say it and expose herself.

"It was all I thought about. I didn't sleep." Now it was happening all over again but it was no good because it wouldn't be just a quick affair and the servant would come to clean the room and disturb them; and that would be dangerous – little things like hair-dye on the pillow could betray them from carelessness.

He turned away because even the damned sun-glasses were no help now. It could be simply that she was trying to delay the fearful moment when she must walk into the open street where the hunt was running. She was not hungry. She did not smoke. Now this. He opened the door and waited for her. She stood by the mirror, trying the cigarette again to show that she wasn't humiliated; then she walked towards him with a beatnik slouch, her hands stuck into her jeans.

"All you thought about?"

"Yes."

She went on to the mezzanine and he locked the door. Over the balustrade he could see that the concierge was not at his desk. Two women were scrubbing the tiled hall. No one was on the steps. He instinctively reached for her hand as they went down, and stopped himself, alarmed by his stupidity. Giselle mustn't exist or even be remembered while he was in the company of this slouching boy.

He told her a little of his plans while they were eating in the most crowded bar he could find.

"There was a man leaving this town to-day, going to England. He might have taken you with him, but when I rang his hotel they said he'd already gone. I know someone with a boat who could take you along the coast, but you wouldn't be any safer in Zacapu or Esmeraldas – they're smaller than Puerto and don't see many strangers. If he took you as far as Peru or Panama there'd be landing difficulties with no passport, and you'd be held there. I have to get you to San

145

Domingo, the airport. I can use some authority there, and we'd fly you out as a Transocean Airlines operational trainee-stewardess, in uniform – simply a matter of switching staff duties."

"And you would come with me."

"I'll be staying on, to see the wreck raised."

"I would want you to come with me." She put her hand on the table towards him and he said:

"Don't do that, Gino."

She looked around her and he knew that behind the dark glasses her eyes were afraid again, so he said: "It must feel strange, not having to go back. Not having to look at your watch any more."

In a moment she said: "There was a little time, last night, along the path when I was waiting for you to come, when I did not know I had done right; but later I knew."

"Yes." It was when she had stood with her hands against her ears, and he had closed the shutters against the glow of the flames. Then she had asked: "Paul, where are you?"

"Now I know that I should have done it a long time before. Now I would do it again, and again."

"Your courage has come back."

"Yes. I feel it. Because I am with you."

She ate the sweet-maize tamales hungrily and he watched her sometimes, thinking it was like seeing a flame brighten at last from the spark that one has been blowing on; but it was not because she was with him; the influence of that house was losing its power.

Afterwards they walked along the Avenida until they came to the Calle Malla, where fishing-nets were strung against the walls to dry. He began looking at every face among the few men who passed or stood in the shade, because he did not know whether Mercer had managed to convince the police or whether the *Sea Queen* would now be under observation by the secret branch.

There should be a cable by now, in reply to his own. Willis knew the need for hurry with the salvage ship, and had probably sent a cable himself after talking to Mercer. There was also a chance that it would be safe to shelter Giselle in the ship if Mercer would agree, until he could somehow get her to San Domingo.

"Where are we going, Paul?"

"To see a man. He's a friend of mine."

"You said you did not have any friend in Puerto –"

"I found him after I found you."

146

It was certain that Mercer had thought up a cover-story; otherwise the police would have searched the harbour and every boat, especially the derelict tender.

The *Sea Queen* was at her berth, the deck deserted. A group of fishermen sat in the shade of a boat drawn up on trestles, talking together. A man sat by himself on a fish-crate, whittling at wood, looking at no one. The bar was noisy, voices rising above the thump of the refrigeration motor of the fisheries store.

It would be less dangerous to come here by dark, but there was the need for hurry. There would be trucks taking fish to San Domingo every day, and Mercer would know about them. She stood beside him as he looked idly around.

The dredger rang out its brute music across the water. The seaplane jetty was almost deserted: the branchliner was not due for two hours and the touts were crowding the bars.

It looked safe. It would be stupid to cross the waterfront himself, because if there were surveillance he would be recognised. A boy in ship's garb wouldn't be looked at twice. If they were here, and so concerned with the boat that they would question anyone going aboard, he would be there first to draw them off: it was a thirty-yard sprint.

He lit a cigarette, for her sake.

"Walk on to that boat, Gino, and ask for the captain. His name is Mercer. Just say it's Jack, and ask him if it's all right for me to come aboard. If not, where can I meet him."

She didn't question it but began looking about them.

"Don't do that. And don't hurry. I'll be here."

"You will not go away?"

"Never in a million years."

He watched her go, scuffing her rope-soles across the hot stones. When she was about half-way he looked at the man who sat by himself, whittling wood; he was lost in his own dream and saw only the white chips coming away on the knife. No one had moved from the group of fishermen.

The bar was noisy, as always at this hour before the torpor of noon fell. A woman – one of the shapeless humps of black old women who worked while their men drank – was splicing rope, her sharp eyes flickering at intervals to watch the fishermen and gather her scandal from their talk.

The paper of his cigarette was uncurling as the sweat of his fingers soaked it, and he dropped it to the paving.

She had reached the gangway, and didn't look back.

Wonderful, wonderful little Gino. His nerves slackened. It had been the din of the dredger that had covered their footsteps so that he had not heard them. They came from the narrow street, some six or seven of them, moving idly as they split up and closed on each side of him, among them the Levantine with the bandaged wrist.

CHAPTER TWENTY-FOUR

THE odds made the situation peculiar. There would be no point in knocking one man down or even two. To break and run was already out of the question; they had quietly made a circle round him. The thing was to draw them away from the boat. They might not have seen her. He began moving up the Calle Malla where the nets were drying but one of them said in Spanish:

"Not that way. This way."

"Very well." It didn't matter where, so long as it was away from the *Sea Queen*.

He fell in step with them. No one spoke. Most of them looked like fishermen. The Levantine pansy walked with a strut. They had gone quite a way when she called his name but he did not turn his head.

"We'll take the *chico* too," one of them said.

"Paul!" She was holding his arm and he said between his teeth:

"*Allez.*"

"Do not stop," one of them told him.

Rayner asked: "Who's this kid?"

"You should know. He was with you."

He said to her: "Sorry, Gino. Was he there?"

"No." They spoke in French. "Who are these men?"

"They want me, not you. Slip them when you can. I'll give you the key of the room when there's a chance. Stay there and don't –"

"Keep it for both of us. The key."

They walked with the men. She scuffed her rope-soles, with the Levantine's eyes on her.

Only two of the men went into the house in the narrow street with Rayner and Giselle, and climbed the stairs behind them. In the big room at the top of the house the heat pressed down from the tiles. In the glare of the window Rayner could see the gantry of the dredger.

The door of another room opened and Rayner looked up.

"Hallo, Lindstrom," he said.

"Who's that?" The man's face was blank and the grey eyes were narrowed as he looked at them in turn. Rayner went over to him.

"You look as if you've had a rough time." Lindstrom wouldn't fly again.

"Oh, I'm all right. Memory's not too hot but I seem to know your face." The nervous spasm passed across his mouth again.

"Rayner. I was station-chief San Domingo when you went into the drink –"

"That's it. But you were at London, before –"

One of the men came to stand in front of Lindstrom, shaking his head slowly.

"Okay, Frisco." He came farther into the room, awkwardly, saying to Rayner, "Let's have a drink. What's London looking like after all this time?" The sentences came in little rushes, as if he had got into the habit of parcelling his speech between the nervous spasms. He didn't seem to know where the drinks were kept.

"Local drizzle. Colder."

"What?"

"London. It's January."

A painful smile came. "Christ, so it is. Look, I've forgotten where we keep the booze –"

"Not to worry. Later." He could hear people climbing the stairs.

Softly in French Giselle said: "He was the pilot."

"Yes."

"Well fancy seeing you here," Lindstrom said, and Rayner smiled and said:

"Life's odd, isn't it?" The man's piteous efforts at light conversation were painful and he was glad when Luis Puyo came in with Colonel Ibarra and another man. Ibarra spoke to one of the men on guard and they went down the stairs without a word. Puyo shut the door and switched on a ramshackle fan in the corner of the room that began fluttering the faded ribbons tied to it for safety.

Ibarra went to the trestle table that served as a desk, where there were a few exercise-books and some ballpoints neatly arranged. "Let us sit down," he said in Spanish. "Who is the boy?"

"A tout I picked up, to show me around the town."

Puyo asked her: "Where is the Hotel Francis Drake?"

Rayner said, "He doesn't understand Spanish because – "

"In English, then – where is the Hotel Francis Drake?"

"On the peninsula," Giselle said.

"Your history's not so good. It's like asking for Napoleon Street in Portsmouth."

Ibarra told Puyo to ask the boy to take off his dark glasses, and Puyo spoke to Giselle. Rayner nodded to her.

"Mademoiselle Vidal, of Paris. A survivor." He looked at Puyo and added very distinctly: "She is in my care. Tell Ibarra, will you?"

Lindstrom said vaguely: "I remember your eyes."

"One could not forget them," Puyo said pleasantly.

"He was with you on the raft?" Rayner asked her.

"Yes."

"And this Spaniard?"

She looked at Ibarra, who told Puyo: "They must speak in Spanish!"

"The colonel doesn't understand English, Mr. Rayner."

"Mademoiselle Vidal doesn't have any Spanish. I'm certain that an officer of the Aguadorean Army will defer to the lady." But Ibarra had jumped up and was facing him.

"The whole conversation will be conducted in Spanish. The *whole* conversation!" He was a short man, standing very erect. The British Consul would not have approved of him at all.

In meticulous Spanish Rayner said: "Colonel, we will conduct the entire conversation in English or French, as you wish, since both are civilised languages. You will forgive this discourtesy, I know – the soil is Aguadorean but the lady is French and she is at the moment your guest. Incidentally I should like to take this opportunity of informing you, Colonel, that in the event of your sending that sloe-eyed little bumboy after me again I shall personally cut off whatever he has in the way of genitals, but only if I am in a charitable mood. Otherwise I shall break his neck instead of his wrist."

Ibarra looked at Puyo, who said: *"El Lavantino."*

"They were not my orders, but that is not to say I may not arrange to have you shot. You will please answer some questions. First, are you aware of the position of the sunken airplane?"

Rayner asked Captain Lindstrom: "How's your Spanish?"

"I get by."

"Do you know why I'm here in Aguador?"

"To find out what happened, I suppose."

"Are these chaps friends of yours?"

"Looey saved my life."

"Luis Puyo?"

150

"Yes. He –"

"You will answer my questions!" Ibarra insisted.

"How did you save his life?" Rayner asked the one-armed man.

"That's putting it too strong –"

"Do you know where the sunken airplane is?" Ibarra asked impatiently.

Rayner looked at him and spoke slowly in English, leaving pauses so that Puyo could translate. He wanted Lindstrom to hear this, and his Spanish might not be too good. "Yes, I know the exact position and I have cabled my company to send a salvage team immediately. There's a ship based at Panama, less than forty-eight hours away, and my company appreciates the need for haste, since there are factions opposed to the raising of the wreck."

When Puyo had finished translating, Ibarra turned away and stood in front of the desk, staring down at it, taking one of the ballpoints and rapping with it like a slow machine-gun. Puyo looked at no one with his blank brown eyes, but sweat began gathering on his face. Lindstrom went to stand at the window and Rayner could not see his expression.

The ribbons fluttered out from the droning fan.

Ibarra burst into rapid speech and Puyo countered him –

"We must cut the time down –"

"They'll need to get permission and that'll take weeks –"

"It's enough for them to *ask* for permission, to bring the navy out!"

"And show their hand? They can't do that –"

"Manoeuvres in the area –"

"With the request for salving-rights already on record at London Foreign Office?"

"You suppose *he* will let that stop him?"

"If it's what you decide," Puyo said more quietly, "you know you can count me in. But not if the rush means failure."

"We can't talk now."

Puyo said to the man who had come in with them: "Let it be known that we must meet." The man went out.

Rayner had one question in his mind. What had she been carrying, the *Glamis Castle*?

Ibarra was speaking to him. "You are wanted by the police."

"That's right."

"It would be simple for us to turn you over to them."

"It wouldn't pay you. We're both on the same side. It isn't that you don't want that aircraft salved – you don't want it salved *yet*."

151

"How do you know this?"

"From what you've just told Puyo. I've given you a forty-eight-hour deadline, Ibarra – not because I'm trying to spike your guns but because I want to see that wreck on the surface. That's what I came to do. And when the time comes, you'll want to parley with my company, because you need that wreck too. You've got the pilot; now you want the plane."

Ibarra turned away again, his shoulders hunched over the problem. Rayner had taken some scattered shots in the dark but they weren't too wide. He asked Puyo in English: "How is your son?"

"He is well." The brown eyes brooded on Rayner's face.

"What are you saying?" Ibarra demanded.

"The *señor* was being courteous."

Ibarra faced Rayner again. "Do you know why the airplane crashed?"

"No."

"You are anxious to find out."

"Not specially. In forty-eight hours I can see for myself."

"You have been asking everyone – everyone! In the doctor's house you asked me what happened to –"

"That was before I found it. I've been here five weeks and I can wait two days more." He decided not to mention that Willis had flown to London with the case finished.

Ibarra looked at Luis Puyo and neither spoke; then he went to the desk. "Where can we contact you, Señor Rayner?" And Rayner knew that he meant T.O.A., not just their representative. He would go through that door safely, with Giselle.

"On board the salvage vessel as soon as she arrives."

"What is your position with T.O.A.?"

"Station superintendent London."

"Have you a bureau in this town?"

"No. San Domingo Airport."

"If you have to contact us, telephone Dr. van Keerls."

"He doesn't trust me."

"We will inform him that for the moment our relationship" – he turned from the desk to face Rayner – "is one of mutual non-interference."

The sun burned on the sea and on the sand. The boats were drawn up with the chocks home and the winch-lines slack; they lay half on their sides like whales washed ashore. The ginger-brown mesh of the nets festooned them. Men lay in their shadows, sleeping, because they worked by night.

Hiawatha Moses sat with his legs astride, a colossus encompassing the small world of a crab the size of a fingernail. The crab was emerald green, and buried itself in the soft gold sand again, whereupon Hiamo scooped it to the surface and watched the trick repeated. The sand might have been liquid gold and the crab a real emerald sinking into it: first it was there and then it was not, and however hard you watched you could not see it happening. It was there; it was not. His hand scooped again.

A man came along the shore from the piled houses of the harbour, walking steadily in the brassy heat. He went to the shack of El Angelo.

The fishermen slept in the shadows of the boats.

The hand scooped the emerald from the gold and let it fall again.

The shack of El Angelo had an opening along the side that served as a window; a flap of timber was raised on a hinge and two supports, making for shade and for air. The shack was built of bleached timber and its shadow was black, an arrangement in monochrome, light silver, dark silver, and now a sudden flare of crimson and saffron as if it had taken fire; but it was only El Angelo draping an Indian rug along the sill of the window.

Hiamo had never seen the rug before. It was beautiful, pouring its fire down the wall of the shack; and he gazed enchanted until the sun's glare hurt his eyes; then he dived for the emerald again, but it was lost for ever in the gold.

The man came out of the shack and went back to the heaped white houses of the town.

The surf rolled a furrow at the fringe of the blue water, leaving honey-coloured scum along the sand. It was the only sound.

In the shade of a boat a man made himself a cheroot with leaf that he kept in a tin; he sat with his back against the boat's keel, his eyes narrowed to a glint as he watched Hiawatha Moses playing with the sand. He lit the cheroot and buried the match, leaning his arms on his raised knees, looking at the world he had left here when he slept, seeing it had not changed, except for the bright colours that hung from El Angelo's window.

"*Hombre* . . ." he said to the man near him, "*Rafael!*" He nudged him with his foot.

"*Que hay?*"

"*Mire . . . mire, hombre! La manta . . .*"

The man near him squeezed his face in his hands to press the sleep away, moaning against the heat and against his

153

friend, who was nudging him again and giving him no peace until he was made to look along the shore to the *manta* that hung from the shack.

"*Ay-ii ... ay-ii ... Hombre!*" Stirred though they were, they kept their voices low, in urgent whispers, as if it were a young woman they had seen.

Rafael begged some leaf for a cheroot and when it was lit from his friend's he got up and trudged through the baking sand to where the next boat lay.

"*Diego ... Chico ... Mire la manta!*"

The surf fell softly, spreading a lace of froth along the shore where one after another the men went from boat to boat – "*Juanito! Mire ... Mire!*" "*Tonio ...*" "*Martin ...*" "*Lopez ...*" "*Rosario ... mire, hombre!*"

Their eyes opened in the shadows of the boats and their voices gathered and called in whispers, running the length of the bay, as if it were the voice of the surf itself that rose and fell upon the word, again and again, *la manta ...*

CHAPTER TWENTY-FIVE

IT was noon and the town was dead and without shadows. The sky in the south had turned copper and a plague of sand-flies was on the wing through the tepid air, clouding towards the river mouth where the reeds would shelter them.

The concierge was not in the hall of the Castillo Marco.

The building, like the whole town, seemed dead as they climbed the curve of the staircase and went into the room.

He had risked going aboard the *Sea Queen* himself on their way back. Mercer was still in the town somewhere, one of the crew told him; but there was a cablegram for him.

Salvage vessel Delver proceeding from Panama. Please assist all ways possible. Harris.

Harris was the chairman's secretary. It looked as though Gates was on his way out again. Willis must have cabled before leaving here.

He had torn up the cablegram.

"The dye has run down," she said in front of the mirror. The sweat from her scalp had left dark streaks on her face. It did not look like stubble; it looked like dye; it was dangerous. While she was in the bathroom he took the chance of checking the street from the window without her seeing. She imagined they were safe. Perhaps they were. He had bolted the door with the massive baroque fastening. The street

154

seemed innocent, so he risked showing himself and closed the
shutters as far as the hinges allowed.

To-night he would go out and try to find transport for San
Domingo, a truck with a driver who would accept money and
a load that would conceal them.

"Let me bathe your arm, Paul." She had been concerned
about it since he had taken off the dressing. He let her wash
the healing skin and dry it with boracic that she had made him
buy on their way here. She treated the cuts on his shoulder,
saying, "You must not hurt yourself any more."

"No."

They went into the shuttered glow of the room and he
asked: "Have you written to friends in Paris yet?"

"Yes. I wrote one letter and did not send it." She leaned
with her back against the mirror. "It is cool, against the mirror."

"Why didn't you send it?"

"Because it is not sure, yet, and if they knew I was still
alive the shock would be worse for them if I never came
home."

"You'll be going home, Giselle." But she had said he
mustn't hurt himself any more, so he stood against her and
did not think about the Paris flight. He pressed into her parted
legs so that she would know it was true: he had thought of
nothing else, last night, but this.

"*Je suis propre*," she murmured, and he began kissing her
so that she couldn't say it again, while the tears fell from her
closed eyes and he forced himself to believe that it was not
going to be from gratitude.

*

His watch said four; they had slept for an hour, and she was
still between sleep and wakefulness, lying still in the attitude
of love, her moist skin shining in the light, her hands loose
and her lips parted, her eyelids moving to the confusion of
images, her dream carrying her as far as the room where the
shutters screened the sunlight and the man sat watching her.
Rayner.

"Paul."

He leaned and kissed her body, then left her before her
hand could move to his, because in two hours it would be
dark and they must be ready.

He came back smelling of soap. She was awake but had not
moved, except to compose her limbs.

"You thought it was only because I felt grateful to you,
Paul."

155

"Yes."

"Now you do not think that."

"No."

"Where are you going?"

"To see some people." He felt cool in his clothes, even in the heat of the room, eased and sure and light of mind, safe again from desuetude. "We have to be in San Domingo to-night."

"You will come with me, on the airplane." She sat up, hugging her knees.

"Perhaps."

"To Paris." She felt a kind of laughter choking in her throat. Paris was a word for a lost world. She watched him, hoping he would turn his head a little so that she could see the light on his quiet Englishman's face.

"Perhaps." He checked his pockets and said: "When I go, fasten the door again. I won't be long."

"If anyone comes?"

"Don't make a sound. The room is empty."

"Be careful, Paul."

"I will."

Outside the door he waited until the bolt swung across; then her voice came softly: "How will I know it is you?"

"I'll say the password: *Je t'adore.*"

Going down the staircase he looked for the concierge, but the man was nowhere in the enormous hall. It was a risk to leave her, but safer than taking her with him through the streets.

He found Mercer on board this time, and gave him an international money order drawn on his own bank, payable in San Domingo at Barclay's.

"Like I said, Jack, the last dive was for free."

"I owe you more than that."

They shared some white rum and Rayner told him:

"I have to reach San Domingo to-night."

"The *Queen's* a good boat but she ain't amphibious, Jack."

"That's nice of you. What about lorries? Trucks?"

"You going alone?"

The crew must have told him about the "boy."

"No. There'll be two of us."

"They truck timber, nights, from the quay here; but you wouldn't want to be hid among that kind of load, case it shifts. Get crushed."

"What about the fisheries?"

156

"Refrigeration trucks. Couldn't hide a dime. You best see one of the Indian boys down by the market sheds. Depends how much you mean to pay. They might go the whole trip just for you. Why don't you come back here say around nine, ten o'clock, see what I can fix? I'll talk to Ibituba – he knows 'em all and maybe we can get a cheap deal."

Rayner left him, making a detour through streets where there was good cover and taking a look round the market sheds near the bull-ring. A few light trucks stood about, but there was no activity; until sundown only a mad dog would be seen on its feet.

Along the Avenida he made no attempt to steer clear of uniformed police; in avoiding them, his tactics might be noticed by men of the secret bureau whom he could not recognise. One of their all-black cars went past him and he lit a cigarette without thinking; but his nerves were better than in the old days, before she had leaned against the mirror.

At the Castillo Marco the concierge was at his desk but didn't see him because he was immersed in a copy of *La Nación*. On the first mezzanine the door of his room was closed but its edge was split near the lock and he swung it open expecting to see the police in there waiting for him, but there was nobody. The baroque latch had sheared at the rivets. He stood in the dim shuttered light, waiting until the wave of sickness passed away; then he went down into the hall.

"Who went into my room?"

The newspaper was lowered. The man was no actor. "Your room, señor?"

He reached over the desk and caught the concierge by the throat, the rage shaking his arm. "*Who went in there?*"

The head began nodding, meaning that he would speak, and Rayner took his hand away and had to wait until the man got his breath, clasping his throat and working his tongue painfully.

"They came. The police."

"And the boy?"

"They took the boy."

CHAPTER TWENTY-SIX

Puyo walked into the bar, looking at no one. Among the few men there was little talking. They had looked once at the Englishman with the tight cold face and burning eyes, then they had not looked at him again. A glass tinkled on the shelf at the back of the bar, vibrating to the thud of the refrigeration motor.

There were rain-spots on Puyo's jacket. The night smelt of metal. He looked at every man in the bar before he said to Rayner: "We will speak English." There was already a white rum waiting for him. "Thank you."

The sand-flies had swarmed into the building so that the corners of the ceiling looked alive. The big spots began hitting the roof.

Luis Puyo stood balanced on his feet and looked again at Rayner. What had happened to this man? There was life and death in his eyes. "Why did you send for me?" Puyo asked him.

"I'm looking for three or four armed men I can hire for the night," Paul told him.

"Why?"

"You remember the woman who was with me to-day. She's been arrested."

Puyo stared at the sand-flies. "And she knows what happened to the plane?"

"She was a passenger." To save time Rayner added: "I'm not thinking of raiding the cells, Puyo." He heard a tone of pleading in his own voice and was disgusted. He had only just lost his independence. It must be like this to lose an arm. "They'll be taking her to San Domingo. She's important to them. I may be too late already – they took her away two hours ago – but they'll have to telephone San Domingo for orders and you know what the lines are like."

"You are thinking of an ambush?"

"Yes. On the mountain road."

"In this?" He stared through the open doorway. Rain was dancing in the light, becoming very heavy. They had to raise their voices.

"There'll be four of them – driver and three escort, at a guess. Each pick our man – they'd have no time to get at their guns. Rocks across the road – they'd have to pull up and get out to clear them."

Puyo stood watching the rain. The scar split his brow with a pink line, dead straight, blade straight. He said: "Have you seen it rain in this town?" The water bounced high on the stones and a man kicked the door shut.

"You think they won't start out?"

"You said two hours?"

"Yes. Between four and five o'clock."

"Then they will not have started out, because we have seen

158

this rain coming since noon. What makes you think I know where to find killers for rent?"

"The Levantine."

Puyo looked at him with blank brown eyes. "That was nothing to do with me. If I wanted you killed I would come to you and do it with this." He lifted his one hand casually.

"You would try."

"I would try."

The door burst inwards and two men came against the rain-bright oblong, throwing the door shut, their clothes shining black; and Puyo looked at them, saying: "What did you do in the war, Rayner?"

"Parachutes."

"Any action?"

"Arnhem."

"What rank?"

"Captain."

Puyo looked away from the two men who had come in, and asked: "Do you love this woman?"

"Yes," in surprise, because he hadn't known it until now.

"Good. A man has to have something to fight for, or he will not pick up a gun. The doc says your arm got hurt."

"It's perfectly usable."

"Where are you sleeping to-night?"

"I'm going to find a room somewhere oposite the first-precinct bureau."

"You will do no good. Listen to me. They won't leave at least before morning and you have no chance in hell of shooting it out with them on the mountain road by daylight single-handed, and I cannot give you any men because if one of them was taken he would be made to give information, and we cannot afford that. There is only one chance that you have. It is to come with me."

In a moment Rayner said: "Give me half an hour."

"Why?"

"I've got to see a man who's trying to find a truck to get me to San Domingo. I've got to tell him it's off."

"Give me his name."

"He might need paying. He might have paid for the truck."

"He will be paid."

"Mercer."

"The *Sea Queen*."

"Yes."

"Wait."

He went to one of the men who stood at the bar in a small

159

pool of water, and spoke to him, and came back. "He is already soaked. He says he will go. He is very reliable. We will tell you if there was anything to be paid." He put his glass on to the bar. "I assume you did not bring your umbrella, Mr. Rayner."

He opened the door and they hunched themselves against the beating rain.

CHAPTER TWENTY-SEVEN

THE sun had burned all day and there was no sign that it had ever rained. The footprints of the fishermen had broken the drying sand long before noon. Many of them had been to the shack where the *manta* hung its colours, to talk to El Angelo's guest; and once Hiawatha Moses had seen this guest in the open sun, walking with some other men along the shore. He was the man with the beard and the wide straw hat.

The boats had not gone out last night, because of the rainstorm, but El Angelo had said they would go out at sundown, which was the usual time. It was an hour from now.

The sun struck at an angle across the sea, casting its fierce light against the boats and the shacks and the fisheries wharf where there was the weighing-machine. Now the fishermen were not walking on the sand, but stood in groups by their boats; and those who had watches on their wrists looked at them often. The others watched the shadow behind the wharf, waiting for it to touch the palm-tree.

The air was still. The sea was calm. There were no voices anywhere to be heard. Then the shadow touched the tree and it was possible to look into the eye of the great red sun as its rim met the horizon and bloodied the sea. Along the shore the men began working at the boats, lighting the big lure-lamps that swung from their derricks; and within minutes the night came and the shore was dark but for the mile-long chain of lights.

The small fleet gathered on the water, to spread out in pairs and groups towards the fishing-grounds; and when they were a few miles to sea it became impossible to tell, from the shore, whether the lamps had been dimmed out by their distance, or whether the fleet was sailing westwards through the dark, with even their riding-lights extinguished.

*

The moon was a quarter full above the black sea when the

boats came back, fifty of them with a thousand men on board. Rayner stood watching them drive on to the sand, remembering how he had asked El Angelo how many convicts were on the Isla de la Paz. "A thousand souls," El Angelo had told him.

He was standing with Puyo's group of "officers" when the first of the trucks came down the road from the river-mouth, its lamps guiding the others. He was surprised at the precision of the operation: the trucks must have been commandeered and drawn up in readiness to wait for a signal from the sea as the boats neared land. The first bunch of men were running up the shore as the leading truck halted and the tailboard swung down.

From the shacks men ran with the ammunition-boxes to the convoy, slinging them aboard. The boats gathered in the gloom along the sand, and men dropped from them to wade through the phosphorescent surf and cross the shore in a shambling trot, their limbs unused to movement, their eyes confused by the distance that had no boundary; they ran surprised that no one shot them down.

The first truck was on the move and the rest were crawling forward; there was confusion, because this was an untrained army and there was little light: men tried to leap into the trucks, afraid of being left behind, before their guns and grenades were passed to them from the hidden stores in the shacks; they were dragged back, to be armed and sent on again while the trucks moved between the tall stems of the palms and turned to join the convoy already grinding north.

Lights sprang up at windows in the town and the siren began blowing from the roof of the police headquarters; when the first police truck met the beach road it hit the ambush of piled driftwood, and flame lit the night as the petrol-bottle grenades went over. Shooting began, but it was wild: the military did not know what was happening, and had no objective. The convoy was clear of the beach before searchlight trucks reached the ambush, to find wrecked transports and crews running with their clothes aflame.

Two closed cars sped up to pass the convoy with Ibarra, Puyo, Rayner and General Gomez in the first of them. Rayner had talked to Gomez earlier in the day: a big spare-bodied man with a close beard, General Vasco y Montalvo Gomez, a name out of an obscure history book of the days before President Maya, long exiled in Spain and summoned home on the promise of a secret army drawn from the Isla de La Paz.

"I am privileged to have a British officer commanding the vanguard, Captain Rayner."

"I wish our causes were the same, General."

"That will make no difference. Once launched, the objective is the only thing an army thinks of."

Colonel Ibarra wore his uniform in the car, and his impatience was gone. He was bare-headed, because his cap had been lost in the sea when the Skyliner had ditched, but the tunic and trousers looked almost smart, with the patches and oil-stains unseen in the feeble light.

Rayner said to him:

"I'm still not sure of my objective – this won't be a general assault on the city, I imagine?"

"The key points are the military barracks – that is the Casa Roja – the arsenal half a mile away towards the Parque Aogusto Gomez, the Aguadorean Radio Building in the Plaza Grande, the police headquarters in the Avenida Isabella, and the airport. These points will come under simultaneous attack. The Government Building is the final objective."

He had looked at Rayner directly. "We have no illusions about you, Captain Rayner. You have told the General yourself that our causes differ. Puyo has explained the curious circumstances in which you are joining us. I believe you already realise that if this woman, Mademoiselle Vidal, has been taken to the capital, she will be held in the Casa Roja. It is therefore the only objective we can give you, isn't it?" He indicated the map. "The Casa Roja has a permanent garrison of some three hundred armed troops; there are searchlights and machine-gun posts on the roof of the main building, and there is a wall some four metres high surrounding the courtyard with a guardpost manned by four armed sentries at every twenty metres. You will have less than two hundred men under your command, but you will have the advantage of surprise if you can deploy your section under cover. Puyo will give you detailed maps of the Casa Roja and you can then plan your campaign and brief your commanders. May I confirm the General's faith in you by saying that we confidently expect this objective to be in your hands before dawn."

The police post on the main highway to the capital had been taken with a certain amount of noise, but no fire had broken out that would make a landmark. They had left seven men dead and had taken no prisoners. The closed Chevrolet sedan had actually been halted at the barrier before the two patrols had been shot dead where they stood and the machine-gun had concentrated on the group of insulators at the top of the tele-graph-post while men went in with Stens and Balista grenades.

The convoy came on at a steady pace, clearing the drought belt and climbing through the foothills. An earth tremor had halted them for ten minutes, while each of the thousand men sat silent and sweating, because a major road-block of rock-fall now would defeat them before they could fire a shot. When the trucks moved off again the men began singing as they jolted their way under the stars, and Ibarra asked General Gomez if they should be ordered to stop.

"Let them sing. It is the way to go to war."

Just before 02.50 hours the fifteen-ton Pegaso-diesel timber truck with forty men and two light machine-guns on board turned from a side street into the Calle Barraca and gathered speed down the slight descent with no lights and the glass already removed from the windscreen, reaching forty miles an hour before it smashed into the iron gates and dragged them bodily from the wall. The machine-guns opened up before the second truck came through, and the guard-posts were lit with grenades.

The scene turned white as the searchlights stabbed down from the roof where the alarm-sirens were already sounding.

CHAPTER TWENTY-EIGHT

THE second truck was tail-heavy because of the ammunition boxes and it came in at an angle and swung wide, hitting the torn hinges of the gates and ripping its timber along one side before the driver lost control and the truck slewed the other way to smash into a guard-post with the fuel-tank split and the packed men dropping clear as the spilling fuel was sparked off by the impact and a wall of flame rose to block the gateway. As the truck slid to a stop against the wall of the building the men ran back to recover the boxes that were strewn across the yard but the flame met them as the fuel poured over the ground. Some of them still went in and found a box and came out or were dragged out with the prize in their arms and their clothes alight. A box had broken up in falling and a thousand live rounds began detonating in a wild fire that drove the rest of them to the shelter of the first truck as the barracks roof-crews opened up with the machine-guns and swept the search-light area with a murderous fan of shot.

A man ran out to bring in his brother but was dropped

across his body with no chance even of a word.

The guard-posts were quiet, with bodies prone in a drift of grenade shrapnel and blood bright in the glare. From the roof the sirens howled and the echoes came back from the volcano range, their lost-soul sound coming thinly against the brute beat of the guns. The second truck was blazing and the flames caught the sun-bleached shutters along the wall of the building where men of the garrison were still trying to jump into the yard with their tunics flapping and their hands fumbling at their guns, their eyes still dazed from sleep and their legs crumpling as the advance group caught them in a spray of close-range rapid fire: waking to a nightmare they died still half-asleep.

A concentrated flock of shot flew black in the higher air from the three grouped guns outside the walls, and the black turned silver as the bullets danced like moths into the glare of the lenses on the roof – then they struck and the glass shattered to spill across the parapet in a drift of icicles and the glare went out. Orange light filled the courtyard, flickering across the walls; the truck had become a skeleton among its own ashes. A convict section-commander and his crew opened up a terrible fusillade against the south door with two machine-guns working together, so that one could watch the timber of the door peeling and flaking away in white slivers round the massive iron locks until it was melted to nothing as if by a jet of acid and the rattle of the guns stopped, and the men went in with revolvers and knives and a honed boat-gaffe and a sabre a man had found in a sunken wreck – they went in like a train into a tunnel, thirty of them, twelve to their death.

A signal lamp shone white above the gates, and those still outside the walls made for the gateway as the unit inside held its fire. With them came Rayner and his three aides-de-camp, running hard across the strewn ground as snipers tried to pick them off from the parapets.

"*Pepito – join Mendoza. Tell him his brother is only wounded and taken to a house for safety.*"

"*Capitán!*"

"*José – find Alviras and tell him to get his men round to the other side of the archway as a rearguard – hurry!*"

A grenade burst and they spun away with their hands against their eyes. The sulphurous blast passed over them, the air alive with shrapnel. They began trotting for the cover of the truck as Rayner caught the boy's arm and guided him through the smoke. "Pablo, there is a prisoner here, a woman, whose name is del Rio or Vidal. Make your way in and take cover when you must. Get to the guard-house and find the keys to the cells. Release all prisoners and if – and when you find this woman, bring her to me."

"Del Rio–"

"Or Vidal–"

Flame blew through the archway, blinding them, as the second truck caught fire.

"Release all prisoners –"

"And give them arms from the dead, but bring that one to me."

He went through the archway and was driven back by blast as a Balista grenade struck ground. He lay with his head covered as the fragments sang above him; then he began crawling for the nearest vantage-point, because Alviras must be found and told to join with Miguel's men. The garrison's answering fire was strengthening, and soon the real fighting would begin.

One wing of the Casa Roja had taken fire from the burning truck and the last of the garrison were leaping from the first-story windows, leaving their guns behind. The corridors were strewn with dead and dying.

The roof crashed, a great length of the parapet going down and standing for a moment like an upright column in the courtyard before it slowly reeled and smashed across the burnt-out truck. The main gunfire was done with, for the garrison was running to join those in the yard where the white sheets waved and where the arms were piled. The sirens on the roof had moaned to silence when the flames had cut the electricity cables.

Men ran through the corridors, the victors, still in their convict garb, some dragging prisoners, some leading friends with bloodied faces. Pablo, his hair singed and his abdomen opened by a grenade, lay near the iron staircase, and Rayner found him and took the keys from him and went back, working at the metal doors with their small high grills, telling one man as he freed him: "Go to that boy by the staircase and do what you can." He swung the doors back and from some of the cells men came out, dazed by the din of the guns, their faces white from the terror of being trapped here by the flames that cut off half the building.

She was not here. All the cells were opened and she was not in any one of them.

He went back, meaning to reach the archway and try the other wing in case there were more cells there. A man screamed as the ceiling collapsed and he started back but was stopped by a wave of flame. There was nothing he could do now for the man so he turned again and made for the north door and the archway, meeting with a boy who had lost his nerve and was pressed to the wall, not knowing which way he must go.

"*Venga – apresurarse!*" But the boy did not understand Spanish and stared at him with wide blue eyes, and he began laughing stupidly as he took her by the hand, realising that he must have let her out of the cell and had not recognised her in the glare of the flames. "*Viens avec moi ... c'est fini maintenant. ...*"

*

Sporadic firing had begun near the airport where a rebel unit two hundred strong was digging in behind an ambush of barriers torn from the concrete-and-wire fence and preparing to hold off a group of transports diverted from the city area, mostly civil police directed by a handful of army commanders.

Rayner crashed part of the wire fence and had to reverse and charge it again, getting through and clear as a volley of shot began getting his range from the ambush simply because the car was black and had no number-plates: he had seized it from the Casa Roja garages.

The glass shattered and he kept shouting for Giselle to keep low between the seats. They slewed on to the perimeter road and made for the main building in a series of lurches with the rear tyre stripped off and the metal rim grinding at the tarmac.

The airport staff had left the aircraft bays and were wandering about in the main hall, ignorant of what was happening. A party of rebels had driven up in a truck to take over the building at key points and mount a machine-gun in the control tower to command the main entrance. Rayner left the battered police car and took Giselle through the Customs room, finding a cluster of air-crew trying to calm a group of some fifty civilian passengers near the T.O.A. bureau. Splinters of glass cascaded from the roof as random shots passed above the ambush in the road outside.

Some brave soul was announcing over the loudspeakers that there was no danger and that Flight 203 would be leaving as soon as possible, but the words could hardly be heard in the crackle of shooting.

"Where's the captain of this flight?"

The passengers were trying to press inside the bureau as if it were some kind of safety-zone and the superintendent was standing on the counter waving them back.

"*Where's the captain?*"

166

A Pekinese ran from someone's arms and went scrabbling down the hall, hysterical with fright; a woman ran after it, her feet slipping on the broken glass. A T.O.A. uniform emerged from the throng – "Who are you?"

"You the captain of 203?"

"Yes –"

"Super, London, taking over here – you're fuelled-up?"

"Yes, but we're waiting for clearance –"

"Hell with that – get airborne!" He began rounding up the passengers, grabbing a steward and telling him to lead them through the departure check, while the captain wanted to know about authority for take-off and crew muster.

"Look, it's going to get worse here because there's a revolution in full swing. My orders to you are to take this flight off the ground while there's still runway lights. You've got British passengers – now get them out of here!"

They moved in a body towards the terraces and the pilot said no more. Rayner hurried Giselle through the swing-doors ahead of the rest. Her face was very pale but her voice was steady again.

"You will come with us, Paul –"

"Not this time. I'll follow –"

"You will be killed here –"

"I don't think so." He took her across the flower-beds and saw some men in overalls and bellowed for the starting-crew. The Skyliner 12 was in darkness but the empty baggage-truck was standing back at the loading-bay and the bowser was down the line. Somewhere on the other side of the building a fire had broken out, perhaps the trucks by the rebel ambush. There were now half a dozen machine-guns clattering and the headlamp beams of arriving transports swept the dark.

The last of the passengers were still boarding the plane when the tail-jets began wailing. Rayner had stood for a minute at the steps, looking into her wide and still frightened eyes, smiling to her, saying, "Now you will be all right. *Maintenant, ça va bien.*"

"You said you would come with me –"

"I only said perhaps. Give my love to Paris."

She looked at him, at the glow of the fire beyond the building, at the open cabin door; her fingers dug into his arm. "I have written my address. Here." He took the scrap of paper. "It was my address in Paris. I will be there when you come."

Carefully he folded the paper and put it away. "*Au revoir,* Giselle."

"Paul –"

"You must go."

The engines had settled; the crackling of the machine-guns was deadened by the scream of the jets.

"Paul," she called against his face, "I owe you my life!"

He smiled and kissed her mouth and made her go up the steps. The captain of the aircraft was flashing his landing-lights on and off, checking them in case the runway markers went out. Rayner stood away and the trolley connected up, moving the steps clear as the cabin door was swung shut. He ran to the wing and shouted to the man there – "Okay, she's cleared!"

They turned their backs as the blast swept over them; when they looked again the Skyliner was swinging for the runway, her silver flank tinged red by the distant flames. The tower was dark, with the snout of the machine-gun poking through a smashed glass panel and already in action.

The Skyliner reached the runway and was braked, gunning-up. In case of a power failure at the airport the landing lights came on, flooding the ground with white. Then she reached peak revs and began rolling, a flickering coloured shape flowing against the dark. As she became airborne, Rayner found the scrap of paper and began tearing it tenderly across and across, because the debt of a life was not love.

CHAPTER TWENTY-NINE

THE winches had been running for two hours on the salvage vessel *Delver* and the main pontoon. The diving-team was still standing-by in case of fouling, but the ocean was dead calm and the two deep-sea anchors were holding well.

"She's not like a ship," said Mercer. "A ship you got to work in thousand-ton figures. She's maybe a hundred, maybe fifty more of dead water inside of her. Only reason they're running slow is not to break her back."

Rayner watched from beside him. Since dawn there had been boats coming out from Puerto and Esmeraldas and Zacapu; now there were a score of them in the area. An hour ago Mercer had been down himself, fifty fathoms in the deep suit, to take a look. "She's dead level, Jack. Handling her like she was a baby."

It was twenty minutes before noon when the sea changed colour between the salvage-ship and her pontoon, and the lookout raised a shout. Rayner leaned at the rail of the *Sea Queen* and looked across the flat bright surface.

Voices called across the water from boat to boat. On the fast launch hired by a major newspaper syndicate the zoom-lensed cameras were focused on the dark patch where the sea changed colour. It was assuming the shape of a great slender fish, and now of a fish with wings, a cross. Water began breaking up along its length, and then the sun picked out detail as the lifting-cables neared the horizontal and the buoyancy of the compressed-air floats took over.

Suddenly the *Glamis Castle* was there, lying on the surface, water streaming off the fuselage and mainplanes and tail-unit; and the winches stopped.

Watching from Mercer's ship, Rayner felt pity. Her lines were still beautiful, but weeds and shell-fish encrusted the once-bright metal, and the tail-unit was strained over at a painful angle. And she was a tomb.

"Say we go take a look, Jack?"

Rayner stood away from the rail. "Yes."

Moving towards the wreck in the *Sea Queen's* boat, he knew what to expect, because already he could see the broken aerial post dangling from the wires. It must have been the first thing to be hit, because there had been no signal.

Mercer held off the boat at a distance, because the *Delver* was weaving her security cables across to the main pontoon; but from here Rayner could see the cluster of holes where the bullets had gone into the control-cabin and the fuselage. The tail-unit had been riddled but the frame had held. Low-incidence shots had gouged the spine of the fuselage; there would be more damage below: they would have come up from under to take advantage of the blind-spot.

"Real shot-up," said Mercer.

"Yes."

"You want to go closer if we can?"

"No."

"Just as you say, Jack."

Rayner lit a cigarette and turned away. He could go home now. The Air Ministry people could have the job of assessing the evidence: the estimated angles of attack, the estimated order of breakdown in the systems as the shots went in, the estimated condition of the aircraft at the moment when the ocean closed over her and buried her dead.

"Okay, Jack, we go now?"

"Yes. We go."

Towards sundown he sat in the bar on the waterfront, where Puyo often came. Perhaps he would be here this evening.

169

He would like to say good-bye to him. To-morrow would be too late. With his last Pernod on the table, he reread the two short items in the report that Gates had given him at the hotel. Most of it was in Willis's precise phrasing.

On the evidence of my contact at the Peón Bar near the Army Barracks at Lago Azul, the two military seaplanes had been repainted during the week prior to the incident, but their identification-numbers and the Aguadorean Army Air Force rondels on the wings and fuselage were not painted in again. It appears that these two machines were ordered up "on patrol" at 15.40 hours local time, that is some twenty minutes before the Glamis Castle was due to land at San Domingo Airport.

On the evidence of the same contact the two seaplanes did not return to base (Lake Azul) until their fuel was low; and this supports the theory that their mission was not only to bring down the Glamis Castle but to circle the area and finish off any survivors. The weather was fine at the time, but the sea too rough to permit the alighting of the seaplanes. Their pilots would therefore have left the area with no certainty that all those on board were dead and could offer no testimony to the attack. See Paragraph 19.

Paragraph 19 referred particularly to the two pilots, Captain Rimez and Lieutenant Torres:

It is to be noted that the personal situation in which these men found themselves was delicate. They had taken-off on a highly-secret mission and were expected to return with a report of unqualified success. Had they expressed any doubts as to the certain demise of the aircraft's complement, an immediate search of the area would have been essential: and it was now nightfall. Three contacts whom I discovered among the strong anti-Ycaza element in the environs of the barracks have stated that the seaplane pilots dared not express any doubts as to the complete success of their mission, since the event of a survivor's reaching land and reporting an attack by military seaplanes would bring about a full inquiry and expose the whole fabric of this heinous crime. The fact that Captain Rimez and Lieutenant Torres reported complete success did not, of course, save them from the attack made on them at the Peón Bar in the guise of a soldiers' brawl, in which they were stabbed to death while seeking to restore calm. I would refer to Paragraph 17, in which there appears testimony of five Army privates and two N.C.O.s to the effect that the "brawl" was engineered by a party of "civilians,"

*in fact members of the secret police, whose orders were to
dispatch the two pilots and thus render them incapable ever of
revealing the nature of their mission over the sea a few hours
earlier.*

The statement by Willis, involving the testimony of some
twenty-five contacts and witnesses available to summons upon
oath, ran to thirty typewritten pages. The statement from the
Foreign Office was longer, and involved depositions from
theorists whose duties brought them close to the person of
Mr. George Platt-Fellowes, Minister-without-portfolio, who
had been the only V.I.P. on board. There was a mass of mat-
erial in support of the theory that was finally put forward
amid a barrage of marginal disclaimers as to the identity of
the theorists: no one wanted to commit themselves irrevocably
even in so secret a document. The entire Foreign Office
would have been aghast at the thought that at this moment
the Transocean Super, London, was reading their report in
a waterfront bar in Latin America.

The nub of the statement lay in Paragraph 76:

*If, as is shown by the depositions in the foregoing, Mr.
Platt-Fellowes professed a friendship for President José-
Maria Ycaza of long standing, it seems reasonable for him to
have flown out to Aguador on his own private mission of
warning the President that in the event of his signing a treaty
with the U.S.S.R. involving the "lease-use" of the three
major seaports as nuclear-armed submarine bases, he (Mr.
Platt-Fellowes) would feel obliged, despite the mutual personal regard between the two of them, to recommend the inter-
vention of the U.N. and the full exposure of President Ycaza's
part in the North American Refineries Group disaster in South-
ern Punjhacitax Province, Aguador, of 1961, certain details of
which appear to have been known in London only by Mr.
Platt-Fellowes. The entire safety of President Ycaza's tenure
in office would therefore have depended solely upon whether
Mr. Platt-Fellowes decided to remain silent on this matter
or to bring it before the U.N. Assembly. It is for Sir John
Sullers, whose remarks in Paragraph 59 are germaine, to propose
whether or not it may be held that President Ycaza might
have been driven to the extreme measure of issuing secret
orders for the shooting-down of the airliner in which Mr.
Platt-Fellowes was known to be a passenger, so as to ensure
his silence, rather than be faced with the painful necessity of
ordering his assassination on the soil of Aguador where he
would have been a personal friend and guest. It is of course
well argued heretofore that even President Ycaza's ruthless*

temperament would not allow of the deliberate killing of ninety-nine innocent people in order to protect his régime and to avoid the necessity of murdering a personal friend and guest upon the President's own soil; yet it should be remembered that this very régime was brought to power by a coup d'état occasioning the death of some thousand of the new President's own country men, some of whom were awaiting political execution at the time of Mr. Platt-Fellowes's proposed visit. The parallel has been referred elsewhere to the death of Mr. Dag Hammarskjöld in circumstances not dissimilar. In the present case, only the salvaging of the Transocean Airlines aircraft and its subsequent inspection by the Air Ministry could confirm or refute any or all of the conjectures here set out; and it must be re-emphasised that their nature is at this stage exploratory and hypothetical in the extreme.

The only other reference to the relationship between Platt-Fellowes and Ycaza was a brief summary of its circumstances: both had been at Sandhurst in the same period, *circa* 1933; their love of horsemanship had furthered their amity and they had both won honours in the equestrian events at the Olympic Games of 1935. Platt-Fellowes had taken part in the Spanish Civil War and had for a few months been Colonel Ycaza's unofficial liaison officer in the field. Ycaza's increasing political ambitions after the Second War had, it came to appear, imposed a certain strain on their relations.

Rayner slipped the papers back into their envelope, re-tying the pink tape round the bifurcated fastener.

Of the many aspects of the affair, one enlightened him particularly: Willis had made his methods explicit. While Rayner had been sticking his neck out in Puerto Fuego trying to find survivors and the aircraft itself, Willis had been sipping his iced white rums at the Peón Bar in San Domingo, profiting from the cooler climate and pursuing his inquiry at the very fountainhead of information sources – in the place where two seaplane pilots had coincidentally died on the day of the *Glamis Castle* tragedy.

Rayner had promised not to let the report out of his sight and to return it by the morning. Their plane was due out of San Domingo at eleven. He had left Gates sending a chain of cables to London.

He sipped his *anis*, watching the sundown. The houses along the peninsular strip were receding into the flameshot nimbus of the west; soon they were dark red shapes against the bright red horizon, and lamps began glistening along

172

the waterfront. He would wait another few minutes, in case Puyo came in.

Talking for a time on the seaplane jetty when the *Delver* was bringing home the wreck, Puyo had told him:

"It started like a lot of things do, on the wrong foot." From his innate courtesy he had spoken in English. "I found them both on the shore, looking like dead – Ibarra and the pilot. We had no trouble with Ibarra, but Lindstrom took time – it was a year before he could talk properly. We had to keep him hidden because a survivor was dead meat if he showed himself or tried to get out of the country."

The *Delver* was coming in slowly, hauling the dead weight of the airliner and the main pontoon. People were coming down to the shore from the town to watch.

"When Ibarra told us it was two Army planes that shot them down, and flying without identification, we got to-gether –"

" 'We'?"

"The anti-Ycaza group in Puerto, mostly fishermen. We said Ibarra and Lindstrom should tell the world – through the foreign press. But they'd have been hunted and shot and their story couldn't be confirmed. Lindstrom was a shock-case, and Ibarra might be making a false charge to get Ycaza out. We needed the wreck, too, full of Army bullets. El Angelo kept going out to find it, with grapples and magnets, but it was no dice. We went on from there, though, because it had got us all stirred up. We were ready for what was going to happen anyway sooner or later: revolution. We changed our plans and got a message to General Gomez. He began getting us cash for arms and we began buying the arms and burying whole crates of them under the shacks. We would go for Ycaza first, and when he was behind bars we could go look for the wreck in safety and find the evidence against him and pin down the bastard for ever – because he had to be taken alive and kept alive, to answer the charges. Some of us said why not just shoot the rat when we got to him, but Ibarra had been on board that plane and he wanted to see him in the dock at an international trial, and hung for a thug. We said okay. Ibarra was the chief of our forces; we didn't argue; maybe he was right, at that. We got the idea of pulling the political prisoners out of La Paz ... that was my own scheme, and you know why: my son was one of them. The governor was a solid anti, and we could rely on him. Then Gomez came over from exile, brought in on a ship. Another two weeks – it was scheduled for the tenth, at full moon – and we'd be ready.

Then Angelo found the wreck, by accident. Okay, we kept quiet about that. Then you showed up, Mr. Rayner."

He gazed for a while at the salvage vessel. Small boats had gone out and were following her in. From the jetty the Sky-liner looked like a great dead whale.

"You showed up, like a spanner thrown plum in the works. Trying to find survivors, trying to find the wreck. Give Ycaza a hint of its position and he'd have ordered a full-scale naval exercise to depth-charge the area, so nobody would ever get to see those bullet-holes. We fixed your deportation." He swung his scarred head to look at Rayner – "How did you ever get out of that fix?"

"I jumped out of the aircraft."

"You did what?"

"It was on the ground."

"For crying out."

The Skyliner was swinging round, to be brought parallel with the quayside where there were float-trestles ready to re-ceive her. An armed police guard was waiting to man the roped-off area.

"We didn't know how hard you'd be to kill, Mr. Rayner. They say the Englishman is a tractable man in peace-time. They say that he is cold, in love." He turned away from the jetty wall; they would go and look at the airliner now that it was close. "I am glad you came through. She would have grieved."

A team of stevedores were lined along the quayside, and the compressed-air engines were running. Floats were to be sunk beneath the aircraft and then inflated to give her buoy-ancy. The Air Ministry inspectors had left London last night.

The chain of lamps was bright now along the Avenida del Mar. Fishermen came in and went out, but Luis Puyo was not among them.

He would go. He meant nothing to Puyo or to anyone here; and they meant nothing to him. A traveller by air must travel light, and there was no room in his luggage for memories. He walked, alone, away from the bar, passing the long grey shape that floated beside the quay, and climbing the narrow street to the Avenida.

Above the buildings to the east he could see the dark line of the volcano range, and the glowing peak that rose higher than the rest. Catachunga. It was all the name had come to mean again: a mountain with a flame on top.

The Ambassador

by Morris West

CRISIS: the bitter and bloody military crisis of South Vietnam; the crisis of Western diplomacy in the Far East; the personal crisis of a United States ambassador who, in moral confusion and tortured by self-doubt, is made arbiter of his nation's destiny, and of life and death for the ruling house of Vietnam.

His unenviable task is made more difficult by the insidious activities of the CIA, of Mel Adams, his liberal progressive aide, and Anne Beldon, the secretary he grows to love . . .

Like its distinguished and best-selling predecessors, *The Ambassador* is the fruit of long research and intimate experience by the author. It brings into sharp, startling focus the moral and political dilemmas of today. It is a challenge, as the world's future is shaped in the deltas and paddy fields of South-East Asia.

FOUR ▤ SQUARE EDITION 7s. 6d.

Trial at Monomoy

by John Masters

Monomoy is a small American coastal town . . . smug, prim, sinful, and ripe for disaster. As Monomoy's inhabitants go about their daily business and nightly intrigues, disaster is gathering as surely as the waves that break on her sandy beach.

For Monomoy is confronted with annihilation as a tornado heads straight for her; for ten dreadful and revealing days her fate hangs in the balance . . . fear, hope, strength and weakness are ruthlessly laid bare. Jim Carpenter is afraid the town will learn he enjoys painting his wife in the nude; John Remington, a coastguard with a brave exterior, is afraid of sexual involvement; Frank Damato, the police chief, is afraid to acknowledge the fact that his son is a vicious hooligan. Joann, the girl who was always available; Lynn, the subversive schoolteacher, and Mrs. Handforth—all their secrets and fears can no longer be hidden.

Can the townspeople survive the threat from nature? Do they deserve to? This is the theme of John Masters' great new novel, written in the vigorous style of his world-famous books set in India. *Trial at Monomoy* is a new venture for this top-selling author, and has been widely acclaimed by the critics.

FOUR SQUARE EDITION 6s. 0d.